Praise for

THE SCORPIONS OF ZAHIR

ALSO BY CHRISTINE BRODIEN-JONES

The Owl Keeper
The Glass Puzzle

THE SCORPIONS OF ZAHIR

ojo ojo ojo

CHRISTINE BRODIEN-JONES

A YEARLING BOOK

Text copyright © 2012 by Christine L. Jones
Cover art and interior illustrations copyright © 2012 by Kelly Murphy

All rights reserved. Published in the United States by Yearling, an imprint of Random House Children's Books, a division of Random House, Inc., New York. Originally published in hardcover in the United States by Delacorte Press, an imprint of Random House Children's Books, New York, in 2012.

Yearling and the jumping horse design
are registered trademarks of Random House, Inc.

Visit us on the Web! randomhouse.com/kids
Educators and librarians, for a variety of teaching tools,
visit us at RHTeachersLibrarians.com

The Library of Congress has cataloged the hardcover edition of this work as follows:
Brodien-Jones, Chris.
The scorpions of Zahir / Christine Brodien-Jones. — 1st ed.
p. cm.
Summary: Eleven-year-old Zagora Pym, who possesses an otherworldly stone, travels to the Moroccan desert with her archaeologist father and astronomy-obsessed brother on a quest to save the ancient city of Zahir.
ISBN 978-0-385-73933-7 (hc) — ISBN 978-0-385-90783-5 (lib. bdg.) —
ISBN 978-0-375-89749-8 (ebook)
[1. Adventure and adventurers—Fiction. 2. Deserts—Fiction.
3. Morocco—Fiction. 4. Fantasy.] I. Title.
PZ7.B786114Sc 2012
[Fic]—dc23
2011026332

ISBN 978-0-385-73934-4 (pbk.)

Printed in the United States of America

10 9 8 7 6 5 4 3 2 1

First Yearling Edition 2013

In memory of Dr. James R. Randall,
founder of Pym-Randall Press and head of the
creative writing program at Emerson College,
who inspired countless young authors.
Mentor, teacher and dear friend.

✿ ✿ ✿

An enormous "Thank you!" to all who have helped me along the way:

My agent, Stephen Fraser, of the Jennifer DeChiara Literary Agency, for your enthusiasm and steadfast support—as always, you are an inspiration! My editors, Krista Vitola and Krista Marino, for your unwavering belief in Zagora and her story, your fantastic editing and your keen insights and tough questions. The staff at Delacorte Press, especially publisher Beverly Horowitz, copy editor Jennifer Black and book designer Jinna Shin. Artist Kelly Murphy, whose extraordinary cover and illustrations perfectly capture the adventure, humor and mystery of *Scorpions*.

The members of my writing group, who critiqued endless drafts and cheered me on: Laurie Jacobs, Donna McArdle, Pat Lowery Collins, Lenice Strohmeier, Christopher Doyle, Patricia Bridgman and Valerie McCaffrey. Also my literary confidante, Heather Wilks-Jones, and my first young reader, Isabella Giordano.

A special thanks to Peter, who introduced me to Morocco during our honeymoon, and to our sons, Ian and Derek, intrepid travelers and companions on our return journey in 1998. Finally, *merci* to Abdul, Mohammed, Ali and the others who welcomed us to Maison Tuareg in Agdz, Morocco, and arranged for our trek into the Sahara, setting fire to my imagination all those years ago. . . .

⟪ PROLOGUE ⟫

The light was beautiful over the walled city of Zahir. Goatherders walked under an immense blue sky; scimitar oryxes grazed in lush oases. Camel caravans and traders on horseback followed a wide road lined with stately columns, leading to the city. High above Zahir rose the Tower of the Enigmas, where guards in silk cloaks sat on their camels, swords pointing skyward.

All of them—men, women, children, camels, goats— moved past the red stone walls that wound through the city like the spines of dragons. Sunlight spilled over terraces and squares and obelisks, and over the confusing maze of streets. At the heart of Zahir was a palace of ocher and dusty pink, built by the mystic poet Xuloc, leader of the Azimuth. Its gardens teemed with peacocks, lemon trees and flocks of multicolored parrots. Turquoise fish swam in the fountains while Azimuth elders strolled along its paths, reading ancient texts.

Through an archway of brilliant colors, within a courtyard bound by high mud walls, stood a small pyramid of unearthly blue stones, infused with light from the planet Nar Azrak. Embedded at the top of the pyramid was a luminous stone no bigger than a robin's egg. And if you observed the stone in a certain light, you could see the image of a gazelle-like creature with long, curved horns—the sacred oryx—that was carved into it.

❀ ❀ ❀

One autumn night, late in the seventeenth century, a lone figure, undetected by palace guards, crept in and scaled the blue stone pyramid. Using a chisel and hammer, the stranger loosened the Oryx Stone, prying it away, and ran off with it into the desert.

Days later, a scorpion the size of a large lizard, its tail hideous and coiled, scuttled across the palace courtyard. More scorpions appeared, each larger and more frightening than the last. Pincers clacking, they crawled into the dark corners and tight crevices of Zahir, poised to strike. Within a month the scimitar oryxes vanished without a trace, leaving the oases empty.

Alarmed, the Azimuth elders convened, fearful that the theft of the Oryx Stone had thrown the balance of nature into chaos. The stone had channeled the power of Nar Azrak, creating a protective barrier around Zahir, keeping away the scorpions. But now the stone was gone, and in despair, the Azimuth left their beloved city, fleeing across the desert.

Month by month, the scorpions tunneled through the sand, hollowing out a colony beneath Zahir. At night they raced over the dunes, shrieking like wild dogs, under the light of Nar Azrak.

Ever vigilant, the Azimuth elders turned to the night sky, studying the constellations, watching Nar Azrak veer off course. They ruminated and pondered, recalling the ancient glyphs and foretellings, the prophetic drawings of Xuloc. Centuries passed and they grew increasingly frightened: their astronomers all agreed that Nar Azrak was moving directly toward Zahir, having been set on its earthbound path the night the Oryx Stone disappeared.

THE ORYX STONE
AND THE SCORPION

Zagora Pym sat with a beat-up leather-bound book open on her lap, dreaming about Zahir. She'd found the book the day before when her father was lecturing at the university and she was snooping around his study. It was at the bottom of his desk, in a drawer crammed with pencils, graphs and navigational charts. On the first page were spidery letters that read *Excavating Zahir: The Journal of Edgar Q. Yegen, Intrepid Explorer.*

She perched on the edge of her bed, slowly turning the pages, which threatened to fall apart at the slightest touch. Zagora was eleven and a bit rough around the edges, with perpetually scraped elbows, a face with sharp angles and a gap between her teeth, and she wore the gaze of a constant dreamer. She knew that while she might not be a ravishing bandit princess or a girl genius with an off-the-charts IQ, she had adventure in her heart, and to her that's what mattered most.

Most of the journal's pages looked chewed up—she guessed by desert beetles—and many were damaged or missing. But that didn't stop Zagora from reading the pages that were left. And although the ink had faded, she could see that the paragraphs had been composed by a precise and scholarly hand, in the language of a particular time.

The book started off with the paragraph:

> I begin this journal on a blustery March day in
> Boston, Massachusetts, sitting in my study overlooking
> Marlborough Street, in the year 1937. In two months'
> time a freighter will leave Boston Harbor for the port
> of Tangier, Morocco—and I will be on it. This expedi-
> tion will be the culmination of ten years of exhaustive
> research, which began the moment I discovered the in-
> famous Oryx Stone.

Zagora had never read anything so thrilling in her
life. Her archaeologist father often talked about his ad-
ventures in Zahir, including his role in the failed expedition to excavate the buried city. But the entries in this
book went all the way back to 1937!

In Edgar Yegen's journal there were accounts of
moonless black nights in the desert, open-air markets
and the bleak Atlas Mountains. She studied his sketches
of mud-walled houses, patterned archways, an underground tomb. It was easy to imagine the sun, the insects,
the heat and dust of the Sahara. She read about the road
to Zahir, with its stone columns, snaking through yellow
sands. What excited her most, though, were the entries
about a mysterious object called the Oryx Stone.

She stopped flipping the pages of the book right where Edgar Yegen first described the strange stone, and read the entry again.

> While roaming the casbah in search of a comfortable pair of slippers, I happened upon a makeshift stall containing the kinds of trinkets one encounters in these bustling markets. Tipping my hat to the proprietor, I was about to walk away when a flash of blue caught my eye. Amid the tangle of evil-eye charms, worry beads and ankle bracelets was the most extraordinary necklace I had ever seen: strung on a ribbon of leather was a blue stone the size of a robin's egg with the tiny figure of an oryx—an animal considered sacred by the ancient tribe of the Azimuth—etched into the center. I held the stone in my hand and my blood quickened. I intuited that this was indeed a long-lost treasure: the infamous Oryx Stone, stolen centuries ago from the legendary city of Zahir.

The description of the Oryx Stone matched that of an object she'd found in her attic years earlier. While searching for an explorer's headlamp to wear in the cellar on a newt-catching expedition, she had opened a

steamer trunk and discovered, under a stack of archaeology magazines, a tattered drawstring pouch.

Tucked inside the pouch was a luminous stone the same ice blue as her eyes. Similar to a small egg in shape and size, the stone was polished smooth and threaded on a worn leather string. If she turned the stone a certain way in the light, she could see the image of an oryx, her favorite desert animal, which had been cut into the surface of the stone.

Ever since that day, late at night, when her dad and brother were asleep, she would creep up to the attic and pull out the stone, mesmerized by its ethereal light. She'd spent hours up there, exploring foreign lands, inventing stories of far-off places, dangerous bandits, magical oryxes and lost desert opals. Riding imaginary camels, she made journeys in her goggles, pith helmet and crocodile boots, which came to a frightening point at the toe. And always, always, she wore the glowing blue stone.

There was a knock at the front door and Zagora guiltily closed the journal, tucking it under her bed. She planned to return it to her father's desk before he discovered it was missing, though it was likely he'd forgotten he even had it. Her dad was absentminded that way.

Bounding downstairs and out to the front porch, she found a huge envelope stuffed in their mailbox. Her father was always getting weird-sized parcels sent from all over the world. This envelope had a weary look, as if it had been traveling for years and years, space-warping to their house from another century.

"Dad, package!" she shouted, bursting into her father's study, where he sat playing *Desert Biome Madness* on his computer.

Charles W. Pym, PhD, DSc, a tall, introspective, first-class archaeologist (in Zagora's opinion) and translator of rare glyphs, was now in the later stages of his career. Zagora bragged to her friends that her father tracked down snow leopards in the Gobi, dynamited a buried fortress in Mali and almost died of thirst while measuring wind patterns in Egypt. His career had been a series of worst-case scenarios, she explained, using his phrase. She didn't know the specifics, but she liked the way the words sounded.

Dr. Pym spun around in his ergonomic bungee chair and Zagora ceremoniously handed him the envelope. It was stamped with the words *Royaume du Maroc,* which she knew meant "Kingdom of Morocco." The handwriting was messy and the stamps were desert themed, with whimsical pictures of lizards, camels, hyenas and insects that she was dying to collect.

"Can I keep the stamps?" she asked eagerly. "They're

really cool." Ever since she was seven, when her dad had brought home a book called *Flora and Fauna of the Sahara,* she'd immersed herself in facts about deserts of the world.

Her father held up the brown envelope tied with string. "What's this, eh?" He squinted at the return address. "Who could be sending me a package from Morocco?"

"Maybe they want you to set up a desert expedition," suggested Zagora. It was always an event when her dad landed a job, especially in some exotic location.

She watched his face carefully as he scrutinized the old-fashioned script through his drugstore reading glasses, the lines around his eyes deepening.

"Good grief." He gave a puzzled frown as he tore open the envelope. "Hmmm. I don't recognize the sender's address—"

Paper crackled and dust flew as the contents spilled out. Zagora caught a sheet of paper as it drifted to the floor; covered with black pencil scribbles, it smelled faintly of limes and spices. She found herself looking at a map; it was gritty and smudged, like something a first grader would draw. Turning the paper this way and that, she tried to decipher the primitive symbols.

"This letter has been forwarded to me by a woman

named Olivia Romanesçu," her father said slowly, looking up with a quizzical expression. "She lives in Morocco. In Marrakech, to be precise. Hmm, very unusual handwriting—"

"Do you think she's an explorer, like Freya Stark?" interrupted Zagora.

Her fourth-grade teacher, Mrs. Bixby, had told her class about Freya Stark: self-reliant, ingenious and plucky, she'd been one of the first Western women to travel through the Arabian deserts. Freya was currently number one on Zagora's Ten Most Admired Heroines list.

"Good heavens, this Olivia is a cousin of an old friend of mine, Pitblade Yegen," said her father, running a hand through his silvery hair. She could see he was making a huge effort to stay calm. "I've never told you about Pitblade, have I?"

Pitblade Yegen? thought Zagora, suddenly curious. *He must be related to Edgar Yegen, the man who wrote the journal!*

Her father paused for a moment, then shook his head. "Pitblade and I met years ago at college and became close friends. He'd grown up on the island of Malta and always struck me as a mysterious figure with a checkered past—insanely brilliant, fluent in at least seven languages. Remember the failed expedition in Morocco I've often talked about? Pitblade organized that dig: he was on a mad search for the Pyramid of Xuloc and wanted me to translate some glyphs."

Zagora could see her dad now, with his geophysical compass, GPS, hydration backpack and snakeproof gaiters, marching into the Sahara to translate some dusty old glyphs. The Pyramid of Xuloc sounded familiar. Hadn't Edgar Yegen been looking for a pyramid, too?

"Why didn't you ever tell me about Pitblade Yegen?" she asked, though she knew her father tended to be quiet and secretive, distracted and overly absorbed in his work. Just the week before, her brother, Duncan, had seen an article in the *League of Archaeologists Review* about an award their father had received for his discovery of petroglyphs inside a necropolis in a Tunisian erg. Yet he hadn't even mentioned it to Zagora or Duncan.

Her father gave a tremulous sigh. "Things went badly in the desert. A few weeks after we started excavating, Pitblade chartered a plane to survey Zahir from the air. The plane crashed in the desert and that was the end of it all: the authorities closed down the site." His face seemed to crumple a bit. "Pitblade's body was never found."

"That's terrible, Dad!" said Zagora, thinking how sad he must have been to lose his friend. The Zahir expedition, she knew, had taken place almost twelve years earlier. That meant Pitblade Yegen had been missing in the desert since before she was even born.

"Pitblade had given me some things for safekeeping," her father continued, "including a journal that belonged to his grandfather, who was also an archaeologist."

The journal had been written by Pitblade's grandfather! Fortunately Zagora's dad didn't notice her face turning bright pink.

"Pitblade also gave me an artifact that he had from Zahir. He always joked that it gave him some kind of mysterious superpowers—but that was Pitblade for you."

Zagora froze. An artifact from Zahir? Was her dad talking about the blue stone in the attic—the Oryx Stone? Then it must be magic after all! What kind of superpowers had it given Pitblade? she wondered. Her next thought was, why hadn't it given *her* any superpowers?

As her father read on, Zagora saw his face light up with delight and astonishment.

"This is unbelievable! Olivia Romanescu says in her letter that Pitblade is alive, and he's somewhere in the desert near Zahir!" He rubbed his forehead and she sensed he was trying to rein in his emotions. Obviously

this startling news had thrown him for a loop. "He managed to contact Olivia and he gave her my address, asking
her to forward this letter and map."

"He remembered your address after all that time?"
Zagora wondered how her dad's friend could vanish into
the desert for eleven years and then suddenly turn up. It
didn't make a lot of sense.

"That doesn't surprise me. Pitblade always did have
a fantastic memory." Her father looked around. "There
should be a letter and a map— Ah, yes." He plucked the
map from her hand and began examining it.

Zagora sidled around his desk, eyeing Pitblade's letter,
tilting her head to read the scrappy writing.

Dear Charlie, it began.

> *I am not dead (I am pleased to say!). Within*
> *reach of Zahir, standing guard against deathstalkers,*
> *but fear situation getting out of hand. Please come,*
> *or I may not make it out of here. Follow the map*
> *exactly. Bring the stone. Trust no one. Your friend,*
> *Pitblade Yegen.*

Zagora's jaw dropped. The blue stone really was the
Oryx Stone! Tears welled up in her eyes at the thought of
relinquishing her beautiful stone. She pictured the dark

fire smoldering inside, the oryx etched into its chilly surface. It was her most prized possession in all the world, and now she was going to have to give it up. Talk about having your life wrecked.

"Dad, what does he mean, 'standing guard against deathstalkers'?" she asked. "Is your friend in some kind of trouble?"

He thought a moment. "Well, Pitblade often communicated using codes, so I'm guessing that's what this is," he said, although Zagora detected worry in his eyes. "Deathstalkers are a type of scorpion, but Pitblade might not be referring to scorpions at all." He squeezed the bridge of his nose with his thumb and forefinger, a habit he had when he was at loose ends. "Guess I'll be checking out flights to Morocco."

"You're going to Zahir?" Something caught in her chest and she found it hard to breathe. Zahir was at the top of another list, Lost Desert Ruins to Discover. She knew about it from years of dinner-table conversations, and even now she could picture its red walls and golden domes, its wise astronomers and sacred oryxes. She'd give anything to go to Zahir.

"No. Yes. I don't know." Her father stuffed the map and the letter back into the envelope, tossed it onto his desk and stepped away, as if the contents might blow up.

"But Zahir's buried under the sand," said Zagora. "Right, Dad?"

"Four-fifths of Zahir is under sand, it's true, but we managed to excavate the city's casbah, including the Palace of Xuloc. There is much more work to be done, obviously." He ruffled through the papers. "Zagora, I need some time alone, if you don't mind."

"What about the stamps?" she asked. "Can I have them?"

"Sure." He leaned across the desk and ripped off the corner of the envelope. "By all means, take them."

She grabbed the stamps, thinking how awesome they were—especially the 3-D one—and dashed up to her room, where she pulled out her Super Duper Magnifier and carefully arranged them on her desk. The 3-D stamp stood out from the others: on it was a shriveled insect with a tail curled like a tiny fiddlehead. How had they made it look so realistic?

When she zoomed in with the Super Duper Magnifier, her mouth went dry. It wasn't a stamp at all. The insect was squashed flat, and it was real—scarily real. Heart thudding, she peeled it off.

That was when she realized it wasn't any ordinary insect. It was a scorpion.

Luckily for her, it was dead.

NIGHT TRAIN TO MARRAKECH

Zagora pressed her face to a window smudged with dust and finger marks as the train clickety-clacked, mile after mile, through the warm Moroccan evening. Villages and towns hurtled past; black edgy shapes loomed up from the land. To the south lay the Sahara, shimmering and off-kilter, an expanse of burning sand—vast, desolate, steeped in myth—and she was heading straight for it.

This was the night train to Marrakech, a ride of eleven hours. She'd been excited to read in Edgar Yegen's journal that he'd taken the night train, too, leaving Tangier in the evening and arriving in Marrakech the next morning.

She caught her reflection in the glass: sunburned cheeks, pale blue eyes, wild black hair tangled down her back. Her father had instructed her to wear modest clothes, in keeping with Morocco's customs and culture, so she was dressed in a white blouse and baggy pants. The train compartment she shared with her dad and brother was cramped and narrow, with bunk beds on one side and a fold-down cot on the other. Overhead were racks crammed with backpacks, blankets and water bottles.

Duncan sat on the top bunk, surrounded by Fruit Roll-Ups, star charts, a Night Star Traveler blow-up globe, his planisphere and two dog-eared paperbacks on astronomy. Her brother was two years older than she, a chubby computer geek who adored astrophysics and space science. Duncan liked his life to be staid and orderly, claiming that any change in routine set off his allergies. He and Zagora had never been anywhere foreign, unless you counted the Canadian side of Niagara Falls, where their Aunt Claire had taken them the past summer. Duncan hated traveling; he was leery of trains, ferries, airplanes, taxis. . . . In fact, Duncan was leery of most forms of transportation.

"What happened to you?" she asked, gaping at the rashes up and down his legs.

"I'm breaking out in hives. My legs are on fire."

When it came to health issues, Duncan tended toward melodrama. "The hives are spreading: my whole body's being attacked!"

"It's just a rash," said Zagora. Contagious diseases and health hazards were high on her brother's mental list of things to worry about, but she didn't give them much thought.

"Yeah, but this place is germy. And in case you didn't know, this train is a perfect breeding ground for death worms." Duncan was trying to sound authoritative, she knew, while at the same time trying to scare her. "Death worms are five feet long and kill their victims by electric shock." He turned to their father. "Isn't that right, Dad?"

Dr. Pym gazed up from a well-thumbed copy of *Morocco on the Run,* his favorite travel guide. "Wrong desert," he said. "You're talking about the Mongolian death worm, a cryptid that supposedly exists in the Gobi. Czech explorer Ivan Mackerle mounted at least two expeditions in search of it."

Zagora grinned, impressed by her father's knowledge of obscure desert facts.

"What about malaria?" persisted Duncan. "Shouldn't we have gotten shots for that?"

"Malaria is rife in countries south of the Sahara,"

murmured their dad, eyes fixed on his book. "But there's a very limited risk of malaria where we're going."

Duncan flopped onto his back, staring at the ceiling with a blank expression.

"No need to hyperventilate," said Zagora, who knew her brother hated being wrong about anything. Duncan was a brainy kid, plodding and methodical, arming himself with facts gleaned from the Internet and their dad's science journals, but unfortunately he had zero imagination—in her opinion, at least. Unexpected situations threw him off balance: he just wasn't wired for change.

"You should get a plastic bubble suit." She bit her lip, trying to keep a straight face. "Then you wouldn't be so paranoid about everything." She liked the sound of *paranoid;* it had a 1950s science fiction ring to it. *Android, trapezoid, meteoroid,* all cool words.

"Don't be obtuse," he huffed. "If you watched the science channel, you'd see how disgusting those parasites look under a microscope. Hey, listen to this." He held up *Scorpions Alive!,* a booklet he'd picked up at the airport in Tangier, and began to read aloud. "'Scorpions feed on insects and spiders, grasping their prey with large claw-like pincers and tearing it apart. They will either crush the prey or inject it with venom, killing or paralyzing the prey so the scorpion can eat it.' How disgusting is that? And there are gazillions of scorpions in Morocco."

"I'm not worried," said Zagora, pretending she didn't care. She was determined not to be frightened. "Anyway, scorpions only come out at night." She'd read the booklet, too. "Guess you should've gone to astronomy camp."

Duncan turned accusingly to his father. "That's right, Dad, I'm missing astronomy camp because you said this would be a golden opportunity! You said we'd track Nar Azrak and do lots of fun things in Morocco."

The rogue planet Nar Azrak—which translated to "blue fire" in English—had been a hot topic in astronomical circles. Zagora's teacher had told her class that two generations earlier, the planet had been barely observable, and now it was brighter than Venus or Mars and several times larger than Mercury. It was thought to be moving nearer to Earth. Because the planet orbited the Earth near the equator, it was highly visible in places like Morocco.

Duncan, who checked the website narazrak.com daily, had said he'd go to Morocco only if he could bring his astronomy instruments to track the planet.

"We *will* do fun things," said their father, doodling in the margins of his book. He'd been out of sorts since the day before, when they had nearly missed their plane because at the last minute he had gone looking for Edgar Yegen's journal, turning the house upside down. Zagora had been too scared to admit she'd taken the book and had hidden it away in her backpack: she worried that her dad might get angry and not let her go to Morocco after all.

Their dad was notorious for making promises he didn't keep, something he referred to as a Personality Flaw. It was just one of many flaws, but Zagora didn't mind. Despite his quirks and shortcomings, she thought him brilliant. In addition to being an academic luminary, he was the only parent they had left. She and Duncan had no memory of their mother, who had died when they were young, and their father had never remarried.

She took another look at her brother's legs and wrinkled her nose. "Eeew, Dunkie, you're bleeding! No way I'm sleeping under your bunk." *That kid better not use up all the bandages our second day here,* she thought. Their father had packed only a limited number, and Zagora might need them once they started exploring the excavated ruins of Zahir.

"See you guys," she said, grabbing her backpack and a bottle of water. "I'll be in the corridor staying up all night to see Nar Azrak and watch the sunrise. It's called *fajr* in Arabic, right, Dad? 'The first light of dawn.'" She remembered the expression from her father's Arabic phrase book—or had she read it in Edgar Yegen's journal?

Her father nodded. "*Fajr,* yes. Such a lovely word."

"Want to come with me, Dunkie?" she asked as she headed for the door.

"Sorry, but I'm wrecked," said Duncan, scratching his legs. "I'll set up my telescope when we get to Marrakech. I even packed my new lightweight tripod."

"Stay in the corridor where I can keep an eye on you, okay?" said her father. "Don't wander off."

Zagora laughed. Sometimes her dad really didn't make much sense. Then, before leaving, she said, "How can I get lost on a train?"

⚬⚬ ⚬⚬ ⚬⚬

Zagora could think of nothing more thrilling than hanging out in the corridor, where the air smelled of peanuts and she was the only kid around. A handful of elderly Arab men in sandals and dusty robes, turbans wrapped around their heads, stood conversing in low voices. One of them opened a window and a fine dust blew in. Probably desert dust, she thought, watching the scrubby flatlands go by. She was impatient to get to the desert, but that was a few days off yet.

An old man, his cinnamon-brown face creased by the sun, passed around a basket of figs. Offering her the basket, he smiled, showing off a front tooth rimmed in gold. Zagora took a fig, devouring it greedily. It tasted fresh and sweet and stuck to the top of her mouth. If only she'd spent more time studying her dad's phrase book, she could have impressed him by telling him in Arabic that she was named for Zagora, a town south of Marrakech, in the Drâa Valley near the desert.

She sank to the floor of the train, inched up against the wall, leaned back and crossed her legs—her favorite position for reading. Reaching into her backpack, she pulled out Edgar Yegen's journal and turned to the first page, drawn once again to his quaint style of writing.

I made my reputation as an archaeologist by discovering some of the first cave paintings in North Africa. My next solo expedition will take me to the ancient city of Zahir, lost decades ago to the dry winds and blowing sands of the desert.

Zahir, home to the Azimuth tribe, was by all accounts a prosperous crossroads city and trading center, known for its great minds in astronomy, its seers and healers, its musicians, poets and architects. Scimitar oryxes, considered sacred by the Azimuth, thrived in

the nearby oases. At the city's peak, its wealth and in-
fluence had no match: Zahir's universities and libraries
lured scholars from all over the world.

Zahir began its downhill slide in the late seven-
teenth century, when the legendary Oryx Stone, embed-
ded in the Pyramid of Xuloc, was stolen. The Azimuth
elders believed that the loss of this stone would precipi-
tate the destruction of a mystical barrier that had pro-
tected the city from scorpions for centuries. Indeed, soon
after the theft, the rise of the scorpions of Zahir began,
as did the slow, painful decline of the Azimuth. Today
few descendants of the tribe remain. Sociologists predict
that within three decades they will vanish forever.

What was a mystical barrier, Zagora wondered, and
how would it protect a city like Zahir? It sounded complicated. She read on.

I intend to uncover the remains of the Pyramid of
Xuloc. Xuloc was the first king of Zahir. Under his direc-
tion the Azimuth constructed a pyramid of blue stones
thought to be meteorites. The pyramid was destroyed
in a cataclysmic upheaval, according to archaeologists.
I am eager to explore this ancient site, as I sense there
are hidden truths waiting to be found within the ruins.

Zagora wondered what sort of hidden truths he was talking about. She had a burning ambition to become a desert explorer like Edgar Yegen. Her plan was simple: she'd pitch a tent in the Sahara and survive on figs and prickly pears, traveling at night by camel, making friends with nomads. Luckily she knew a thing or two about nomads. First, they were minimalists. All they needed were goods to barter with, stars to navigate by and a few sturdy camels. Nomads were fierce and super-smart. They kept daggers tied to their wrists and knew spells that gave you bad luck for the rest of your life.

Yawning, Zagora closed the journal and dropped it into her backpack, the Oryx Stone floating dreamily through her mind, brimming with Azimuth charms and desert spells. Yet she felt a deep sadness, knowing it wasn't hers anymore. Two days earlier she'd followed her dad up to the attic, where he'd retrieved the stone from the steamer trunk; then she'd watched him pack it away. The stone, she'd realized then, was lost to her forever.

She stood up, leaning out the open window, listening to the clickety-clacking of the train. *One day,* she told herself, *I'll have a tooth all shiny gold, just like the man with the figs. And I'll get a tattoo, a tiny one—well, maybe two of them: interlinked magical Arabic symbols.* That was what you'd expect an explorer to have, along with a backpack filled with hand-drawn maps of uncharted deserts, an electromagnetic compass and a tiny headlamp for exploring tunnels.

A fierce wind struck her face, whipping her hair into knots. She breathed deeply, hoping she wasn't sucking in any bugs. Maybe that night she'd see omens. A shooting star would be good, a moon eclipse bad; comets could go either way, depending. She felt a delicious shiver run through her, thinking how she was following in the footsteps of Edgar Q. Yegen, intrepid explorer.

Through the window she saw a sun dipped in bronze, sinking behind the trees in a blaze of crimson and orange. For a moment Zagora heard a different kind of wind, low and haunting—she sensed it was coming from the desert—and a shimmer of what looked like sparkling sand fell before her eyes. Her breath caught as she glimpsed a line of reddish-gold shapes poised on the distant horizon and silhouetted against the sky.

In the light of the dying sun, she could just make out the long-legged gazelle-like creatures: scimitar oryxes, standing motionless, with elegant curved horns.

She told herself she was imagining them, because oryxes had died out a long time ago. Her dad said that the scimitar oryx was now classified as EW—Extinct in the Wild—and the only ones left were in captivity. Yet she had the oddest sensation, as if the oryxes had stepped out of time and were actually standing there in the Moroccan dusk, waiting.

Heart pounding, Zagora stepped away from the window, unsure of what she'd just seen. She glanced over at the men opening suitcases and sharing olives, cold meats and bread, talking quietly among themselves, and felt calmed by the sight of such ordinary gestures.

When she looked out the window again, the oryxes had vanished. All she saw were the darkening sky and a moon shaped like a half-melted coin, rising over the flat empty landscape.

((☉ "WELCOME TO MARRAKECH" ☉))
IN ENGLISH AND ARABIC

The train suddenly screeched to a halt, jarring Zagora awake. She had been dreaming about fantastical creatures with curved horns and the lost city of Zahir. Bleary-eyed, she sat up and looked around: she'd fallen asleep on the floor of the train. The men with their suitcases had vanished, leaving dusty footprints and the remnants of their figs.

Scrambling to her feet, she realized she'd missed Nar Azrak—and the sunrise, as well. Disappointed, she looked out the window to see where they had stopped. Outside, people were spilling off the train, shouting and laughing, lugging suitcases and parcels tied with string.

With a sigh she wiped her hands down the front of her white blouse. Almost every article of clothing she'd packed was white, because her dad said white would reflect the desert sun and keep her cooler. But she knew she'd never blend in, because nobody in Morocco was dressed like her.

The crisp whites of her clothes had already faded to dingy grays, and she'd ripped a hole in the knee of her pants. Her hair stuck out like a comic-book scribble. She looked a real mess, but suddenly it didn't matter. She was in Marrakech!

She heard her father mutter something incoherent as he lurched out of the compartment, Duncan clumping behind him, looking confused and half-asleep. She grabbed her backpack and followed them off the train. Climbing down the metal steps, she was hit by a wall of heat that took her breath away. Beyond the crush of passengers, a crimson sun floated behind a row of cypress trees, casting a golden light on the city, turning its ancient walls a deep shade of rose. *This is so incredibly beautiful,* she thought.

Seeing her father's safari hat bobbing above the crowd, she ran to catch up with him, thinking how excited he must be, returning to Marrakech after eleven years and traveling to the desert to see his long-lost friend.

"Hey, wait up!" shouted Duncan. "Don't leave me!"

She glanced back to see a familiar stocky figure in a bright yellow shirt and shark-themed Bermuda shorts, weighed down by an overloaded bag. On his feet were thick socks and hiking boots with flapping laces. Along with his tip to dress in white, their dad had advised them to pack minimally. But predictably, Duncan hadn't listened. He'd crammed his backpack to bursting, filling it with junk food, astronomy books, stargazing instruments, moon charts, *Sky & Telescope* magazines and a hundred other useless items.

Pointing a finger at the sky, Duncan stumbled over to Zagora. "See that sun?" he said. "Watch out, because any minute now it's going to spit out lethal death rays and melt everybody into puddles on the street."

"Cut it out, Duncan," she said, annoyed. Why was he making silly comments when he should be noticing all the amazing things around him?

"Welcome to Marrakech, also known as the Red City," said their father, placing a hand on each of their shoulders. "There's quite a crowd here, so let's keep together." He winked at Zagora. "Aren't you glad you brought a light rucksack? Less is more, right?"

She grinned, feeling warm and fuzzy inside, thinking

how she and her dad were savvy travelers, perfectly in sync. All they carried were backpacks purchased from an online sports outfitter: his idea. Her father prided himself on being a minimalist. She loved the way he used the word *traveler* instead of *tourist,* and the British term *rucksack*. It made her feel more foreign and explorer-like.

"Dad, could you take a photo of me and Duncan?" she asked, pulling out her digital camera. "How about over there?" She pointed to the edge of the platform, where the words MARRAKECH and ص‌اكش were painted in bright colors on a large sign. The English word looked rough and chunky next to the Arabic one, which was written in a delicate flowing script.

Pulling Duncan along with her, she laughed out loud, feeling light-headed with excitement as they stood beneath the sign.

"Smile, Duncan," she said as their father aimed the camera.

"What's to be happy about?" he muttered. "We're at the ragged end of nowhere, I've got hives all over my legs and this is exactly the kind of place to get food poisoning."

Forget the desert, thought Zagora, rolling her eyes, *Duncan might not survive Marrakech.*

As their dad snapped the photo, Duncan sneezed so hard he dropped his backpack and bags of chips and pretzels fell out, followed by a box of candy bars. All were quickly crushed underfoot by people hurrying from the train.

"Oh no!" he cried, trying to rescue everything at once. "Hey, everybody, stop!" He held up one hand like a traffic cop. "Guys, go the other direction, you're messing up my stuff!"

Embarrassed, Zagora started to walk away, but her brother looked so upset she bent down and salvaged some of the least crushed candy bars. Then they were on their way again, weaving through the hordes of people outside the station. She imagined Edgar Yegen, sweaty and exhausted, climbing off the night train from Tangier and striding into the crowds of Marrakech, dressed in khaki clothes, weathered boots and a rumpled fedora.

As her father stepped into the street to hail a taxi, Zagora experienced a jolt of excitement. This was what her teacher, Mrs. Bixby, would have called a Historic Moment: arriving in a centuries-old city a day's journey from the Sahara, where anything at all could happen.

The world seemed to twist dizzily around her, and she felt her life spinning off in unexpected directions.

Zagora, Duncan and their father rode in a taxi down a boulevard lined with orange trees. Zagora's eyes widened as they entered a vast open square in the city center, surrounded on all sides by wooden hotels and whitewashed arcades. Figures moved to and fro in a chaotic profusion of zingy, vibrant colors.

"This is the infamous Djemâa el Fna," announced her father, "one of the oldest marketplaces in the heart of Marrakech. Take a look around, kids, it's a sight you'll always remember."

Zagora was instantly enchanted by the riot of colors, the garbled voices of people buying and selling, the exotic smells of burning spices and the relentless blue of the sky. She stared at women balancing baskets on their heads and dark-eyed, copper-skinned men in pale robes with pointed hoods. Tall, stately nomads pulling camels glided past, wrapped in black turbans with only their eyes showing. Merchants spread out their wares on worn strips of carpet. And dust swirled everywhere, adding to the confusion.

"Behind those hotels at the edge of the marketplace lies the city's ancient quarter, the casbah, or medina," said their father, "an enormous honeycomb of streets and

markets. In centuries past, casbahs confused and slowed down invaders because of their narrow, twisting nature."

Zagora had seen *casbah* in her father's phrase book. *Casbah, qahwa, al-qasr*—all mysterious-sounding Arabic words. And of course, Edgar Yegen had written at length about it in his journal: the casbah of Marrakech was where he'd discovered the Oryx Stone.

She told herself it was important to follow Edgar's trail. If she could find the place where he had first seen the Oryx Stone, she might come closer to unraveling the stone's darkest, innermost secrets. One way or another, she was going to investigate the casbah.

The crowd pressed up against the taxi, some selling handmade goods. Louder-than-life sounds reverberated in Zagora's head as Berber tribesmen dangled bracelets, scarves and necklaces. Barefoot children waggled their hands, grinning at her, and she waved back. The Djemâa el Fna, she decided, was definitely moving at warp speed.

"Oh, gross," said Duncan, pointing to a grizzled man holding a snake. Tongue flicking, the snake slithered up the man's arm and coiled around his neck, its diamond-patterned skin metallic in the sunlight. Zagora shuddered. Snakes, she knew, were definitely bad omens.

Leaving the hectic marketplace behind, the driver turned down a street lined with hotels, restaurants and teahouses, then maneuvered through alleys where cats fought amid piles of garbage and hissed as the taxi rumbled past.

"I hope our hotel has air-conditioning," wheezed Duncan, leaning back in his seat, gasping a little.

Zagora turned to her brother. His face was paler than usual, and sweatier—not surprising, she thought, since he tended to panic in hot, noisy places. But what if he had an asthma attack right there in the taxi? Sure, Duncan got on her nerves, like, 99 percent of the time, but he was her brother and she didn't want anything bad happening to him.

"It's okay." He held up his inhaler. "I can breathe."

"Are we almost at the hotel?" asked Zagora, anxious to get Duncan out of the taxi.

Seated in the front, waving *Morocco on the Run,* her dad shouted directions to the driver, but Zagora could see that the man was having trouble understanding. At last the taxi stopped before a whitewashed building with turquoise shutters and double wooden doors.

"We're here," announced their father. "This is the place!"

Zagora clambered out of the taxi. The hotel looked welcoming with its gleaming walls and bright flowers entwined around the shutters. The front doors were gigantic, all arches and panels and hand-tooled wood. There was a brass knocker shaped like a turtle and a huge keyhole, before which their father crouched to peer through.

"Look at these marks, Dunkie," Zagora said, sliding her finger over the grooves in the wood—probably made by the blades of scimitars. It gave her a funny feeling inside. She'd learned about scimitars from Mrs. Bixby's class: they were long sharp swords, curved like the horns of oryxes. "I bet they had all kinds of battles and sword fights here."

"Yeah, about six centuries ago," said Duncan, fiddling with the zipper on his backpack. At least he didn't look quite so pale anymore.

"It's still creepy to think about," she said. "I mean, people ended up *dead*." Death by scimitar, how gruesome was that?

"This building was a *riad* before it was a hotel," explained their father, clearly steering the conversation in a new direction. "It's a traditional Moroccan house with an interior garden inside a courtyard. Apparently quite a few *riads* in Morocco have been converted to hotels."

Zagora grew even more excited at the prospect of staying somewhere traditionally Moroccan. Her father could easily have booked one of the chain hotels, but he said those were for tourists.

A door swung open and a tiny wrinkled woman in a head scarf peered out. With a toothless smile she ushered them inside, into a courtyard with lemon and lime trees and a burbling marble fountain in the shape of an octagon. The floor was a pattern of enameled tiles in gold and ice blue, forming geometric designs, none of them repeating.

Inhaling the fresh cool air, Zagora gazed around at the brightly colored mosaics, the rich carpets and polished furniture. Tropical plants grew everywhere, bursting through cracks in the tiles. All the rooms opened onto the courtyard, and there was no roof overhead—only sky.

"Wow, what an awesome hotel," she said.

"My book gives this place four stars out of five." Her father beamed down at her. "You kids wait here. I'll go check in."

Zagora wandered over to the fountain and sat on the marble, watching birds flit through the trees. Suddenly she remembered her scorpion—the dead one she'd mistaken for a 3-D stamp—and reached into her secret zippered pocket, relieved to find that it was still there. She'd sneaked it into Morocco thinking it might be useful in case anything went wrong. You never knew when a dead scorpion might come in handy.

Duncan clomped over, dropping his backpack on the floor and sitting down next to her. She slipped the scorpion back into her pocket.

"I'm beat," he said, wiping his brow with the back of his arm. "Hey, is there a *turtle* under that tree?" He leaned forward. "Holy cow, that's totally unhygienic."

Zagora watched a prehistoric-looking creature with orange markings and a domelike shell move slowly across the tiles. "I think a hotel turtle is cute," she said. Its eyes were crusted over, as if it had just woken up. The turtle looked old but it was nothing like the wise, magical turtle in *Magic by the Lake,* a fantasy book Mrs. Bixby had once read to the class.

She wondered if Edgar Yegen had taken a room here, since it seemed like the kind of hotel where explorers would stay—though she couldn't recall reading anything about turtles in his journal.

"Shoo!" said Duncan to the turtle. "Go away."

Duncan, who had an aversion to animals, usually found ways to avoid them. He'd totally freaked out when it was his turn to bring home the classroom hamster, Galileo, and he always came down with sore throats or stomachaches on the days his class visited the zoo. It

seemed to Zagora that her brother was interested only in things he could ponder from a distance, like planets and constellations and galaxies.

The lady with the toothless smile guided them up a staircase tiled in deep greens and blues. Their dad had reserved two rooms connected by a door, and Zagora, to her delight, was given a room of her own. She unlocked her door with an enormous key imprinted with the hotel logo (a turtle, what else?) and rushed inside. The bedroom was simple, white and minimalist. She nodded in silent approval at the rickety ceiling fan overhead, the plain white bureau and the venetian blinds drawn at the window against the glare of the sun.

Flopping onto the white bedspread, she opened Edgar Yegen's diary, skimming through the pages until she found a description of Marrakech.

A dazzling light falls through the window of my hotel room as the acrid odor of burning oil from braziers drifts up from the street below. Ah, Marrakech! Evenings I stroll through the teeming marketplace, enthralled by the frenzied madness of it all, winding my way through the casbah to the tiny, brightly lit rooms of my favorite café, where I order mineral water and a plate of roasted lamb. Concealed inside my shirt is the Oryx Stone, safe from the pickpockets who roam this city.

In two days' time I will be setting off for the town of Sumnorum, where I will procure a guide and make preparations for crossing the Sahara, in search of the buried ruins of Zahir and the pyramid of blue stones.

Flipping to another page, she read:

According to eighteenth-century explorer Alexander Serifos, the Pyramid of Xuloc was built of meteorites from Nar Azrak, which contained otherworldly powers. The Oryx Stone, also from Nar Azrak, was especially powerful, as it had been blessed by Azimuth elders. These elders were known throughout the desert as formidable seers, and claimed to possess an ancient magic that came from the stars.

Zagora sat very still, taking in these words, remembering the intense energy of the Oryx Stone. The stone came from another planet! She knew from Duncan's science fiction comic books that superpowers from outer space were totally different from earthly superpowers, and more mysterious, too. Could the Oryx Stone give humans the outer space kind of superpowers? she wondered.

If only she could have the stone again, just for a little while—maybe then she'd know.

✂ ✂ ✂

Zagora found Duncan in the lobby, sitting in a tapestry-backed armchair, absorbed in *Constellations of the Southern Hemisphere* while working his way through a bag of peanuts. Turtles crowded around his feet, and she could see him pretending not to notice them.

"Want to explore the hotel?" she asked. Duncan was boring company, but he was better than nobody. When he didn't answer, she said, "Do you think this is where they filmed *Casablanca*?" *Casablanca* was her dad's favorite movie. "I don't see a piano."

"Nope, no piano. No elevators or Internet, either, so I can't check the Nar Azrak site. This hotel is so retrograde I give it minus three stars." Duncan glanced down at the turtles, quickly tucking his feet underneath him. "I've got a bad feeling about this place. . . ."

Zagora frowned. It seemed that no matter where they were, her brother always had a bad feeling about things. But hotels weren't the real issue here: Morocco was just

\mathcal{C} 48 ✑

too far off the grid. Nothing here matched Duncan's version of reality, not even the constellations.

"Come on, Dunkie," she said, "we can go exploring."

"Go-away-I-am-busy," said Duncan in his robot voice, the voice he used when things got unpleasant and he wanted to zone out. "Don't-call-me-Dunkie-it's-very-annoying."

"Hey, space boy," she said angrily, "forget your books, we're in Morocco!" She snatched *Constellations of the Southern Hemisphere* out of his hands and danced away with it.

"Give that back!" hollered Duncan, jumping out of his chair. She watched with grim satisfaction as peanuts, pencils and star charts went bouncing across the tiles. The turtles ran for cover, moving surprisingly fast.

Hearing the desk clerk shout, Zagora dropped the book and raced away, running up the stairs, certain that Duncan—consumer of doughnuts, cheese curls and sugary cereals—was too out of shape to catch her.

Three flights later, feeling overwhelmed, she stepped onto an outdoor terrace, inhaling a heady scent of grilled lamb, perfume, spices and burning oil. She gazed out over the uneven rooftops, across patios and lines of wash flapping in the sun, watching the golden city unfold on all sides. In the distance rose the high minaret of the Kutubīyah, one of the city's most revered mosques.

With a start she saw her father sitting at a wrought-iron table beneath a sun umbrella, studying his Kummerly & Frey map. He'd had that map forever. It was even older than his guidebook. He peered up at her over his plastic-rimmed reading glasses, but she could tell he wasn't focusing on her. A part of him was still inside his map, exploring the far reaches of the desert.

"Hello, Zagora. Are you kids having fun?"

"Duncan's in the lobby with his star books and a gang of turtles, but he's in a bad mood," Zagora said. "He keeps talking in his robot voice and it's annoying."

"Duncan has a few social behaviors to iron out, that's all. I was like him at that age, shy and bookish. Right now he's hit a rough patch, but that's normal."

Zagora raised her eyebrows. Somehow *normal* wasn't a descriptor she'd apply to Duncan. *Nerdy,* yes. *Dorky,* yes. *Paranoid,* absolutely. But adults viewed him differently. Duncan was the brainy toad in the family: the geeky golden boy, adored by teachers and camp counselors alike. Aunt Claire called him "brill" (magazine-speak for *brilliant*), and his room was filled with science fair ribbons, debate club trophies and awards for programming a computerized depiction of the universe.

"But he's got no life and no friends," she argued.

"Well, you worry about Zagora, okay?" said her father with a chuckle.

She looked down at the map, torn at the creases, taped and retaped, red Xs marking the strange and important places her father had visited in Morocco. She never tired of hearing his desert stories, especially the ones about eating sheep's eyeballs and seeing a camel go mad.

She tapped a red X two-thirds of the way down. "Is this Zahir, Dad?" Her mind was overflowing with questions.

"Ah, Zahir, a place of strange and frightening beauty," he replied dreamily, "its hidden treasures lost beneath the sands. The most unforgettable of ruins, and the most mysterious."

Zagora smiled to herself. He'd lifted those sentences straight out of Edgar's journal.

"In Arabic, the word *zahir* means 'sparkling' or 'luminous'—and also 'obsession,'" he continued. "Zahir supposedly has the terrible effect of being unforgettable."

"Why is it terrible to be unforgettable?" she asked, curious to hear more.

"According to Bedouin tribes who roam the desert, whoever looked upon the city of Zahir could think of nothing else," he said in his egghead professor's voice, "and the image only sharpened with time. In the end, the memory of Zahir drove them mad." He gave one of his philosophical sighs.

"Hmm, that's really interesting, Dad." Zagora's mind went back to the ghostly oryxes she'd seen from the train the night before. "Do you think there are still scimitar oryxes around?"

"Scimitar oryxes have been extinct in Morocco for many years, unfortunately." He smoothed out the map. "Unless, of course, you choose to believe the old legends."

Zagora looked up. He'd never mentioned any legends before.

"According to my friend Pitblade, the Legend of the Oryxes says that one day the oryxes will return to Zahir and the city will rise again, but only after great chaos."

"I hope it's true," said Zagora. She thought a moment. "Did he say anything about the Oryx Stone?" It surprised her that the stone wasn't famous throughout the world or, at the very least, locked up in a museum somewhere.

"Pitblade once told me the stone has the power to attract oryxes," said her father. "The stone also has the power to repel scorpions. Not bad, eh?"

"Cool, Dad. And does the stone give its wearer superpowers?" she asked. "The stone's magic, right?" Silence. "Dad? Is the Oryx Stone magic?"

"Hmm," he murmured, leaning over his map. "Something like that, yes."

But the moment was gone. Her dad was lost in his map again.

Noticing her father's backpack on the floor, she nudged it with her foot, and it toppled sideways. A tattered drawstring pouch fell out and she glimpsed the Oryx Stone, winking in the sunlight, grains of sand spilled around it. Why hadn't he tucked the stone safely away in one of his zip-up compartments? Then she remembered that her dad sometimes got a bit distracted when he packed, especially if it was for a last-minute trip.

Feigning a yawn, she reached out, bending down, her fingers closing around the stone. It radiated a dark, intense energy and felt as smooth as a nomad's compass, as perfect as an Arabic symbol. It felt, somehow, right.

"See you later, Dad," she said, casually pushing the backpack under the table with her foot.

"Sure thing," said her father, uncapping his pen. "Have fun."

Clutching the stone, she beat a hasty retreat downstairs to the lobby. There was no sign of Duncan, so she sat by the fountain, water splashing over her hair and shoulders. She opened her hand and looked down at the Oryx Stone, rubbing her thumb over its surface; the shape of it was as spare and elegant as the poetry Mrs. Bixby called haiku. The oryx shimmered, light-struck and mystical, as if it were alive, moving in time with her heart.

Zagora placed the stone around her neck, wishing she could keep it forever.

The stone had belonged to Zahir, then to a thief; then it had vanished for centuries, until Edgar Yegen found it in Marrakech. Now it was hers—well, not really, but it was fun to pretend. Pitblade Yegen was the stone's true owner, but he'd been missing for years.

What had happened to him out in the desert? All she knew was once you went in, there was no turning back. Hadn't her father told her that a hundred times? That was the desert's secret rule, from Desert Survival 101: the desert always changes you, no matter how strong you are, no matter how smart.

No matter, even, how brave.

ᚖ THE CASBAH OF MARRAKECH ᚖ

Slamming the door behind her, Zagora stepped out into the dazzling light. Freshly scrubbed after a hot bath and smelling of soap and watermelon (a lady in a silken head scarf had given her a slice), she was dressed in a pale pink T-shirt and Capri pants. A spangled scarf, wrapped twice around her neck, fluttered in the wind. Hidden beneath the scarf, the Oryx Stone lay snug against her throat. Edgar Yegen's comment about pickpockets had made her extra cautious.

Her dad had promised to take her and Duncan to the casbah, but right then he was busy planning their journey to Zahir. Too impatient to wait, she'd decided to go solo—and secretly—instead. Nobody needed to know, and anyway, she wouldn't be gone long.

When she thought about her dad, with his quirky smile and humble nature, she knew he really was her hero—even if he was different from her friends' fathers. *Her* dad was an explorer, and he had weightier things on his mind, like translating glyphs and setting up expeditions to faraway places, so he wasn't always free to do father-daughter-type things. But that was okay with her.

Though sometimes, just sometimes, she wondered what it would be like to have a mother to do fun things with: someone she could confide in, who would take her shopping and help pick out clothes for school, someone who'd fix her hair so it didn't always look so messy. It saddened her to think that it would never happen.

Traipsing through the zigzag alleys, Zagora darted around piles of garbage and hissing cats, imagining Edgar Yegen walking down these streets. She pictured him in the casbah, bartering for a blue stone that looked almost supernatural. Edgar had described it this way:

> I happened upon a shabby backstreet square in the magnificent city of Marrakech, crowded with so many wooden stalls it was almost impossible to thread one's way through.

Now, eager to discover more, Zagora was intent on retracing Edgar's steps.

She charged across a dusty road to the Djemâa el Fna, dodging taxis, bicycles and horse-drawn carts. In the packed marketplace, the sun beat down and the air vibrated with nonstop babbling. Trying to get her bearings, she hurried past tarot card readers, snake charmers and a waiflike girl drawing henna tattoos on the arms of tourists. Three small children tugged at Zagora's arm, refusing to let go. Unsure what to do, she handed them each a coin.

At the far end of the marketplace stood hotels made of weather-beaten wood, painted in pale colors. Men wearing turbans and long robes she knew were called djellabas sat at outdoor tables with cups of coffee. Behind them, light sizzled on the walls of the cafés.

Taking a deep breath, Zagora stepped out of the sun-drenched square and into a labyrinth of streets, into the ancient quarter: the casbah. She scampered along alleys no wider than footpaths, enchanted by the green-painted doorways, the flat-roofed shops, the jumbled houses and clay walls jutting out above her head. There were tiny stores no bigger than closets, where merchants hawked perfumes, olive oil, pistachios, salt scrubs and caftans. So many odd and offbeat things were for sale she didn't know where to look. Everything in the casbah seemed to be exactly as Edgar Yegen had described.

Turning a corner, Zagora heard a low, haunting wind—she was sure it was coming from the desert. Sparkling grains of sand drifted down to the street. She felt the hairs on her neck rise as she saw a hazy copper glow ahead, at the far end of the alley. More curious than frightened, she stepped forward. The light, altogether a different quality from sunlight, was turning the air a powdery gold.

A shadow moved toward her and she saw—or thought she saw—a glowing oryx, its long, lithe body filling the alleyway. *This is crazy,* she thought, staring at the curved horns and golden fur. *Oryxes are extinct.*

The oryx threw back its head and snorted, blowing plumes of dust through its nostrils. Somehow its presence calmed her, lifting away her fears, and she felt her heart melt just a little. The creature was beautiful beyond description, airy and translucent, like the oryxes she'd seen from the train. She longed to throw her arms around its neck.

"Oryx?" she whispered, certain that she was seeing a ghost. "Why are you here? Hey, do you want to see the Oryx Stone?"

As she reached for the stone, shouting and laughter

echoed through the alley, along with the sound of running feet. Startled, the ghost oryx backed away. Zagora watched as the golden light dimmed. The outline of the creature grew smoky, then it began to fade, as if a giant eraser were rubbing it out. Moments later the oryx was gone—as if it had never been there at all.

Somewhat dazed, she tramped down the alley. From nearby came a high-pitched giggling, and with a chill of unease, she walked a little faster, feeling alone and vulnerable. As she navigated through the dark warren of streets, she heard the giggling again. The sound seemed to be coming from all around her. Unable to shake the sense of being followed, she began to run, surprised to discover that she was truly frightened.

She sprinted around a corner and up a flight of crooked stone steps. Here the mud houses were built so close together that no light fell between them. Ducking through a gateway with puzzle-shaped carvings, Zagora stumbled into a courtyard of whirling red dust. The small square was crowded with shoppers, vendors and wooden stalls.

This could be where Edgar had found the stone! He'd written about going through a gateway, and this matched the bustling marketplace he'd described—more or less. Excited, Zagora hurried from one stall to the next, mouth watering as she breathed in the smells of roasted peppers and grilled fish. Her stomach lurched as she spotted the head of a sheep swinging from a plastic rope and, next to it, an eel swarming with flies.

At the center of the square a bearded man knelt on the ground, hammering out silver bracelets, each one with a different design. He set down his hammer and gave her a kind smile.

"Please, have a look at my beautiful silver," he said.

Reaching into her pockets and finding them empty, except for the dead scorpion, Zagora realized she'd given away all her coins. She eyed the bracelets longingly and said, "Next time I'll bring my money."

Once again she had a sense of being followed. Her scalp prickled when she saw a gang of kids scuff through the dust, throwing savage glances her way. In the lead was a tall, skinny girl, robes billowing, hair swirling, arms whipping at her sides.

Leaning forward, the silversmith whispered: "Take care, my little friend, they have their eyes on you." He nodded toward the band of children, who were dawdling from one stall to the next. Goggle-eyed, they sniggered and pushed one another, stirring up the dust; a woman selling fruit shouted and they danced away laughing.

The man went back to hammering bracelets. Zagora

noticed the tall girl staring at her with a cold, hard gaze. Determined not to act frightened, she glared back, taking in the sharp cheekbones, the copper skin and inky eyes. Coils of henna-red hair floated around her face, not quite covering a purple bruise on her forehead. There were tiny silver stars sewn into the girl's veils and robes.

She stepped forward, grinning, and Zagora caught a strong whiff of mint.

"Give it over," demanded the girl, holding out her hand.

"I don't have any money," said Zagora, trying to sound brave. She saw that the bruise on the girl's forehead was a tattoo: a scorpion with its stinger in the air. The image made her shiver in spite of the warm sun.

With a crooked finger the girl pointed to the scarf wrapped around Zagora's throat. "There is something there," she said darkly, "around your neck."

Zagora felt a thrill of fear. There was no way the girl could know about the Oryx Stone—or could she? *If she goes near it, I'll scratch her eyes out,* Zagora thought fiercely.

"I am not here to take away your treasure," said the girl, as if reading her thoughts. "I only want to have a look." She smiled, showing a row of small, uneven teeth.

Those teeth could use a good brushing, thought Zagora. Then she tried to unthink it, just in case the girl really

was a mind reader. "Why do you have that tattoo?" she blurted out, pointing to the scorpion.

"Because I am not like the others." The girl pushed back her hair with long fingers. "I have powers that others do not. I know how to tame scorpions and I keep spells in the palms of my hands, like a sorceress. I can speak to swarms of bees. Sometimes I see great distances through the eyes of the oryx."

Impressed, Zagora stared wide-eyed at the girl. What did it mean to see through an oryx's eyes? She supposed magic was involved. This girl was a wild card, as her dad would say, unlike anyone she'd ever known: super-wired, edgy, ready to fly apart—maybe even slightly insane.

"I have more scorpions. See?" The girl lifted her foot, wriggling her mud-caked toes. Around her thin ankle were tattoos of scorpions and oryxes, interlinked. "Evil and good, good and evil," murmured the girl. "It is important to balance the two."

Zagora stared, transfixed, thinking of Marietta von Stollen, a girl who had worn dresses with frilly collars to Mrs. Bixby's class and had a dragonfly birthmark on her wrist. Some kids said Marietta was a prophet, and others swore she knew antigravity spells. Marietta had once predicted the flattening of a chicken farm by a hurricane and the next day it had really happened.

This girl was mysterious, too, but in a scarier way.

"Who are you?" asked Zagora, feeling her mind grow foggy, as if the gears inside her head were jamming. "Do you know magic?"

"My name is Amina Ash-Shaulah," said the girl. "Yes, of course I know magic." She rolled her eyes, as if Zagora had asked a silly question. "Please, call me Mina. Mee-na. I am named after an ancient Muslim princess," she added in a haughty tone. "It is an Arabic word meaning 'trust-worthy.'"

Zagora wasn't so sure about that. She thought she remembered a character named Mina in Duncan's comic-book version of *Dracula*. Not wanting to be outdone, she boasted, "My dad named me after a town in Morocco, and nobody in the whole U. S. of A. has my name."

Mina's eyes shrank to dark holes. "You are Zagora, yes?"

Zagora's mouth fell open. This girl was ten times freakier than Marietta von Stollen.

"I know many things." Mina's lips curved into a thin smile. "I learn from my grandmother, who is a seer; her magic comes from the stars." Her voice fell to a whisper. "We are a desert tribe, very old, very powerful—we are beyond memory."

The raggedy group of kids crowded behind Mina, smirking and elbowing one another.

Magic from the stars sounded strangely familiar to Zagora. Then she remembered: she'd read it in Edgar Yegen's journal. She leaned forward, intrigued. "You mean you're off the map?" Her father used the phrase *off the map* when referring to remote desert settlements never charted by cartographers.

Mina lifted her bony shoulders. "Not on the map, no." Then a greedy look crossed her face and she snapped her fingers. The kids shuffled in closer, throwing off waves of horrid smells—unwashed clothes and dirty feet—that settled over Zagora in a cloud of dust.

"Give me the stone," said Mina in a quiet voice. "I must take it to Grandmother. She will know if it is the one we seek."

Zagora, frightened, sensed she was in over her head. "You can't have it," she said defiantly. "I borrowed it from my dad and he'll hit the roof if anything happens to it."

Mina's eyes flashed. "If it is the stone of the oryx, it belongs to my tribe." Mina's hand flew out and she grasped the leather ribbon. "You have no right to keep it."

"Let go!" shouted Zagora, giving the girl a push.

Mina lost her balance and one of the boys crowding

around her caught her before she fell. Swiftly she righted herself, hissing through her teeth, her eyes going black, and for one heart-stopping moment Zagora glimpsed a face that was light-years from human. She backed away, her stomach twisting into knots.

"Get it!" Mina shouted to the boys.

Zagora screamed as they flew at her, tackling her to the ground, dust flying. Eyes shut, she clenched the stone, thinking, *I'll never give it up, never. . . .* Before they could grab it, she heard shouts and the thud of bare feet on the ground. Opening her eyes, she saw Mina and her gang tearing through the marketplace, the bearded silversmith chasing close behind.

Moments later he returned to Zagora. "Go quickly, little one." He helped her up off the ground. "You are not safe here. They will be back."

Clutching the precious stone to her chest, Zagora darted out of the square and under the gateway, racing through the maze of streets, anxious to return to the fever-spiked chaos of the Djemâa el Fna.

ᴏᏀ ᴏᏀ ᴏᏀ

"Where the heck have you been?" asked Duncan as Zagora burst into the hotel lobby. He was sitting on an overstuffed divan, leafing through *Sky & Telescope* magazine. "Dad thought you got kidnapped! He's a nervous wreck."

"I wasn't gone long—was I?" she said, feeling her heart sink.

Duncan peered over his magazine. "Long enough."

On her way back she had gotten lost. Surprisingly, the name and address of her hotel had flown completely out of her head. A fatal mistake when you were an explorer: if you lost your way, your expedition was doomed.

Upstairs in her room she fell onto the bed, exhausted. How had she gotten mixed up with an off-the-wall girl like Mina? It was obvious that the girl had intended to steal the stone.

To calm herself, Zagora dug Edgar Yegen's journal out of her backpack and began to read.

We leave the town of Sumnorum at the crack of dawn, the fajr, when the sky is turning an ashen pink. Mohammed, my guide, has dark eyes and a quick smile; he wears a turban, a homespun burnoose and sandals of goat leather. Our camels raise clouds of red dust and the sand crumbles underfoot, shifting as we make our way deeper into the desert. Mirages float in the distance, suspended between sky and earth.

We reach a tract of sand where the earth has been

baked by the wind and sun. The sky is the deepest blue imaginable. In the distance I can make out a stone tower, high on an outcropping: the infamous Tower of the Enigmas, built looking over Zahir, guarding the city. I can see what look like scimitar oryxes, luminous and glowing, ranged around the base of the tower—as if waiting for me to arrive. Their appearance is unearthly.

Edgar had seen oryxes in Morocco, too? His phrase *luminous and glowing* described exactly her ghost oryx! How freaky was that?

Suddenly there was a pounding on her door. "Zagora, open up!" boomed her father, sounding like a crime scene investigator.

She sprang to the door and he strode in, looking distraught. "Where on earth have you been? Duncan and I were searching all over for you! I was about to call the police."

Staring at her feet, Zagora tried to imagine what a Moroccan jail cell looked like—worse than the third-floor girls' bathroom at school, she was pretty sure.

"You didn't go to the casbah, did you?" Her father was using his blustery chief inspector's voice, and it was clear he was seriously upset. "You're covered in dust and you smell like spices. Zagora, those winding dark alleys go on for miles! That was extremely reckless of you."

"I know, I know, but I really wanted to go." She felt terrible, knowing she'd let him down. No use trying to defend herself; her father always caught her making things up. Sometimes she wondered if he had a lie detector machine wired into his brain. Still, she knew he'd get over it.

"I wasn't really lost," she said in a meek voice. A turtle appeared in the doorway, looking like it wanted to ask a question. "And I didn't stay there very long at all."

Her father gave a weary sigh. "Duncan and I were both worried when we couldn't find you." He reeled back, his foot just missing the turtle.

Zagora frowned. Duncan had been worried about her? That seemed highly unlikely.

"Any more shenanigans like this," her father added with a severe look, "and you'll be on the next plane home—to Auntie Agnes."

Zagora cringed at the thought of grim Auntie Agnes, who worked in a mustard factory and had moon-pebble eyes. Agnes, her least favorite aunt, was one of many relatives she and Duncan stayed with when their father went on expeditions.

"It won't happen again," she said earnestly. "Hey, guess what, I met this—" She started to say *weird girl,* then stopped. Telling her dad about Mina might not be a good idea. He'd ask questions, and if he found out she'd sneaked off with the Oryx Stone, she'd be in big trouble.

Luckily he hadn't been listening.

"I haven't forgotten the Galileo incident, you know," he said, closing the door behind him with a definitive *clunk*.

When Duncan had brought Galileo, the class hamster, home for the weekend, Zagora, feeling sorry for it, decided to let the hamster stretch its furry legs. But when she opened the cage door, it darted down a heating duct. Weeks later Duncan had found Galileo, by then a hamster mummy, behind the washing machine. At first Zagora denied any wrongdoing. When she finally admitted she might have opened the cage accidentally, she lost two weeks' allowance and missed going to the Big Top Circus. Worst of all, her credibility rating in the Pym household had plummeted to zero. Now it seemed she was going to have to prove herself all over again.

Looking befuddled, the turtle peered up at her. Its vacant expression reminded her of Duncan.

ꙮ DINNER AT THE CAFÉ MEKNES ꙮ

Zagora lay stretched on her stomach beside the fountain in the hotel lobby, coaxing a turtle (nicknamed Duncan II) to climb over an empty candy box. Her brother sat nearby, polishing his telescope lenses. Hearing someone whistling "If I Were a Rich Man," she looked up to see her father coming down the stairs. He wore a crisp yellow shirt with blue parrots and multi-pocketed safari pants—his idea of dressing up. Zagora considered his taste in clothes part of his unique personality.

"Ready for dinner, kids?" he called. "I've booked the Café Meknes for seven o'clock."

"Man, I'm so hungry I could eat a camel," said Duncan.

Zagora glared at him. "Don't say that, Dunkie." As a little girl she'd been devoted to a toy camel named Lila, which she'd carried everywhere she went, and even now she adored camels. On her list of Favorite Desert Animals, camels were second only to oryxes.

"Olivia Romanesçu, Pitblade's cousin, will be joining us," their father added.

"Wow, fantastic!" said Zagora, imagining a wiry, sunscorched woman in khaki who rode camels all over the desert, looking for buried cities. "I can't wait to meet her."

"Hey, hear that, guys?" Duncan set down his telescope. "They're talking about Nar Azrak on TV!" Jumping out of his chair, he lumbered through an open archway.

Zagora and her father followed him into a room with velvet-upholstered chairs ranged around a tiny black-and-white television with rabbit-ear antennas on top.

"One country which has come under scrutiny regarding the rogue planet is Morocco," a British announcer was saying. "Astronomers at the Royal Observatory in Edinburgh have determined that Nar Azrak's orbit is shifting significantly closer to Earth, and today issued warnings that the planet is moving at an increasing speed."

A picture flashed on the screen, showing Earth and the surrounding planets, with a broken line depicting the path of Nar Azrak. "As this drawing illustrates," the announcer continued, "Nar Azrak is moving at an unheard-of rate. Astronomers are trying to gauge how near it will come to our planet. Some predict that it may even collide with Earth. If their views prove correct, Morocco, which lies directly in Nar Azrak's path, risks complete destruction."

Duncan fell into a stunned silence. Zagora couldn't quite believe what she was hearing.

"Can we go home, Dad?" asked Duncan quietly. "Like, *today*?"

Oh no, thought Zagora. What if her dad was having second thoughts about bringing his kids to Morocco?

"Don't worry, nothing's going to happen," said their father reassuringly. "These astronomers are alarmists, Duncan. They thrive on worst-case scenarios. And I for one don't believe them: this is media hype, pure and simple. Trust me, we have nothing to fear."

ა ა ა

In the cool of the evening, the Pym family made their way through the serpentine streets of Marrakech. Zagora sniffed the spice-filled air, feeling the dry wind against her face. All around her rose deep voices from the shadows and sounds of children playing in the alleys. None of the Pyms mentioned Nar Azrak, and Zagora pushed any negative thoughts out of her head. She wasn't going to let those doom-and-gloom astronomers wreck her visit to Morocco.

"Notice how you can't see any stars?" said Duncan. "That's light pollution, same as we get at home. Lights from the city wash out the night sky."

Looking up, Zagora realized that it was impossible to see even one star overhead. That meant all Duncan's astronomical charts and instruments were useless. She felt a little bit sorry for him: stargazing was the one thing he'd been looking forward to on this trip.

Moments later they were sitting at a table on the terrace of Café Meknes, overlooking the bustling torch-lit markets of the Djemâa el Fna. Zagora could hear music from street performers drifting up, mixed in with shouts of vendors and the babbling crowd.

Tense and impatient, she was eager for Olivia Romanescu to appear. The Oryx Stone lay discreetly hidden beneath the folds of Zagora's silky purple blouse, and she was wearing her fanciest clothes, including her floral-print harem pants, a gift from trendy Aunt Claire.

(She sometimes found herself wishing Claire could be her mom, because it would be nice having a mom with such cool taste in clothes.)

Their father cautioned her and Duncan not to ask any impertinent questions. "Let me do the talking," he told them. "After all, Ms. Romanesçu is a total stranger. We don't want to overwhelm her."

"But there are things I want to ask," said Zagora, watching waiters hurry past with trays of jasmine-scented couscous and grilled meat on skewers. "Like where did she travel in the desert and did she meet any nomads and sleep under the stars—stuff like that."

Her father threw her one of his stern looks. She knew he worried about her becoming noisy and overexcited, which often happened when she talked about the desert.

"What makes you think Ms. Romanesçu spends time in the desert?" he asked.

"This Olivia has to be an explorer, I just know she is." Zagora was dying to meet a fellow adventuress who shared her passion for the desert. "Why else would she be in Morocco?"

"Lots of reasons," said Duncan. "She could be a tomb robber or an illicit trader—did you know there's a huge black market trade in meteorites these days?—or she could be spying for the Russians, using Romanesçu as her nom de guerre."

Ignoring Duncan, who in her opinion watched way too many spy movies, Zagora went on: "So, Dad, does the Oryx Stone really belong to Pitblade Yegen?" After reading Edgar's journal, she was bursting with questions. "Is he the true owner?"

Her father nodded. "The stone was bequeathed to him by his grandfather. And as there are no Azimuth left to claim it, Pitblade is indeed the rightful owner."

Hmm, thought Zagora. *Mina was trying to trick me, saying the stone belonged to her tribe. She was probably planning to sell it.*

"Did you bring the stone with you, Dad?" asked Duncan. "To show to Ms. Romanesçu?"

Zagora froze. She'd meant to sneak the stone back into her father's pack, but she hadn't been able to resist wearing it one last time.

"You know, I've been so caught up planning our trip to the desert I totally forgot," said her dad, looking sheepish. "It's still in my rucksack." He grinned.

Zagora gave a secret sigh of relief. He hadn't noticed it was missing—not yet, anyway.

Their father frowned. "A pity I couldn't find Edgar Yegen's journal. I was certain I'd left it in my desk drawer.

Oh well, it'll turn up eventually and I'll give it back to Pitblade."

Zagora squirmed in her seat, feeling a trifle (but not too) guilty, for sneaking off with the journal. She had every intention of giving it back to Pitblade Yegen— once she'd finished reading it.

"Was Edgar Yegen famous?" she asked, eager to change the subject.

Her father slipped on his reading glasses and opened the menu. "Edgar made many important discoveries in North Africa and was highly respected in archaeological circles. Zahir, sadly, was his final expedition. It was there he met his untimely demise."

"Edgar Yegen died in *Zahir*?" asked Zagora, shocked by this revelation. "But . . . how? Did the stone have a curse on it or something?" She hoped that wasn't true, because she loved the Oryx Stone so much.

Before her father could answer, a woman's voice cut through the air. "Halloooo, Dr. Pynn? I'm looking for a Dr. Pynn! Anyone here by that name?"

"Uh-oh," said Duncan, slouching down in his chair. "This doesn't sound good. . . ."

Zagora gave a little gulp, seeing a stout woman approach their table in a flurry of vibrant colors, moving with a careless elegance. Olivia Romanesçu was big boned and heavily made up, her wheat-colored hair swept high into a topknot. In the light of the overhead lanterns she looked not so much like a desert explorer as like an aging film star from a wacky comedy film.

Striding behind her were two men in dark glasses: the taller one had a goatee and shaved head; the shorter, toadlike man had a thin mustache that looked drawn on. Zagora noted that both wore cream suits, what appeared to be authentic snakeskin shoes, and serious expressions.

"Hey, cool, she's got bodyguards," said Duncan. Turning to Zagora, he whispered, "Olivia must be the brains behind a Moroccan crime syndicate."

"Charmed, I'm sure, Dr. Pynn," said Olivia Romanesçu in a throaty voice, extending a thick freckled hand garnished with rings.

Dr. Pym looked up into the woman's wide, pale face. "The name's Pym." Zagora noticed that his eyes looked startled behind his reading glasses. "Charles Pym."

Her dad probably hadn't been expecting such an imposing presence. It seemed when Olivia sat down next to Zagora, she took up all the breathing space at the table.

"He's Dr. Charles W. Pym, actually," said Zagora shyly. "Our dad has two doctoral degrees."

The woman gave a faint smile and arranged her voluminous robes. "Is that so? Most impressive." A rich scent of lime and lavender drifted off her shoulders as she turned to address their father. "We are birds of a feather, Dr. Pym, are we not? Both of us are scientists, one working to unlock the secrets of the past, the other investigating medicines of the future. A perfect balance, wouldn't you agree?"

The stone-faced guards took up positions behind Olivia's chair. Zagora thought her makeup was amazing—terra-cotta lipstick and eyes outlined in black, like Cleopatra—and her dazzling clothes, cut from expensive fabrics, were straight out of a glossy magazine. *Glamorous,* that was the word: Olivia Romanesçu was glamorous.

"Toxins," she heard Olivia say as the woman launched into a summary of her career as an entomologist, "and the effects of insect venom on human nervous tissue."

She talks so fast, thought Zagora. *Sounds like she has an English accent—sort of.* She listened with rapt attention while Olivia talked about cutting-edge experiments with snake poison and scorpion venom, and perilous journeys to remote areas of Senegal, the Maldives and the jungles of Brazil.

"I'm taking my experiments to a completely new level," Olivia told them. "By manipulating toxins through genetic engineering, I intend to create a new class of

drugs: painkillers based on scorpion venom, to treat severe pain from trauma, extreme injuries and even organ transplants."

Olivia was talking so fast that Zagora had trouble keeping up with her. Chin in hands, Zagora sat thinking how Mrs. Bixby would have a fit listening to all those run-on sentences. Even so, she was impressed: Olivia was obviously a top-notch scientist. The details of her experiments were fuzzy, but she had a way of making her work sound dramatic. Zagora wondered what it would be like to have such a smart and sophisticated woman for a mother.

"When my cousin first went missing, I thought, *How absurd,*" said Olivia, moving on to a new topic. "Pitblade is a formidable explorer, a genius at desert navigation." Zagora watched the woman's eyes grow moist with tears. "But lost he was—for eleven years."

"I wanted to thank you for forwarding Pitblade's letter to me," said Dr. Pym. "The good news is he's alive."

"Alive, yes, but is the man sane?" snapped Olivia. "Of that I am not so sure."

Zagora could see her dad frowning.

"Did he indicate that he was in any sort of trouble?" asked Dr. Pym.

Olivia pushed a loose strand of hair back into her

topknot. "His letter was cryptic, very brief. Between the two of us, I fear my cousin has gone mad—quite mad indeed. As the saying goes, 'The desert consumes the reckless and destroys the weak.' Not to mention that insanity runs in the family."

Uh-oh, thought Zagora, *this conversation's going downhill fast.*

"I do not believe for one moment that Pitblade is insane," said Dr. Pym tersely, glowering at Olivia across the table. "Disoriented, perhaps . . . but who wouldn't be? And Pitblade tends to write messages using code and metaphor, which can be quite confusing."

"Ah, *merci.*" Olivia gave the waiter a regal nod as he set down a plate of braised lamb with dates. "Pitblade sent his letter by falcon to the American embassy in Marrakech. Can you imagine, *falcons* in this day and age?"

In her mind's eye Zagora saw a falcon land on the embassy roof, a rolled message tied to its claw with camel-gut string. Better yet, maybe it would be fitted out with a mini backpack.

Duncan scooped up a forkful of *tagine,* a rich stew of meat and vegetables. "Hey, I saw this BBC program about pigeons on top-secret World War II missions, delivering messages to Allied troops behind enemy lines."

He stuffed the food into his mouth, chewing fast. "Now-adays you could send messages by remote-controlled model helicopters. Right, Dad?"

"Yes, that's possible," said their father, tapping a finger against his front tooth. Not a good sign, Zagora knew. "Did you bring the letter Pitblade wrote to you?" he asked Olivia.

"No," she said, shaking her head, "because I didn't want to risk having it lost or stolen. Simply put, he wants the Oryx Stone. If you prefer, my men could deliver this artifact to him. Save you the trouble of going to the desert."

"Thanks, but it's no trouble at all," said Dr. Pym. "I'm looking forward to this journey."

Olivia sniffed, as if she found the subject distasteful. Zagora had a funny feeling that she wasn't all that fond of her cousin Pitblade.

"About this stone . . . I'm anxious to have a look at it, if I may, to check its authenticity." Gem-studded brace-lets clashed together as Olivia held out her hand. "You do have the Oryx Stone with you, don't you, Doctor?"

Zagora noticed that Olivia's eyes were unusually bright and that an eagerness crept into her voice every time she mentioned the Oryx Stone.

"I assure you, the stone is quite safe," said Dr. Pym.

If only she knew, thought Zagora, feeling a bit smug, *the Oryx Stone's right here under her nose!*

"Like you, Ms. Romanesçu," Dr. Pym continued breezily, "I prefer not to take chances."

Duncan kicked Zagora under the table and they exchanged looks. *My dad's one cool character,* Zagora thought, watching Olivia press her lips into a tight line.

"Should anything happen to my cousin," said Olivia when her mint tea arrived, "this artifact—the Oryx Stone—would revert to next of kin. That would be, of course, yours truly."

Stirring his cardamom-scented coffee, Dr. Pym narrowed his eyes. "Nothing is going to happen to Pitblade."

Zagora could almost see sparks flying between the two adults.

"How about if I send my men around to your hotel on Rue Moulay Ismail tonight, to collect the stone?" Olivia gave an odd little laugh that made Zagora wonder if she was somehow threatening her father.

She noticed her dad glancing nervously at the bodyguards. Why was Olivia sending bodyguards to pick up the stone?

"That won't be necessary, Ms. Romanesçu. I'll deliver

the Oryx Stone to you myself," said Dr. Pym in a brisk, confident tone. "I'll be at your apartment first thing to-morrow."

Suddenly Zagora was struck by a wild notion. She reached into her trousers for the dead scorpion, stiff and springy at the bottom of her pocket. *Nobody threatens my dad and gets away with it,* she thought. *I'll show her.* She slid her hand across the top of Olivia's glass of tea, which was sitting untouched next to her plate.

She looked around quickly, making certain that no one was watching, and dropped the dead scorpion into the tea. It landed with a soft *ker-plunk* and sank to the bottom of the glass.

Duncan suddenly gave an earsplitting shriek. Mouth quivering, he pointed to Olivia's glass. "Sc-scorpion!" he stuttered.

Zagora watched the scorpion paddle in circles, candlelight bouncing off its shiny black carapace, and her heart started to thump. It was *alive*! To Zagora's surprise, Olivia didn't bat an eye. She looked more disdainful than terrified by finding a scorpion in her tea.

Leaning over, Olivia hissed into Zagora's ear: "You'll pay for this little prank, my dear, don't think you won't."

Feeling a shiver go through her, Zagora pulled away.

"It's getting bigger!" shrilled Duncan. "Look!"

Zagora looked back at the table and nearly choked. Pincers waving, the scorpion was very much alive—and at least four times its original size, its angular body filling the entire glass.

ᑖᑐ ESCAPING MARRAKECH ᑐᑖ

In her dream, Zagora was Freya Stark, spirited adventuress and desert navigator, perched high on a camel, swaying to the rhythm of a snake charmer's flute, plodding across burning sands. A line of camels trailed behind her, followed by Duncan on his bicycle, tires popping. Overhead sailed Nar Azrak, turning the stars an icy blue. The constellations were shaped like oryxes. No need for a map: the Oryx Stone was guiding them straight to Zahir.

In the distance stood a shadowy figure, face hidden under a brimmed hat: Edgar Yegen. Time was running out, and Zahir was in mortal danger. Galloping across the dunes, Zagora grew frantic as the dream dissolved around her. Edgar looked ghostly, fading into the sand, taking his journal with him. The stone around her neck turned to dust.

She awoke, startled, finding herself in a bed with white pillows and a thin white blanket. She had no idea where she was—until she heard the *whickety-whick* rhythm of the ceiling fan, pushing around the dusty air. Marrakech!

Switching on the bedside lamp, she opened Edgar Yegen's journal, carefully turning the fragile pages to find the place where she'd left off.

> The Tower of the Enigmas is magnificent, with inscriptions and glyphs and finely detailed reliefs portraying the history of Zahir. Some reliefs are cleverly hidden in the stone architecture of the tower, making them difficult to find. Yesterday I discovered a foretelling I recognized as the Circle of Four, set inside a niche within the tower wall, hidden in the shadows where no light fell. Extraordinary.
>
> As we leave the tower, the sun beats down upon us, violently bright. From beneath the hood of my burnoose I see the red-walled city of Zahir rising up at the end of a small, narrow valley, even though the city has been gone for centuries. Mohammed and I stop to drink warm goat's milk, thick with fat, and chew

crushed dates mixed with bitter desert herbs. We plan
to set up camp near the Palace of Xuloc, which is still
buried beneath the sand.

Zagora couldn't bear to read any more. It was too painful, knowing that by the end of the journal, Edgar Yegen would be dead.

Her thoughts turned to Café Meknes and an icy shudder ran through her. She had no idea how the scorpion had come alive or had suddenly grown so large. Duncan said he'd never seen anything so abnormal in his life; their father had quickly paid and hustled them out of the restaurant. Sneaking the scorpion into Olivia Romanesçu's tea hadn't been such a clever idea after all. Still, Zagora wasn't sorry she'd done it.

She checked her glow-in-the-dark Indiana Jones travel clock: four-thirty a.m.—the perfect time to return the Oryx Stone. Hopping out of bed, she grabbed Duncan's super-small titanium Teknik-mini flashlight, which she'd borrowed without asking, and opened the door connecting the two rooms. Predictably, her brother lay snoring under the covers. Her father's bed was empty, but that wasn't surprising: he often had trouble sleeping and wandered around the house during the night.

She found her dad's backpack under his bed and

fished out the drawstring pouch. With a pang of regret, she dropped the stone inside. If only she could keep it a little longer.

As she zipped up the bag, her father's leather wallet tumbled out. Like many of his possessions, it had a for-lorn, ready-to-fall-apart look to it. Opening it up, Zagora rummaged through the credit cards, documents and dir-ham notes, until she found two interesting items: a photo and a newspaper clipping.

Curious, she unfolded the clipping and read:

> Pitblade Yegen, a resident of Malta, has been re-ported missing in the Sahara. Mr. Yegen was last seen in a Piper Cub plane south of Marrakech, where he was carrying out excavations of the buried city of Zahir. Fol-lowing a three-week search, he remains missing, pre-sumed dead. Mr. Yegen is the grandson of renowned archaeologist Edgar Quince Yegen, who perished in the desert in 1939 after

The rest of the article was torn off. Edgar Yegen died in the desert after . . . *what?* Being attacked by hyenas? Trampled by wild camels? Her father had said Yegen's demise was untimely, but what did that mean? She had a creepy feeling that Edgar hadn't met a peaceful death.

She beamed her light on the photograph: a man on a dune, dressed in white trousers and a flowing shirt, stood with arms outstretched, as if embracing the sky. He had a short beard and wild curly hair. A huge sun loomed up behind him. There was, she thought, something Zenlike about his gaze, the way he looked straight into the lens of the camera. Some cool Batman type of guy. Pitblade Yegen: missing, presumed dead.

Quickly Zagora put everything away, worried that her dad might show up. Leaving Duncan's flashlight on his bed stand, she hurried back to her room, where pale gray light filtered in through the open blinds. It was almost dawn! Throwing a shirt over her nightgown, she raced upstairs to the rooftop terrace, hoping to catch the sunrise.

As she reached the top step, she heard her father's voice, sounding angry and frustrated. Puzzled, she crouched down to listen.

"I don't understand," he was saying. "You're a desert guide; this is what you do. So why exactly can't you take me to Zahir?"

"It is regrettable," replied a man with a thick accent. In the muted light Zagora saw a shaggy-haired figure cloaked in brown robes. "Monsieur, Zahir is far too dangerous. Scorpions, dust storms, sinkholes—there is a long history of unpleasant things. You will not find anyone to take you to Zahir, for the reasons I am telling you."

"Look, I'll pay you double." Her father paced back and forth. "I've come all the way from the United States and I don't intend to turn back now. I'm returning an artifact to a friend, and it is essential that I see him."

"I understand what you are saying," the man replied, but Zagora could tell by the tone of his voice that he didn't understand at all. "Artifacts fetch excellent price in the casbah."

"It's actually a meteorite. Not quite the same thing."

"Very popular, meteorites." The man pulled up his hood. "I can find a buyer for you."

Zagora thought she remembered Duncan saying something about a black market trade in meteorites, but she knew her dad would never get mixed up in anything illegal. He was too honest a guy.

"It's not for sale," snapped her father. Placing his hands on the back of a chair, he said in a weary voice, "All I need is a guide, a desert guide. It's that simple."

The stranger bowed his tousled head and said, "I regret I cannot be of more help. Good day, monsieur."

His rough cloak brushed Zagora's arm as he hurried past her and down the stairs.

"Hi, Dad," she said, standing up. "I wasn't listening in, I was just—"

"Zagora!" Her father looked surprised. "What are you doing here?"

"I wanted to see the sun come up." She walked over and leaned against him, gazing out over the rooftops and terraces, to the kerosene glow of the Djemâa el Fna. The smell of Moroccan soap wafted through the folds of his shirt.

"Why was that guide here so early?" she asked.

"Because I want to leave Marrakech. Quickly." She could hear the tension in his voice. "But that's how things are in Morocco: everything takes longer than you think."

"We're on a *quest*," she said with certainty. "And quests take time."

"The problem is that Olivia Romanesçu is determined to get her hands on the Oryx Stone. I'm afraid that any minute now her henchmen will turn up here at the hotel."

Henchmen. That sounded scary. "We can't let them take it, Dad," she said fiercely. "We have to keep the stone safe." She wondered how much Olivia actually knew about the stone. "Is Olivia Romanesçu dangerous?"

Her father shook his head. "I have no idea. She talked

about saving the world with her medicines, but her experiments sound rather questionable to me."

Zagora realized she hadn't quite grasped all of that conversation. Not surprising, since Olivia had turned out to be a nonstop talker. "Nothing bad is going to happen, Dad, don't worry," she said, noticing new wrinkles around his eyes. "Remember Mrs. Bixby?"

"White hair, round glasses? 'Reimagine the world,' she told you kids. Introduced you to Byron and Yeats and had you reading poems in haiku, is that the one?"

"That's her." Zagora smiled, enveloped by a warm feeling. Mrs. Bixby had been, during the school year, a sort of motherly type, advising her on what clothes to wear, encouraging her to be kind and brave and to take on the world—all the things her real mother would have taught her, she was sure.

"Mrs. Bixby's motto was 'Dream big and dare to fail.' Sometimes you have to take leaps in the dark, even if they're scary or hard." For once, Zagora realized, her father was actually listening to her. "Your friend Pitblade was a risk taker, right?"

Dr. Pym chuckled. "Hmm, I guess Mrs. Bixby had it right." His voice turned serious. "'From a certain point onward there is no longer any turning back.' Kafka, of course."

Zagora nodded. She was determined not to be frightened of anything, not even the elegant, unsettling Olivia Romanesçu.

The two stood, silent as stone carvings, faces to the wind, watching the red-gold rim of the sun—*fajr,* the first light of dawn—as it rose over the slumbering streets of Marrakech, over the squares and gardens, the mosques and palaces, over the rose-colored walls. Hearing the muezzin's haunting call to prayer floating upward across the city, Zagora secretly thanked all the invisible forces at work around her for bringing them there.

∽ ∽ ∽

Keeping pace with their father, Zagora and Duncan pushed through the frenetic crowds of the Djemâa el Fna, past vendors selling pottery, peanuts and slippers woven with tiny beads. Stalls were crammed with leather and iron goods, silks and textiles worked by hand. They couldn't stop to buy anything, though, because their father had to find the car rental agency, and judging by his speed and the way he kept glancing over his shoulder, Zagora was beginning to think he really *was* frightened of Olivia.

It seemed to her that her dad was becoming more anxious by the hour. At breakfast he had noticed two men outside the hotel and told her and Duncan to pack up at once. After paying the bill, he had ushered them out the back door, James Bond–style—a thrilling getaway, in Zagora's opinion, though she hadn't had a chance to say goodbye to the turtles.

She was keeping a close eye on the crowd, as well. So far they'd been followed by a water seller wearing crimson pantaloons and ankle bells and holding out a brass cup, and two little boys asking for coins. She fervently hoped she wouldn't encounter Mina again.

"See Olivia's goons anywhere?" asked her brother, blinking at her with pink-rimmed eyes. A small boy with dreadlocks tugged at his sleeve and Duncan handed him a stick of gum.

"Don't worry," she said, not wanting to admit that her nerves were jangled, too. "Once Dad gets the car sorted out, we're on our way to the desert."

"I wish we were going to Essaouira instead." Duncan kicked an empty soda bottle. "It's an ancient fortress city by the sea. We'd be safe there. And, oh yeah, there are goats along the roads that climb the argan trees."

"Goats in *trees*?" said Zagora, intrigued. Still, there was no question that Zahir won over tree-climbing goats. The Pyms had an important mission to carry out in the desert.

"Here we are," said their father, pointing to a squat pink building at the edge of the marketplace. Over the door she could see a blinking AUTO RENTALS sign in English and Arabic.

"I'll wait outside," she said. "Someone has to stand guard."

"Fine, Zagora," said her father, "but please, don't wander off."

"Copy that," she replied, using one of Duncan's expressions. She would never go off and leave them, not when Olivia's henchmen might burst on the scene at any moment.

This city sure looks unreal, she thought, hearing the door bang shut. She lapsed into a dreaming silence, watching people and buildings shimmer in the heat, looking as if they might float off into the air. A voice drifted up over the crowd, shouting her name. Spinning around, she saw a skinny figure in blue robes carrying a wooden cage.

"Mina?" she called out, squinting into the light.

It was Mina, all right. There was no mistaking her pretzel-thin body, zingy tattoos and fiery hair. Behind her, a troop of kids slapped barefoot through the dust, snickering and tripping one another. One boy was swinging a lizard by its tail.

"If you're looking for the stone, I don't have it!" yelled

Zagora, shrinking against the wall, watching Mina's cage bob up and down.

At least the Oryx Stone was safe with her dad—well, sort of. When she had returned it early that morning, she'd placed the stone at the bottom of his backpack, where it wouldn't fall out. Hopefully he hadn't moved it. Anyway, these kids wouldn't dare attack her father . . . would they?

Mina ran to the window of the car rental office and peered inside. Zagora could smell mint in the air. Inside the cage a bird with a pointed tail was making *tseep, tseep, tseep* sounds.

"Why are you renting a car? You are going south?" Mina asked, flicking an insect from her hair. Zagora's stomach did a little flip when she saw that it was a locust.

"My dad's taking us to the desert," she said excitedly.

Mina's face brightened. "My grandmother will be pleased to know this." Then she added, "I don't want to be your enemy, Zagora. We can be friends, yes?"

Zagora frowned. *Mina just wants the Oryx Stone,* she thought. On the other hand, she'd already made an enemy of Olivia Romanesçu. Mina was volatile, maybe even dangerous, but it might not hurt to have Mina on her side.

"I'll think about it, Mina." She glanced at the gang of urchins, scuffling next to a fruit stand. "But first tell those kids to go away. If you do, I won't tell my dad they jumped me."

Whirling around, Mina shouted to her gang in Arabic. They froze, looking at one another with bewildered expressions; then they scattered. Zagora wondered what Mina had said to them but decided not to ask. It was a relief just to have those kids gone.

"Look around this city," said Mina. "Traders, nomads, warlords, thieves, bringing every kind of spice and camel and silken robe." With one arm she made a sweeping gesture. "Marrakech is the center of the Arab world," she said proudly. "Centuries ago sultans rode camels out of this city and fought battles in the desert—terrible battles. Sometimes they buried their enemies alive."

Zagora nodded, eager to hear more history, though she hoped Mina was mistaken about that last part.

"Come," said Mina, pulling her into the crowd.

"Mina, I can't," protested Zagora, "I have to get back—"

"You must come," said Mina. "This is very important."

With a shrug Zagora followed her. The lure of the

marketplace was too irresistible. They threaded past women with kohl-rimmed eyes carrying baskets of medicinal herbs, merchants hawking ostrich eggs and pomegranates, a blacksmith forging pots. As they hurried along, Zagora could hear the tinkling of Mina's copper ankle bracelets.

"You see the Tuareg?" whispered Mina, nodding toward a group of men. Each one wore an indigo-blue cloth, resembling both a veil and a turban, wrapped around the head and face. "These are desert nomad warriors: *blue men*. They wear the *cheche,* to protect them from sand—and to keep away evil spirits." She pronounced the word "shesh."

Enthralled, Zagora stared at the Tuaregs' fierce eyes and dark skin, their long thin legs. Their children had blue-tinted hair worked into fine braids. They all looked dignified, straight-backed and desert-savvy.

"Here is my grandmother!" said Mina, pulling her past a row of stalls.

A slight, spare figure in veils and blue robes was crouched beside a small burning fire surrounded by birdcages stacked one on top of the other. The figure turned its head and all Zagora could see was a pair of scorching black eyes.

Mina embraced her grandmother and handed over

her wooden cage. *That's some cool granny,* thought Zagora, noticing the scorpion tattoos on her hands. The old woman unhooked the door to one of the cages, setting free a burst of silvery birds. Watching them swirl around their heads, Zagora thought how at last she was seeing good omens.

"Grandmother's name is Noor. It means 'light' in Arabic," said Mina. "I do not know her age, but she is terribly old. Her bones crack when she moves."

Noor sounded kind of mysterious, like Zagora's own name. "Hello, nice to meet you," she said politely, wishing she could recall the words in Arabic. "I'm Zagora."

From behind the shadowy veils, Noor glared at her. The woman's eyes held a mix of something ruthless, wild and powerful—and maybe something not quite human. Noor pushed aside her veil, revealing a gaunt, weather-lined face the color of burnt copper, as creased as one of Zagora's father's maps, and a nose pierced with a gold ring. Zagora saw with surprise a tattoo above the woman's eyes: it was an exact replica of the scorpion on Mina's forehead.

"Why are you named for a desert town in Morocco?" asked Mina. "My grandmother wants to know."

"My dad named me." Zagora decided to tell the short version of how she got her name. "He's an archaeologist, and when he came to Morocco to translate glyphs, he stayed in Zagora."

Mina gave her a funny look and translated. The old woman's thin lips cracked into a smile. Seeing her small crooked teeth, Zagora relaxed a little.

"Do you know what is desert sight?" asked Mina. Zagora shook her head and she continued: "Certain people are born with this talent, and when they travel to the desert, they find they have this power. They see into the past: they see all things of the desert that have vanished over time." She paused, staring at Zagora. "Grandmother thinks you have this gift."

Zagora stared back, confused. Was that the reason she'd seen the ghost oryxes? But the idea of oryxes suddenly appearing out of the past seemed fantastic, like something from a time-travel book.

"Why does she think I have desert sight?" she asked Mina. "I mean, I'd know if I had an amazing talent like that, right? I think your grandmother's got it wrong."

Noor stood with her shoulders thrown back, regal as a desert queen. Her wizened face grew solemn and she uttered a string of words, short and clipped, with a frantic undertone. Zagora grew uneasy again.

"Grandmother had a vision," said Mina in a half whisper. "A vision of you in Zahir."

"But I haven't even been to Zahir," Zagora whispered back.

"I do not know Grandmother's heart; she does not tell me all things," said Mina, sounding a bit sad. "You have traveled many kilometers over the sea, here to Morocco. Grandmother says the stone has found *you,* and you must show us the path through the desert—not the old path, the one we were lost on, but the new path. You could help free the Azimuth from a terrible fate."

"The Azimuth? But the Azimuth are extinct!" said Zagora. Seeing Mina's baffled look, she added, "You know: *dead, gone.* My dad told me, and he knows about those kinds of things."

"No, not all Azimuth are dead," said the girl. "Our tribe still lives in the desert, in a hidden place, a half day's camel ride from Zahir."

Zagora's eyes went wide. "Are you serious? The Azimuth are actually living in the desert, near *Zahir*?" Her father would go bananas when he heard this.

"When the stone of the oryx was taken, many Azimuth fell sick, and their beloved oryxes vanished. The scorpions grew stronger. The Azimuth were forced to leave Zahir." Mina's eyes filled with tears. "Our city was lost to the scorpions."

What a sad story, thought Zagora. In comparison, her

life seemed easy. She wondered if Mina had a mother or a father. Maybe Noor was all she had.

"The stone of the oryx belongs to the Azimuth," said Mina with a fearsome look. "Grandmother says it must be returned to Zahir—because of the foretelling. The prophecy."

Before Zagora could say anything more, Noor began to sway on her feet, whispering under her breath, her face oddly radiant. Her bones seemed to be glowing beneath her skin. Zagora watched, fascinated, drawn to the woman's terrible magic, the fever of her dark tattoos. Yet although Zagora believed in prophecies, she also worried that Noor might be confused. Sometimes elderly people's minds were fragile.

With brass tongs, Noor picked embers from the fire and placed them in a brightly painted clay incense burner shaped like the head of an oryx. Then she added crystals—"Frankincense," whispered Mina—which glowed brightly, and soon a fragrant, smoky plume enveloped the three of them, cutting them off from the rest of the crowd.

A spidery hand darted to Zagora's neck, searching for what could only be the Oryx Stone.

"I don't have the stone!" she whispered, terrified of what the old woman might do.

For an instant something older than the Earth itself showed through the creases of the old woman's face. Then the light went out of Noor's eyes and from her lips fell words Zagora couldn't comprehend, whispering away into space, until, with a shudder, Noor sank to the ground.

Zagora backed away, watching the smoke dissolve around her. What language had the old woman been speaking? She hoped Noor hadn't cast some kind of freaky spell over her.

Then she heard a different voice, shouting her name. It was Duncan!

"Oh no, I forgot!" she cried, spinning around in a panic. She'd messed up again! "I'm supposed to be watching out for Olivia's goons!"

Above the stalls she could see the flashing auto rentals sign and what looked like her father's safari hat.

"I've got to go—*now,*" she said. "See you later!" Waving to Mina and Noor, she dashed off toward the squat pink building, a hundred questions tumbling through her brain.

"Until the desert!" she thought she heard Mina shout after her.

〰️ THE HIGH ATLAS 〰️

Zagora sat in the front seat of a rusted Mercedes-Benz with bug-spattered windows and faulty air-conditioning, thinking about Mina and Noor, mulling over the things they'd told her about the Azimuth and the Oryx Stone. She was astonished and bewildered to think she might actually have desert sight. Was it possible that she had the power to see into the desert's past?

They chugged up a narrow winding road with crumbling edges along a steep-walled valley. She couldn't wait to tell her dad the Azimuth were still alive, but at the moment he was too preoccupied with driving—and intent on getting as far away as possible from Marrakech.

Her father shifted into a lower gear, and they just managed to make it up the gradient, which was getting steeper and steeper. He sat hunched at the wheel, jaws clenched, pressing the pedal to the floor as they wound higher into the Atlas Mountains, braking for goats and donkeys. Occasionally a bus or a taxi or some beat-up vehicle whizzed by, missing their car by only inches. Zagora's heart was in her mouth every time.

Even with the windows rolled down the upholstery gave off a gamy odor; the smell reminded her of the tinned food Auntie Agnes fed her Manx cat. Zagora noticed that it was getting harder to breathe, but she knew the reason: thin mountain air.

"Dad, have you ever heard of desert sight?" she asked.

"As a matter of fact, I have. *Desert sight* is an ancient term referring to visionaries and seers: gifted people of the desert who have the innate ability to see into the past. Very rare, of course. Why do you ask?"

Being a desert visionary sounded pretty amazing, but she didn't want to give too much away, especially with her brother listening to the conversation.

"I met a girl in Marrakech who told me about it. Her name's Mina and her grandmother sells birds," Zagora said, avoiding the whole truth. "Do you think someone with desert sight could see animals that are extinct?"

Her father considered. "Yes, of course, it makes perfect sense."

"I'll ask Pitblade Yegen about it when I see him," said Zagora dreamily. Maybe she really had seen oryxes from the past. "And about the legend of the oryxes returning to Zahir." She was sure her father's friend would have the answers to all her questions.

At this elevation there was little traffic on the narrow, twisting mountain road, although Zagora had already counted two near collisions: one with a bus, and the other with a turquoise spray-painted car that Duncan said was circa 1960 and that nearly ran them off the road. Sometimes she could almost see, or imagined she could see, oryxes in the far-off hills.

"My guts are all shook up!" hollered Duncan as they rounded another hairpin curve. "I think I'm going to be sick!"

Zagora twisted around in her seat. "You'd better not be," she said in a threatening tone. "In the desert the weak ones get left behind."

"We'd never leave Duncan behind," said her father, giving Zagora a comical look.

"But in the desert you can't let the weak ones drag you down," she argued. "If Duncan gets sick, he puts us all in danger. He could doom our expedition! Ask Freya Stark."

"Danger?" said Duncan, and she sensed a dramatic moment coming on. "What about Nar Azrak, do you call that safe? Think about it: we're in Morocco and we're going to the Sahara, to the exact same place where the astronomers are saying the planet might crash!"

"They're fanatics, Duncan. All that talk is nonsense," said their father, slowing on a turn. "You'll be glad you went to the desert. It's the experience of a lifetime."

A boy in a T-shirt jumped in front of the car, holding up a giant quartz crystal. "Special price, not tourist price!" He thumped his hand on the hood. "Crystals and fossils, very special!"

Zagora thought it would be cool to buy a Moroccan fossil, but she knew explorers and archaeologists didn't do that sort of thing. In fact, they were the ones who *dug up* the fossils.

"Windows up!" cried Duncan in a panicky voice.

"Chill out, he's just selling sparkly rocks," said Zagora irritably.

"Not today, thanks!" called their father, swerving around an elderly man wearing a ski cap and holding a jar of honey. "If we stop now, we might not get going again."

She watched the peddler grow smaller in the rearview mirror. *These people almost don't seem real,* she thought. *What if they're, like, high-altitude mirages?* The road grew steeper, with no barriers along the sides. She gnawed on her knuckles as a bus overloaded with passengers whipped around a bend, one wheel suspended over the edge.

"I knew we should've rented a four-wheel drive Jeep," said Duncan. "The car rental guy said it's reliable on mountain roads, plus you can drive all over the desert with a four-wheeler."

The car swerved and Zagora glanced out the window at a hundred-foot drop, her stomach fluttering. "Jeeps are for tourists," she said. "And we're not tourists, we're travelers."

"For centuries explorers have been drawn to the desert," mused their father, shifting to his egghead professor voice. Zagora loved when he got philosophical and off topic. "Some travelers set off on spiritual quests, in search of mystical revelation, while others seek treasures beneath the sand, remnants of ancient cultures—"

"I'd just like to find a Burger King," muttered Duncan, irritation filling his voice yet again. "I'm telling you guys, we cannot drive over sand in this clunker."

"Who said anything about driving?" Zagora's dad looked over at her and winked.

She smiled back. In a heightened state of exhilaration, she wiggled her feet on the dashboard, staring out at the red earth and distant trees and heart-stopping drops.

A gloomy silence settled over the backseat. Deprived of creature comforts like air-conditioning and indoor plumbing, Duncan was shutting down. Zagora knew he was desperate for cyberspace, online chat rooms, the science channel, Twinkies and lemon-filled doughnuts. He missed sitting on the couch, tearing open bags of chips while he flipped the remote, watching endless reruns of *Star Trek, The Outer Limits* and PBS's *Star Gazer*.

As for Zagora, she didn't miss anything. She was prepared to abandon it all.

∽ ∽ ∽

"Here we are. We're at the highest point, the Tizi-n-Tichka pass," announced Zagora's father, pulling up to a square mud-brick building at the edge of the road. "Rumor has it that the last lion in Morocco was killed here in 1942."

"I wish there were still lions here," said Zagora, who loved all kinds of wild cats.

"You know, I think we have enough to deal with at the moment," her dad replied with a chuckle. "Time for a break. Let's see if we can order chebakia here."

"Is that an Arab dessert?" asked Duncan, who could never resist anything sweet.

"It sure is, and I think you'll like it."

Zagora jumped out of the car, thinking how the word *chebakia* sounded warm and plump and golden. *Chebakia, chubby, cherub,* all fat words rolling around inside her head. She breathed in the dry mountain air, her nostrils sticking together as if someone were pinching them. Her dad had said that might happen, because there wasn't much oxygen in the High Atlas.

She looked out at the dry mountain landscape, the red-tinted houses scattered in the valley below. It would be another day before they reached the desert. Smells of fried meat and vegetables drifted out of the café, where colored plastic strips hung in the doorway; she could hear an Arabic song playing on a radio. To one side of the building the scrubby land dropped off into a ravine. It seemed like a sad place, maybe because it was so isolated.

Zagora suddenly remembered that Edgar Yegen had taken a bus from Marrakech to Sumnorum, following this same route. In his journal he'd written:

*The ancient creaky bus winds slowly through the
narrow twisting roads of the Atlas Mountains, stop-
ping along the way at roadside cafés so passengers may
stretch their limbs and partake of a cup of tea or perhaps a small meal.*

Maybe Edgar had stopped at this café and ordered
chebakia. How awesome would that be?

Their father chose a table outside and opened his
map. A man wearing a long brown-and-white caftan,
smelling of tobacco and strong coffee, greeted them with
"As-Salāmu `Alaykum" and took their order.

"Here's our route so far," said their father, his finger tracing a road through the Atlas Mountains. "After
the Tizi-n-Tichka pass, we'll be driving downhill out
of the mountains and across the Drâa Valley." His finger
hovered over a line of tiny dots, and Zagora grew excited, seeing that one town was marked *Zagora*. "We can
stop in Zagora for a break. I'll show you the famous sign
there."

"Great, Dad, I can't wait to see it," she said, smiling.
The town of Zagora was old, she knew, dating back to
the thirteenth century, with caravan routes from the Sahara winding around it.

Duncan tapped a black X that was in the middle of

nowhere on the map. "This can't be Zahir—there's no road to get there!"

"Roads don't last long in the desert," replied their father. "They get swept away."

"That's where the camels come in," said Zagora, grinning.

"You know, if we were normal tourists, we'd rent a four-wheel drive Jeep with super swamper tires—but I guess the Pym family isn't what you'd call *normal,*" grumbled Duncan. He looked at Zagora. "No way I'm riding a smelly old camel."

"But camels are so cool, Dunkie." When was he going to shape up? Zagora wondered if her brother was tough enough to go to the desert.

"Chebakia?" said a voice.

She looked up to see a barefoot boy with copper skin and a jaunty smile. Dressed in baggy shorts and a T-shirt patterned with guitars, he carried a tray with glasses of mint tea and a plate of steaming pastries, kicking up dust as he scuffed along. He seemed awfully young to be a waiter.

"Right here, buddy," said Duncan, thumping the table in front of him.

I wish my brother wouldn't act so ridiculous, thought Zagora. *It's embarrassing.*

The boy placed the chebakia in the center of the

table. He looked to be around her age, and his black hair, sticking out in fuzzy knots, was even messier than hers. She could see nicks on his elbows, scars on his knees and dirt between his toes. His eyes were dark, bordering on mysterious: the kind of eyes that held secrets. A real cool misfit type.

Their father took a bite of chebakia. "*Très délicieux.* Delicious," he said.

The boy gave a wide toothy grin. "My auntie makes this. Chebakia is everybody's favorite."

Zagora thought it truly delicious, too—it tasted of honey and butter—and reached for another. If she didn't move fast, she knew, her brother would eat them all.

"We'll be arriving in Sumnorum late this afternoon." Her father folded his map with swift, precise movements. "I was unable to arrange a guide ahead of time, but I'm sure we can find one in Sumnorum. So plan to leave for the desert early tomorrow morning."

"Fantastic, Dad!" said Zagora, jumping up and hugging her father. "This is going to be so amazing!"

It was hard to believe this was happening. For so long she'd envisioned going to the desert—all those imaginary treks she'd taken on imaginary camels as she'd conjured up ancient cities lost beneath the sand—and now her dream of Zahir was becoming a reality.

"Hey, there goes that turquoise spray-painted car again," said Duncan, finishing off the last piece of chebakia. "You don't think anybody could be following us, do you?"

"No. No, of course not," said their father, looking a bit pale. Zagora had a funny feeling he might still be worried about Olivia's henchmen. "Time to pay the bill," he said, pushing back his chair, "then we can get back on the road." He headed for the café, Duncan loping after him.

Zagora looked at the boy, who was standing beneath an orange tree, turning a beetle over with his toes. Around him the ground was littered with feathers, crumpled napkins, melon rinds and rusty cans. She noticed holes in his shorts, and the way his big toe overlapped the one next to it.

"You are going to Zahir?" he asked, giving her a curious look. "Nobody lives in Zahir." He flicked the beetle into the air with his big toe. "It is a strange and dangerous place."

"I know that," she said, a bit defensively. "You're like the millionth person to say that."

"Things happen in Zahir, things nobody can explain," the boy went on. "My cousin's falcon was attacked there and was badly hurt."

"Oh, that's really sad," said Zagora, who hated to see animals of any kind suffer. "But we have to go to Zahir to find my father's old friend. He was missing in the desert for eleven years! We're sort of on a quest to rescue him."

The boy listened with a grave intensity, as if he'd heard this kind of thing before. "Many travelers are lost in the desert—and many never come back. Your friend is lucky." Using a stick, he drew a squiggly line in the dust, stirring up insects. "Here is the road to the desert. And here is Zahir." He marked an X in the dust, just as her father had done on his Kummerly & Frey map. "I hear many things about Zahir, and always they give me nightmares. My uncle Jamal says unnatural creatures live there, and he is not the kind of man who tells stories."

"I'm not scared," said Zagora, but she felt a sudden chill, wondering what he meant by *unnatural creatures*.

With a shrug the boy let his stick fall to the ground.

"I'm going to be an explorer when I grow up." She swirled her foot in the dust. "I want to spend my whole life in the desert."

The boy looked surprised. "You will give up your country? That is very brave."

Zagora blushed. No one had ever called her brave before.

"One day I will live in the desert again," said the boy,

his voice filled with longing, "because that is where I was born." He straightened his shoulders, clearly trying to appear dignified despite his ragged clothes. "My name is Razziq Q'na Nasir. And you? What is your name?"

"I'm Zagora," she said, smiling shyly. "Zagora Maeve Pym. Maeve was my mother's name—but I never knew her."

The boy nodded, as if he understood perfectly. She gazed hard at him, with his lean wiry limbs and solemn eyes, and knew he was a dreamer—like her. He had courage, too; she could see it in his eyes and in the way he stood with his back very straight.

"Come, Zagora Maeve Pym," said Razziq with a grin. "I will show you something."

She followed him behind the café to a scrubby yard where chickens and goats picked through the garbage. Two wooden crates covered with wire mesh had been pushed against the wall of the building. "Go, look inside," he urged, pointing to one of them.

Running up to the crate, Zagora pressed her face against the mesh door. The interior was dark, and it smelled of dirt and straw. She heard a rustling at the back, where a shadow seemed to be moving; then she gasped, seeing a bird unfold its wings.

"A falcon," said Razziq proudly. "My cousin trains

him to deliver messages." He unlatched the door and reached inside, stroking the bird's head. "I am helping to train him. This falcon is strong and smart. And he is very beautiful, no?"

"He's super," said Zagora, staring at the bird's fierce white face and glittering eyes. She imagined Razziq riding a camel over the dunes, the falcon tethered to his wrist.

"He flies through the desert like the wind," the boy went on, his eyes growing brighter as he talked. "He also is my friend. I leave his door open sometimes because I know he will not fly away."

"I'd give anything to have a pet like that," she said, "but my brother's allergic to feathers and dander. We had goldfish but they died, and once Duncan took care of a classroom hamster, but that died, too." She didn't add that she'd been responsible for Galileo's sad exit from this world.

"What's in there?" she asked, peering into the other crate, pinching her nose because it smelled so bad. Feathers littered the floor, and she could see a shadowy mass huddled in the corner. "Is this the falcon that got attacked in Zahir? Poor thing, his feathers are all droopy."

Razziq gave a sad nod, and Zagora felt a chill go through her. Hadn't Olivia told them that Pitblade Yegen sent his letter by falcon? But before she could say more, an earsplitting shriek cut through the air.

"Duncan!" she cried. Had he fallen down the ravine?

Zagora and Razziq sprinted around to the front of the café, where Zagora saw her brother hopping from one foot to the other, shouting crazily. Her father, looking distraught, was wrestling with the lid of the trunk.

"Duncan!" she called, running over to him. "What happened?"

"Snakes!" His face was flushed and his eyes were wide with terror. "Three snakes, right there on the front seat." He pulled out his inhaler and took a puff. "I almost sat on one!"

For once, Zagora realized, Duncan wasn't being paranoid. This was real.

"Dad, do we have a snakebite kit?" her brother shouted.

"I packed a medical kit, but I'm afraid it won't be of much use," said their father. "There's no antidote for desert horned vipers."

"Vipers are very dangerous," said Razziq, looking a bit queasy. "They are deadly creatures."

The café owner stumbled over, gripping a heavy pot. "Vipers jump quickly," he said to Duncan and Zagora. "If one bites, you turn black—and you die very fast."

Zagora felt her stomach go cold. Where were the snakes now?

"Who the heck would put killer snakes in somebody's rental car?" wheezed Duncan.

Recalling that she'd been sitting in the front seat, Zagora wondered uneasily if the snakes had been meant for her. Or . . . had they been intended for her father?

From beneath a chair came a soft rasping, like water sizzling on a hot plate. Zagora froze. The sound rose and fell in soft waves; it might have been the wind, but somehow she knew it wasn't. A long, thin shape slid by, moving almost impossibly fast. To her horror, a snake the color of dust coiled around Duncan's leg.

He let out a shriek. "Get it off me, get it off!" he howled, shaking his leg. But the yellow-gray snake squeezed tighter, flicking its tongue and hissing.

Staring at the creature's pale eyes, Zagora screamed.

"Viper!" shouted the café owner.

Zagora stood trembling with fear, waves of nausea rushing through her. The snake had weird horns like a snail's, only bigger, and its skin was smooth and iridescent. Swaying to and fro, the creature fixed her with its eyes, which were vertical slits.

Placing two fingers between his teeth, Razziq gave a high whistle. The viper reared up, hissing wildly,

whipping its triangular head from side to side, poised to strike at any second. Zagora stopped breathing, not daring to move, watching Duncan's mouth open wide with terror. No sound came out.

Looking anxiously toward the café, Razziq whistled again, the sharp sound reverberating in the air around them. The viper ceased its frantic rhythm, as if sensing danger. Then, without warning, from behind came a loud *whoosh* and a flash of brown-and-gray feathers. Zagora saw the falcon plummet swiftly, take hold of the snake with its hooked beak and shake it violently. Moments later the snake went limp and thumped into the dirt.

With a triumphant cry the falcon soared skyward, blood dripping from its beak.

"My falcon killed the snake!" yelled Razziq, jumping around excitedly. "I whistled for my falcon and he killed the snake!"

Zagora watched the falcon in awe as it wheeled high above their heads, wings flashing in the sunlight. Relieved and overwhelmed, she turned to her brother. His face was a chalky gray, and his mouth hung open in an expression of horror. Tears filled Zagora's eyes. Duncan had never gone through a life-threatening experience like this before. The worst thing she could remember happening to him was falling off his bike and dislocating his shoulder.

The thought that Duncan had been inches from death made Zagora's heart crack wide open. Sobbing, she threw her arms around him. "I thought you were a goner, Duncan!" she said, hugging him hard, astonished to find how precious her brother really was. Sure, he was annoying, but in a way, he couldn't help it, because, well, he was Duncan.

"It's all right, son," said their father, gripping Duncan's shoulders. "The viper's dead. And I've checked the car: there's no sign of the other snakes." He turned to Razziq. "Calling your falcon was a stroke of genius—you saved my son's life."

"I know he would have done the same for me," said Razziq humbly.

Wide-eyed, Duncan stepped up to Razziq. "Hey, I owe you my life."

"His name's Razziq," said Zagora.

"Thanks, Razziq. Thanks for what you did," said Duncan, awkwardly shaking the boy's hand. "I don't know how I can ever repay you." He stared admiringly at Razziq, as if he'd just discovered a new superhero. Zagora supposed that, in a way, he had.

As her father and Duncan headed back to the car, she

saw Razziq kneel down beside the snake, stroking its belly and black-tipped tail. Zagora stared at the viper, thinking how it seemed almost elegant in death, and strangely beautiful. The sight of it lying there saddened her, even though she hated it for almost killing her brother.

"I know your falcon isn't supposed to be a killer, Razziq," she said, kneeling down next to him. "But if he hadn't killed that snake, my brother would be dead now."

The boy nodded, and she thought she saw a tear glistening in one eye, which made her like him even more.

❧ WELCOME TO MAISON TUAREG ❧

Zagora's father drove down, down the mountain, and as they bumped along the road, she felt a rush of vertigo. In the distance she could see dry riverbeds and oases filled with palm trees shimmering in the heat, as if floating underwater. The incident with the snake had left her exhausted. Her stomach somersaulted every time she thought of the viper, with its icy cold eyes and space-invader horns.

Houses flew by, squat and chopped off, reminding her of the milk carton villages Mrs. Bixby's class had glued together for their Colonial New England diorama. But the towns here in Morocco, with their one-story adobe houses, wide dusty streets and lack of traffic lights, were different from American towns. There were no malls here, either, no billboards or megastores along the road. Zagora loved how each town had its own distinct archway, painted with trapezoids, diamonds and oblong shapes, and how all the signs pointed south to the desert—as if east, west and north didn't count.

She could hear Duncan and Razziq chattering in the backseat, discussing cowboy movies, video games and how to train birds to carry messages. Her dad had offered Razziq a ride to Sumnorum, where he was delivering a package for his uncle and visiting cousins. In return, Razziq had promised Dr. Pym that he'd find them a desert guide. Zagora was incredibly happy to have this cool misfit hero riding along with them. It was a shame they couldn't have brought the falcon, too.

"Did you know scorpions kill more people than any other predator except for—guess what?—snakes!" she heard Duncan say.

"'Beware small scorpion, waiting in the dark,'" murmured Razziq. "This is an old Arab saying."

"I guess you should know, right, Razz?" said Duncan. "My book says scorpions can adapt to anything: freeze 'em, nuke 'em, whatever, they won't die! If they lose a leg or pincer, they grow a new one. We'll all get blown off the planet and scorpions will still be here, hah!"

Hmm, thought Zagora. Maybe that explained why her scorpion hadn't actually been dead: it had adapted to the outside of the envelope. Twisting around in her seat, she asked, "What about scorpions growing bigger, like when you put them in water?"

Razziq gave her a quizzical look. "I have never heard of such a thing."

"An old Berber once told me that to kill a scorpion you have to trap it inside a circle of fire," said her father. "The scorpion will sting itself to death to escape the heat and flames. Fire is the only thing they fear."

Desert Survival 101, thought Zagora: *Carry matches to protect yourself from scorpions.*

"Where are your parents, Razziq?" her father asked, clearly trying to make conversation. "Do they live in the High Atlas?"

"I have no parents anymore," said the boy.

Razziq was an orphan? Zagora bit her lip. That was so sad. She found it hard to imagine a life without any parents at all.

"I was very young when my parents died," he told them. "We were living in the desert. My uncle

Jamal came for me and brought me back to his mountain café."

"Geez," said Duncan in a low voice. "Sorry, Razz."

Zagora saw her father nod sympathetically. Maybe that was why the café had seemed so dreary. Razziq had been taken away from the desert, the place he loved most, and now he lived in a run-down house in the mountains on the edge of nowhere, waiting tables in a café. Not exactly a fun life.

They ate lunch at a restaurant in the town of Zagora, ordering veggie kebabs and fresh orange juice, and took pictures of one another next to Zagora's famous road sign. The sign read TOMBOUCTOU 52 JOURS, which, loosely translated, meant "fifty-two days by camel to Timbuktu." Although her namesake city was an ancient crossroads, Zagora was disappointed to find that hardly any old buildings had survived. Her dad said the town was a stopover for people going to the desert. They could buy maps and stock up on supplies, or rent quad bikes or camels for desert trekking.

On the road again, she watched the landscape grow more desolate: stone and sand and windblown trees, a white-hot sun overhead. Leaning back, she closed her eyes, imagining the desert, described by Edgar Yegen as "vast and endless and crackling with light."

She must have fallen asleep, because the next thing she knew, her father was announcing, "Sumnorum ahead!"

She sat up, wide-awake and alert, staring at a green-and-blue archway with yellow diamonds painted down the sides. She sensed her vision growing clearer, heightened, as if she could see beyond Sumnorum, miles and miles into the desert. *The heat's having a strange effect on me,* she thought. They rolled into town on a wide street, past terra-cotta houses and arcaded shops grouped around a square, veiled in a haze of dust.

Had Sumnorum looked like this in 1937, wondered Zagora, when Edgar Yegen arrived?

Without warning a metallic *zing!* ricocheted under the hood, and the car swerved, tires squealing. She stifled a scream as her dad just missed a woman on a donkey.

"Steering's locked!" he shouted, jamming on the brakes. The car kept going. He pulled the emergency brake and they shuddered to a stop.

"I knew it," said Duncan. "Faulty brakes and an antiquated engine."

"At least we made it to Sumnorum," said Zagora. *And Dad didn't crash the car.*

Flinging the door open, she tumbled out into the scorching white sunlight. The heat was all sharp edges. She could see the woman on the donkey disappearing down a side street. The square seemed to be deserted. Her dad jumped out and opened the hood, peering at the engine with a worried expression.

"I go now to see my cousins," said Razziq. "Tell your father many thanks, and please assure him I will find him a guide. My older cousin perhaps; he is a desert guide." He glanced at Zagora. "Okay, maybe he will not go all the way to Zahir—but close enough."

"Hold on," said Duncan. "You're coming with us to the desert, right? Come on, Razz, we need you in case we run into any more vipers. It's only for two days."

"No, no, I cannot," said the boy, shaking his head.

"Please, Razziq," said Zagora. She'd envisioned the three of them as a team of explorers in the desert, guided along by her archaeologist dad. "We'll have a real desert adventure!"

"Don't worry, Razz," said Duncan, "nothing dangerous is going to happen. We can go hiking and explore stuff together. It'll be mega cool."

"Okay, I will think about it," promised Razziq. "So long, see you!"

Watching him run off, Zagora wished she could meet his cousins. There were many questions she wanted to ask them. She'd love to find out what kids who lived near the desert were like.

Now the place was filling up with people, mostly men in caftans, talking in low voices, eyes fixed on the smoke billowing out of the tailpipe. At the other end of the square she saw the turquoise spray-painted car nosing its way through the crowd, and a creepy feeling came over her. What if somebody really was following them?

"I think the electric system blew," said her father. He looked up, and for a second Zagora saw panic on his face. "And the radiator's leaking. Everything seems to have overheated."

Duncan didn't say anything, but his round face looked ready to cave in. *No wonder he's a mess,* thought Zagora. *Imagine being attacked by a desert horned viper and almost dying.* She wished Razziq were there to cheer them up.

"Don't worry, Dunkie," she said, forcing a smile. "How many kids from America get to go to the Sahara? Not many, right? When you get home, you can tell your friends how you narrowly escaped death." Not that Duncan had many friends; he was a pretty solitary kid.

"Yeah, I guess." He wiped his sweaty face with the back of his hand. "But I should be at astronomy camp now, and gearing up for debate club and—hey, who's this character?"

A tall, delicately featured man with a walnut complexion was making his way toward their father. He wore a soft-looking hooded white caftan and a black turban. Perched on one shoulder was an iridescent green bird— exactly the kind Zagora imagined a pirate would own.

"Monsieur! One moment please!" called the man, hurrying across the dusty square. "Hello, I am Abdul." She watched him bow slightly. In a smooth, silky voice Abdul said, "I speak English. Perhaps I can help you, yes? My cousin, he will fix your auto good as new."

"Nice to meet you. I'm Charles Pym." Zagora could see that her father was doubtful. "Is your cousin a trained mechanic? This is a rental car, so I have no idea—"

"Please, do not worry." Abdul smiled, showing a set of dazzling white teeth. *He looks like a sultan,* Zagora thought, *or maybe a rock star.* "Come out of the sun, my friend. Please, come to my house with your family. I will make you a nice couscous and you will have a place to stay for the night."

"Tell him yes, Dad," said Duncan. "We have to eat something!"

"Duncan's right, Dad," added Zagora. "We need to get out of the heat and rest."

"Come, have a glass of tea," insisted Abdul. "My cousin will fix your auto, no problem."

Their father gave a defeated shrug. "Hmm. Guess I haven't much choice...."

Zagora and Duncan gave each other high fives. *Awesome,* she thought, *we're going to the home of a real Moroccan.*

Tall and rangy, Abdul led them through the crowd of curious onlookers, out of the square, past fruit trees and date palms that grew wild along the streets. Zagora was mesmerized by the parrot hopping on Abdul's shoulder. It cackled madly as they passed beneath archways and shadowy arcades. She wondered if the bird knew any swear words.

Abdul stopped before an adobe building with a sign above the door that read BIENVENUE/WELCOME TO MAISON TUAREG. She grinned, remembering the fierce blue men she'd seen in Marrakech.

Brushing dust off her sandals, Zagora followed Abdul into a shop filled with all sorts of amazing treasures: beaten copper pots, necklaces strung with coins, bowls of colored beads, jewel-encrusted bracelets. Enchanted by everything she saw, she decided that these things must have come from the desert: incense burners, woven silver headbands, a mirrored-glass globe, carpets woven with arabesque designs. This was definitely the kind of shop a desert explorer would own.

"An astrolabe," said Duncan, holding up a gold disc with inscriptions on it. "I've always wanted one of these.

It was used in ancient times for astrological measurements."

"Neat," said Zagora, half listening as she rummaged through a jar of coins, hoping to find one with an oryx stamped on it—an impossible search, she knew, since her dad said oryx coins from Zahir were priceless and found only in museums.

"Is this your shop?" she asked Abdul, wondering why he'd brought them there.

He smiled. "Yes, it is." He gestured toward the hanging carpets. "Authentic Berber wool, very good price. And over there is Uncle Ali. He is my favorite uncle and he helps me in the shop."

Across the room she saw a man in white robes and a white turban sitting cross-legged on a mat, his face as wrinkled as a dried fig. With a start she noticed that one of his eyes was opaque.

Duncan paid for the astrolabe and Abdul motioned for them to follow. Uncle Ali nodded as they all trooped past. "As-Salāmu `Alaykum," said Zagora's dad, and she repeated it, smiling at the old man. He lifted a gnarled hand in greeting, his one good eye twinkling.

They entered a room furnished with luxurious cushions, tapestries and rugs. Fragrant incense wafted through the air. Carpets of every shape and texture hung from the rafters and were piled in corners, some rolled up, others folded into tall stacks. There was no ceiling; when she looked upward, all Zagora could see were rows of carpets, sunlight filtering down between them.

Abdul gathered an armful of cushions and placed them on the floor around a low table. "Rest here. I will make tea for you."

"It better not be mint," Duncan whispered to Zagora. "I'm really sick of mint tea."

"Quite a place, eh?" murmured their father, raising an eyebrow at Duncan. "Serving mint tea is a customary ritual with the Arab people. If you are offered tea, you should always accept."

"Yeah, you have to say yes to everything they give you, no matter how disgusting," said Zagora, trying to sound knowledgeable. "Even if it's fried octopus suckers or boiled sheep's eyes."

Duncan fell silent.

High above the carpets floated a lonely patch of sky. Zagora stretched out on a green cushion embroidered with gold camels and imagined Edgar Yegen stepping off a bus, hoisting his bag over one shoulder as he strode into the dusty square of Sumnorum, blinking in the sunlight.

Flourishing an ornate brass and silver teapot, Abdul poured with his arm held high. The tea landed perfectly each time. Zagora kept an eye on the parrot, nodding sleepily on his shoulder. She expected it to fall off any minute.

"My wife and daughters are taking our goats to the mountains." Abdul handed them each a glass of steaming mint tea. "Many days they are gone."

Zagora tried to imagine climbing mountain paths with a mother who was smart and adventuresome, sort of like Freya Stark, and sisters, too, herding goats and sleeping in tents. What a life that would be.

"I stay here at the shop with Uncle Ali." He settled on a leather hassock and she watched the parrot doze off. "Our kilim carpets are tapestry woven by desert crafts-people."

Abdul launched into a history of his family's business and Zagora sat, chin in hands, listening. His father and grandfather had been traders, crisscrossing the desert by camel caravan, bartering with nomads for jewelry, carpets, pottery, whatever. Back then they'd navigated by the stars, using hand-drawn maps and dead reckoning to find their way around.

"I too traveled many years through the desert," he concluded, "but now I run my shop with Uncle Ali, while my younger brothers travel to distant parts of the Sahara. Only there is one difference: they have satellite GPS, ha-ha!" He gave a hearty laugh.

"Have you heard of the Oryx Stone?" Zagora blurted out. He was bound to know something, she thought, having traveled all over the desert. "The stone belonged to the Azimuth, but it was stolen, and then the scorpions invaded Zahir."

Abdul threw her a piercing look, the kind her vice-principal, Mr. Porter-Jones, used to give, and she felt color rise to her cheeks.

"Ah yes, the Azimuth are a part of Moroccan folk-lore." Abdul's smile looked pasted onto his long, bony face. "In Morocco we have many desert myths, such as the Legend of the Oryx Stone. My uncle Ali knows many of these stories. Perhaps you should be asking him."

"The Azimuth tribe isn't a myth," said Zagora. "They're totally real. And the Oryx Stone is real, too." She turned to her father. "Ask my dad. He studies ancient desert tribes and he knows a lot of stuff."

Dr. Pym gave a scholarly nod. "The Azimuth once inhabited the city of Zahir and there is evidence that such a stone existed. Anthropologists believe, however, that the tribe has died out."

"No, not true, Dad!" said Zagora, jumping up excitedly. "Remember I told you about Mina, the girl I met in Marrakech? She told me there are Azimuth people living in the desert—near Zahir!"

"Azimuth?" Her father leaned forward with a wide smile. "This is truly amazing news, Zagora. Extraordinary. You may just have made a groundbreaking discovery."

Zagora beamed. "I know, Dad, I know."

"Is Mina the girl you met in the marketplace?" asked Duncan. "The one with the freaky grandmother and the scorpion tattoos?"

"Yeah," she said, nodding. "That's her."

Abdul fell quiet, as if piecing this information together. "In this part of the world scorpions bring bad fortune," he said darkly. Zagora watched as he scrunched his beetle-shaped eyebrows together. "Have you not heard of the Time of the Scorpions?"

She sat up, suddenly alert. The phrase sounded slightly ominous.

"In the Time of the Scorpions, the world as we know it will change," he continued in a gloomy voice. "Uncle Ali has often spoken of this foretelling. A great battle will take place in the desert between oryxes and scorpions. Uncle Ali believes the oryxes will be defeated and the desert will fall into eternal darkness. If such a thing happens, scorpions will rule the desert."

Zagora went clammy all over.

"So it'll be night twenty-four-seven and scorpions will be in charge?" said Duncan. "Sounds pretty grim."

Lacing his fingers together, Abdul moved on to the next topic. "You are here on tourist holiday, taking in the sights of Morocco?"

"We're not tourists," huffed Zagora. "We're travelers! We're going to the desert on camels. To *Zahir*," she added, hoping to impress Abdul. "Our dad was there eleven years ago, translating glyphs."

Abdul turned to her father. "And you go a second time to Zahir? I think you must be very brave, my friend, or perhaps very foolish. Has no one told you about this ruined city beneath the sand? There are dark creatures in Zahir, and they do not sleep. No one goes to the buried city, for what lies in Zahir is beyond imagining."

Zagora heard Duncan suck in his breath next to her. She listened with growing apprehension, wondering for the first time what kind of trouble Pitblade Yegen had gotten himself into—and what exactly they would find when they got to Zahir.

"Threats and warnings won't stop me from going to Zahir," said her father determinedly. "This journey is about friendship, and I suppose you could say loyalty, too."

Zagora smiled. She'd always admired her father's steadfastness. Right then he sounded like an olden-day knight entrusted with a sacred duty.

"We're on a mission to rescue our dad's friend," she said importantly. "We have to return an artifact."

"You have a Moroccan *artifact*?" Abdul fixed his dark eyes on her and she winced, realizing she'd spoken without thinking. "We are growing tired of losing our treasures to outsiders," he went on heatedly. "Europe, America, Russia, they fill their museums with Moroccan artifacts that do not belong to them."

Realizing she might have just made a mistake, Zagora looked to her father. He gave her a reassuring nod, as if to say he knew sometimes her emotions got away from her and she said things she regretted later, but not to worry.

"People travel here from all over the world," said Abdul, "and we are pleased to take their money—because, as you have no doubt seen, in Morocco life is difficult. But we are not so happy when they take away our treasures."

Zagora thought of the ragged children begging for coins in Marrakech, and of Mina and Razziq, whose lives were impossible to comprehend. Life was hard, all right, for lots of people.

"You have a point, Abdul, artifacts are stolen all the time, and it is wrong, absolutely," said Dr. Pym. "But this particular object has been in the Yegen family for generations."

"It's not really an artifact," said Zagora. "It's a meteorite." She heard Duncan clear his throat and realized too late that hadn't been a smart thing to say, either.

"There is a black market here in Morocco for meteorites," said Abdul in a cold, quiet voice. "There has been much looting of meteorite sites in the desert. It is, of course, illegal."

An awkward silence fell over the room. Zagora started to feel panicky, wondering if Abdul would report them to the authorities.

"Perhaps Zahir is best left under the sand, its dark secrets forgotten," murmured Abdul, rising to his feet.

Zagora watched as he left the room in a flurry of white robes, the green parrot clinging to his shoulder. *Uh-oh,* she thought, *I hope we still have a place to sleep tonight.*

ᴄ SCORPION DREAMS ᴐ

In the evening Abdul was calm and pleasant, serving Zagora and her family a delicious meal of chicken and al-
monds wrapped in phyllo pastry, with spicy roasted plums
to finish. They dined in an upstairs salon where the walls
were filled with tapestries of nomads, camel caravans and
desert scenes. Over the fireplace hung a curved sword
that Zagora recognized as a scimitar.

They sat on cushions on the floor, eating at a low
table of dark wood inlaid with ivory. The atmosphere was
friendly and relaxed. Dr. Pym talked with Abdul about
American baseball and Abdul explained how to roast
plums, while Zagora and Duncan heaped their plates

with food and, encouraged by Abdul, took seconds (and thirds, in Duncan's case).

"Excuse me, but do you have any new information on Nar Azrak?" asked Duncan, digging into his bowl of plums.

Abdul stared intently at Duncan. It looked to Zagora as if he didn't have good news.

"You have not heard?" he said. "I thought Americans were always *in the know,* as they say, ha–ha."

"Yeah, but our dad's BlackBerry doesn't work this far south," said Zagora, bristling. "And our car radio doesn't get English stations."

"Since we left Marrakech, we're, like, off the grid," said Duncan. "Way off."

"There is much fear in Morocco at the moment, and much confusion." Abdul's voice was grave. "It seems there are changes in the night sky over our desert—changes no one could have predicted in the planet Nar Azrak."

Zagora, Duncan and her father leaned forward, hanging on his every word.

"They are saying Nar Azrak comes closer each day, and at a speed that is increasing by the *hour.*"

Zagora heard a sharp intake of breath from Duncan, and she herself nearly choked on a plum.

"You mean Nar Azrak really is heading for Earth?"

said Duncan. "But our dad said the reports are bogus. The planet's light-years away!"

Dr. Pym set down his fork. "I find it hard to believe that the effect of the Earth's gravitational field on Nar Azrak is changing."

Zagora couldn't quite interpret the expression on her father's face, but she was sure Abdul had it wrong. *He's just a gloom-and-doom kind of guy,* she thought.

"Well, this is what our astronomers are now telling us." Abdul lowered his voice and Zagora had to strain to hear what he said next. "No one knows precisely how near to Earth the planet will come, but it is a fact that Morocco lies directly in its path. In five days Nar Azrak will cross before the moon, and our astronomers worry that this will be the defining moment."

"A lunar eclipse?" said Duncan. "Oh man, this really is like a science fiction movie!"

"I don't believe there's any need to panic," their father reassured them. "Not all the evidence is in, but I don't believe it would ever . . ."

Zagora wasn't convinced.

"Exactly how serious do you think this is, Abdul?" asked her father.

Abdul dabbed his mouth with a silk napkin. "Extremely serious. Permit me to take you to a café tonight where there is a television. We can listen to our national astronomer on the BBC. We will find out more, yes?"

"Sounds good," said Dr. Pym.

"Can we go with you, Dad?" asked Zagora, not wanting to be excluded.

"Sorry, but it's already past your bedtime," he told her. "We leave at the crack of dawn, and you both look exhausted. I'll give you the details on Nar Azrak tomorrow."

"Upstairs we have a rooftop courtyard for sleeping," said Abdul, rising from the table. "Come, I will take you."

Until then Zagora had been wide-awake, but her eyelids felt suddenly heavy. She kissed her father good night and gave him an extra hug, and Duncan hugged him, too. Grabbing their backpacks, the children followed Abdul down a hallway and up a twisting staircase. Abdul carried a metal container he called a brazier, which smelled of hot oil and smoke. *I remember those,* thought Zagora sleepily. *Edgar Yegen wrote about braziers in his journal.*

At the top of the stairs, Abdul went through a curtain of wooden beads, ushering them into the coolness of the evening, onto a walled-in terrace. Zagora was impressed by the beads: they clattered around her like small insects as she walked through them. Out on the terrace she stood listening to the distant wail of a radio and the hum of crickets. The town looked mysterious in the moonlight, its wide streets dark and deserted. She felt a warm wind, smelling of desert flowers, on her face and was thrilled to be spending the night in such an exotic setting.

Duncan looked over the terrace and said, "Hmm, interesting, no streetlights. Wow, fantastic—I can see constellations! Look, Zagora!"

She gazed past rooftops and a stately minaret at a confusion of stars. "Where's Nar Azrak?"

"The planet of blue fire will show itself later," said Abdul, unrolling two carpets. "After the moon has risen." Zagora noticed that his manner had become almost formal again.

"We have no lights in Sumnorum," Abdul continued. "We prefer to see the stars."

"I'm with you there, Mr. Abdul," said Duncan, smacking his leg. "I find the night sky totally fascinating." He swatted at mosquitoes buzzing around his head.

"My brother's crazy about planets and constellations," said Zagora proudly. "He's won all kinds of computer science fair ribbons for his astronomy projects."

She was about to ask if they had computer science fairs in Morocco when Duncan said, "Any chance we could have some spray for bugs?"

"*Forbugs?* I do not understand this word." Abdul was quiet a moment; then Zagora saw him reach into his robe and pull out a small bottle. "Ah, I understand. . . . Here is cedar oil, to keep away the insects. It comes from cedar trees in the High Atlas."

"Great," said Duncan. "Thanks, Mr. Abdul."

"Laila sa'eda wa ahlaam ladida," said Abdul. "Good night, and pleasant dreams."

Zagora whispered the phrase. She loved hearing the enigmatic sounds of the Arabic language. Abdul raised a hand in farewell, and Zagora listened to the wooden beads clacking behind him as he glided away.

"Man, there are bugs all over the place. I hope this stuff does the trick," said Duncan, opening the vial and rubbing the oil into his arms. "Hmm, smelly stuff."

Zagora stretched her arms high, arching her back like a cat.

"Do you believe what Abdul said about Nar Azrak?" asked Duncan, handing her the bottle. "I think he's an alarmist."

"Maybe he wants to scare us a little," said Zagora, inhaling the sweetish scent of the oil. "Or he likes to exaggerate. Don't worry, Dad's going to find out what's really happening."

"I wish my pal Razz was here," Duncan muttered drowsily.

"Me too," Zagora said, thinking how Razziq's light-hearted nature might calm them down.

Smoothing oil into her skin, she began to worry. Their father had clearly looked upset, and she knew how brave and unflappable he usually was. Edgar Yegen had written about Nar Azrak: even in the 1930s, the planet had been acting strangely. She was tempted to tell her brother. But no, maybe later. Right now it seemed important to keep the journal a secret.

"I'd set up my telescope, but I'm too wrecked," said Duncan, crawling under his blanket.

Two seconds later he was snoring. Snapping on her mini flashlight, Zagora dug Edgar's book out of her backpack. Things had been too hectic since their dinner at Café Meknes even to open the journal. She read:

> Mohammed tells me that certain desert nomads
> are superstitious about dreams. Some believe that who-
> ever appears to you in a dream, whether from the land
> of the dead or from the living, is seeking you out be-
> cause they have a fervent desire to communicate.

That was an odd little entry, she thought, flipping to another page.

Last night, in the soft glow of moonlight, I saw a shadow outside the window. My heart thudded; my knees quaked. I saw a face that was not human, with multifaceted eyes. The creature peered in through the window and our eyes locked. Mohammed and I fled to the room of ancient inscriptions and barred the door. The most frightening thing about the scorpion was not its size, but my sense that the creature possessed an intellect.

I am convinced that the scorpions have been drawing energy from an unworldly source, namely the blue stones that were used to build the Pyramid of Xuloc. It is common knowledge these stones were meteorites from Nar Azrak. And so, infused with the planet's dark powers, the scorpions have grown larger . . . and more intelligent.

Zagora shuddered. *Intelligent* scorpions? That sounded a bit weird. Yet she didn't think Edgar would make something like that up. He struck her as too old-fashioned, a bit of a fuddy-duddy, in fact.

She listened to the rustle of palm leaves above the occasional low sound of the wind, carrying the dry smells of the desert. In the quiet of the night, she heard tiny feet pattering: lizards. Crossing her arms mummy style, she took a deep breath and settled into the rug. Images whirled through her head: a small pyramid of blue stones in Zahir, golden oryxes, the mysterious tribe of the Azimuth. She saw Nar Azrak and the scorpion in Olivia Romanesçu's tea, Mina and her strange grandmother, Abdul and Uncle Ali.

Was there a chance that, in some inexplicable way, all these random things were linked? This was her last thought as sleep suddenly overwhelmed her.

༄ ༄ ༄

She dreamed of a thin figure wrapped in gauze robes, hair shooting out like fiery cobwebs. Mina! The girl sprang from the shadows of an alley, crawled up the side of Abdul's house, swift as an insect, and vaulted over the terrace wall, her scorpion tattoo glistening.

"I don't have the stone!" Zagora cried out. "Go away, Mina, I don't have it!"

"The treasure belongs to Zahir!" Mina hissed, reaching out with spidery hands.

Then Mina was gone, and Zagora was standing in the lobby of their hotel. She could see Olivia Romanesçu, dressed in bright robes, holding a glass box filled with scorpions, which were scuttling up and down the sides. A moment later the box exploded and the scorpions rained down, tails coiled into tight knots, landing on Zagora's shoulders and arms, tangling in her hair, sliding down the back of her neck. Screaming, she tried brushing them away, but more and more came falling down.

"Hey, I'm trying to get some shut-eye here . . . ," mumbled Duncan. His eyes flew open and he jumped to his feet in a kung fu stance. "What's all the noise?"

Zagora stood up, trembling. "I dreamed about scorpions," she whispered. "They were in a glass box and it blew up and they were crawling all over me. It was so scary!"

"Oh man," said her brother, "I hate scorpions, worse than desert horned vipers, even."

Zagora was comforted to know that Duncan sympathized with her. In the past he would've been rolling on the floor laughing.

Turning her head, she saw the flicker of a lantern behind the beaded curtain.

"Please, what is wrong?" shouted Abdul. "Why are you screaming?"

Holding the brazier high, he moved, phantomlike, onto the terrace, cloak blowing in the night air. The parrot fluttered at his shoulder. Behind Abdul, Zagora could see Uncle Ali, his eye gleaming like a pale marble.

Her screams must have been really loud—maybe loud enough to wake up the whole neighborhood.

Abdul stood over her, swinging the brazier and looking concerned, his skin an eerie blue.

"I had a nightmare," she whispered, her teeth chattering. "First I saw Mina, then she turned into Olivia, and then—" She knew she wasn't making sense, and she wished her dad were there instead.

"Then a box of scorpions blew up," said Duncan.

"Scorpions were crawling all over me," said Zagora with a shudder. "Hundreds of them. It was horrible!"

Uncle Ali moved nearer. Looking into his blind milky eye, Zagora wondered if she'd made a mistake telling them about her nightmare.

"These people in your dream," said Abdul in a quiet voice, "who were they?"

"Mina Ash-Shaulah," she told him, sounding out Mina's entire name. It had a strange ring to it. "She's a kid, like me." She could see Uncle Ali frowning. "And Olivia Romanesçu. They're just people I met in Marrakech." Edgar's words came back to her, about people in dreams trying to communicate. "Do you think they were trying to tell me something?"

Abdul and Uncle Ali huddled together, conversing in hushed tones.

"In Arabic, *ash-shaulah* means 'raised tail of scorpion.'" Abdul seemed to glare at Zagora. Behind his angry countenance, she caught a glimpse of something else. Was it fear?

"Nobody gives a child an unlucky name such as this," he went on. "Scorpions bring bad fortune, always. Dreams of scorpions awaken old curses. Years ago Uncle Ali had such a dream and the following day my cousin Josef was attacked by a scorpion."

Zagora, her mind full of dark questions, stared first at Abdul, then at Uncle Ali. They both appeared to be extremely nervous. Was Abdul saying her dream was connected to some bad-luck curse? And what about Josef: had he survived the scorpion attack?

"Dreams of scorpions," said Abdul, shaking his head. "This is very worrisome."

He and Uncle Ali strode off, murmuring to each other, leaving Zagora and Duncan in the glowing blue darkness. Why were those two acting so strange? she wondered. It was only a dream.

"Zagora, look," whispered Duncan, pointing to the sky.

She followed her brother's finger, shocked to see Nar Azrak. Vast and glimmering, it loomed over them, shining so brightly it seemed almost supernatural. The planet was so much bigger than she had envisioned, its light intense—not at all like the pictures she'd seen on TV back home.

She took a deep breath, trying to calm herself, but as she stared at it, fearful and disbelieving, the planet seemed to loom larger by the minute, expanding to a monstrous blue globe on the distant horizon.

∿ ∿ ∿

Early the next morning Zagora watched her dad as he loaded their packs into the trunk of their car. She'd hardly slept the night before, thinking about Abdul's cousin being attacked by a scorpion, and worrying about Nar Azrak. It had looked awfully big for a planet.

"All set to go. The car's running like clockwork," her father announced. "We're renting the camels from a fellow by the name of Badi al Raman, just a ten-minute drive from here."

Zagora grinned, forgetting her worries. Today was the big day, and more than anything, she was deliriously excited.

"Dad, what did the astronomer say on TV last night?" asked Duncan, loping over to the car. She could tell by his bloodshot eyes that he hadn't slept much, either.

"Sorry, kids, Abdul took me to the café, but

unfortunately they couldn't get the television to work. Never mind—we'll get the details when we're back in Marrakech."

Duncan's face fell.

"It's okay, Dunkie," said Zagora, seeing her brother's expression. She felt anxious, too. "Nar Azrak was kind of big last night, but it's still like a zillion miles away." At least, she hoped it was; unlike Duncan, she had no idea how to estimate distances in outer space.

"Hello, good morning!" shouted a familiar voice. "I bring you an excellent guide!"

Zagora whirled around to see Razziq hurrying toward them, along with a young man wearing a baseball cap and a white burnoose bleached by the sun.

"Razz!" shouted Duncan, his face breaking into a wide grin. "Razz, you made it, buddy!"

"This is Occam," said Razziq. "He is my uncle's second cousin, and he has much desert experience. His English, okay, maybe not so good . . ."

Occam shook hands with each of them. *Looks kind of skinny,* thought Zagora, *but maybe he's real tough underneath.*

"Razz's coming with us, right, Dad?" said Duncan. "He can be our translator."

Zagora saw her father hesitate, no doubt thinking, *Oh no, one more kid to worry about.*

"Please, Dad," she said. "Razziq was born in the desert."

"Yeah, and if anything goes wrong, Razz is our man," added Duncan. "He knows how to kill snakes and stuff."

"You might call me a desert rat." Razziq flashed his toothy grin. "You'll have no worries about me. My family does not worry, either. They know I am with Occam."

"Hmm. Well, I suppose so," said Dr. Pym with a sigh.

The three of them—Zagora, Duncan and Razziq—grinned excitedly and gave one another high fives. *Now we really are a team of explorers,* thought Zagora.

The next moment shouts filled the air and Abdul ran out from under the arcade, waving his arms and shouting: "Please, come quickly!"

Everyone raced to the shop. Zagora was the last to enter, calling after Duncan and Razziq, but they'd already disappeared into the gloom. The air hung thick and smoky, laced with smells of incense and musty carpets—and, she realized, something else: the electric smell of fear. From the back of the shop came a low keening wail and she felt a prickling down her spine.

"Abdul!" called Dr. Pym. "What's happened?"

In the murky light Zagora saw Abdul on his knees, struggling to lift Uncle Ali. Face twisted with pain, Ali gave a low moan. The parrot on Abdul's shoulder cried out as if its tiny heart were breaking.

"My uncle has been attacked!" said Abdul. "He is stung by scorpions."

Zagora felt her stomach drop.

"Let's get him out of here," she heard her father say. "Hurry!"

"Oh no!" croaked Duncan. "What's that on the floor?"

Zagora stamped one foot and heard a crackling beneath her sandal. "Scorpions!" she cried, wheeling on Duncan and grabbing him by his shoulder.

His face was deadly white. "They're all over the place!"

Spinning around, Zagora saw one scorpion, then another . . . and another. Terror engulfed her. She felt as if she'd been here before. Then she realized that the scene was just like her dream the night before. There were dozens of scorpions, dropping from the carpets and walls, crawling down cabinets, scuttling across the floor. A scorpion the size of a mouse leapt onto the counter, knocking over the basket of coins. Zagora was terrified.

Duncan gave her a push and they bolted for the door. Trembling, she waited outside with her brother and

Razziq, who both seemed as dazed as she was. Soon the door flew open. Her father and Abdul carried Uncle Ali out of the shop and set him down in the shadowy arcade.

"Is Uncle Ali okay?" asked Zagora, staring at the welts on the elderly man's neck.

"Did I not tell you scorpion dreams awaken old curses?" Abdul glared furiously at her. "*Ash-shaulah:* 'raised tail of scorpion.' You bring into my house a plague of scorpions!"

"That was just a dream!" she cried. "Those scorpions weren't real!"

Duncan stepped forward. "This isn't my sister's fault, Mr. Abdul," he said, surprising Zagora with his boldness. "My sister hates scorpions. She wouldn't go near one if her life depended on it."

She threw her brother a grateful smile.

"Your accusations are unfair, Abdul," said her father calmly. "You are talking about old superstitions from the desert."

"Think again, my friend." Abdul's eyes were filled with cold fury. "This girl is not like us. She sees things that we cannot." Zagora stiffened, hearing his words. "Perhaps she has the power to call up scorpions, who knows?"

What was he talking about? Desert sight was one thing, but he was talking about an evil kind of power.

"This is ludicrous!" shouted Duncan. "My sister doesn't have a mean bone in her body!"

Zagora blinked hard; she still couldn't believe her brother was actually defending her. He never would have done this back home.

Abdul rose slowly to his feet and she shrank from his withering gaze. The parrot hopped and chattered on his shoulder. Even that silly bird seemed to be accusing her. "Please go, all of you," said Abdul in a weary voice. "You are no longer welcome at Maison Tuareg."

☙ THE GOLDEN LIGHT ☙
OF THE DESERT

Zagora sat in silence as the car sped southward, tires hissing on the road, heading for Badi al Raman's compound. She wanted to enjoy the desertlike scenery, but all she could see was Uncle Ali's terrified face and scorpions coming out of the walls.

"There must be a scorpion nest in that shop somewhere," said Duncan, clearly trying to explain away the strangeness of what had just happened. "There were hundreds of those things! They could've attacked us in our sleep!"

"Thanks for defending me, Duncan," said Zagora.

"I can't believe Abdul said all those things." She felt a new warmth toward her brother—not just because of the snake incident, but because of the way he had stood up to Abdul.

"I can't believe Abdul kicked us out of Maison Tuareg," Duncan muttered. "Why did he accuse us? We're just tourists! And all that stuff about artifacts and black market meteorites, like we're this gang of international smugglers or something."

Abdul's harsh accusations had hurt Zagora—and she still couldn't help finding him a bit mysterious. She knew he'd sensed that she was different in some way, but he'd guessed wrong, thinking she had the power to call up scorpions. Even if it turned out she had desert sight, that was a different sort of power. Desert sight was seeing into the past, not attacking people with scorpions.

"This man, Abdul, was angry," said Razziq, "but I think also he was fearful."

"Abdul was distraught," said their father. "He said things he didn't mean. But I suspect you're right, Razziq: he was afraid. I think perhaps Uncle Ali has influenced him—and Ali is superstitious, fearful of many things."

Zagora remembered the creepy feeling she'd had the night before when she told Abdul and Uncle Ali about her dream.

"We'll never know if Uncle Ali has made it or not," she said, wondering if there was such a thing as anti-scorpion medicine. "I hope he'll be okay."

"I will return to Maison Tuareg," promised Razziq. "I will find out and tell you."

"Thanks," Zagora said, throwing the boy a wan smile. It seemed she could always count on Razziq. "I'm going to worry about him until I hear."

Noticing a basket on the seat beside her, she remembered that Abdul had packed them a lunch. She passed around sandwiches of potato, egg and peppers on flatbread, and they munched quietly. Duncan dropped pieces of egg on the upholstery, but Zagora didn't mention it—not after he'd turned out to be her ally.

Gazing across a treeless plain, watching sunlight bounce off the stones, she suddenly realized she was forgetting all the things she'd left behind. She could hardly recall her trilobite collection and Tintin comics, her collection of Harry Potter figurines and her new five-speed bike. The faces of real people, like Aunt Claire and her Latvian email pal, Doña, were fading. She tried to remember, but couldn't recall, the smell of pickles and fly spray in Aunt Agnes's kitchen.

She was alarmed at first, but as she leaned out the window, breathing in the sunbaked earth, she felt oddly serene, as if those things didn't matter or had happened in another lifetime. There was a reason she was forgetting: because something much larger loomed ahead. Events she couldn't explain were taking place, things she never could have predicted. She would be going home eventually—but not to the home she knew.

"Occam says we turn here." Razziq pointed to a narrow sand-blown track. "This road will take us to Badi al Raman."

Zagora saw a palm grove floating in a wavy green line and, beyond, a square building with a low thatched roof. This was it: the camel place! Her father pulled into a courtyard surrounded by acacia trees and she bolted from the car.

"Where are the camels?" she yelled, kicking up yellow plumes of dust.

"First we drink tea and barter for dromedaries— what you call camels," said Razziq, climbing out after her. "Then we will go to the desert. This is the order of things."

Zagora recognized *dromedary* from one of her books about camels in the Sahara. The word had a solid ring to it, like a term from one of her dad's geology books. *Dromedary, lapidary, sedimentary.*

"Hello, my friends, welcome!" A round-faced man

with rimless glasses and a black mustache appeared at the doorway. "I am Badi al Raman. Please, come inside."

Badi al Raman came out and took them into the cool, darkened building. Everyone sat on the fuchsia-and-gold carpet while their host bustled around, making jokes as he poured tea from a copper pot, putting them all at ease. Zagora thought he looked like a cross between a garden gnome and a Buddha. The dirt floor had been swept clean, but she had a funny feeling that this was where the camels slept. It smelled sort of like, well, camel.

Dr. Pym bartered with Badi al Raman for camels, a tent, food and supplies. Zagora could tell from his confident manner that her dad had done this plenty of times before. After two rounds of tea and some good-natured arguing, her father ceremoniously handed over a stack of dirham notes to the camel owner. Then the two men shook hands.

Badi al Raman took them outside to a dusty square. Three camels, each with a leather harness and saddle on a brightly colored blanket, stood chewing the tall weeds. Heart pounding in excitement, Zagora ran around each camel, laughing as they snorted and showed their leathery gums and square yellow teeth.

"Hey, guys, where's Razziq's camel?" asked Duncan. "He needs one, too! So where is it?"

Zagora saw Razziq place a hand on her brother's arm.

"I will walk into the desert," said Razziq. "Do not worry, my friend, for me it is not a hardship."

"But it's hot out there. It's over a hundred degrees!" Duncan thought a moment. "Listen, Razz, if you get tired, you can take a turn on my camel. I don't mind walking."

Had she just heard Duncan offer Razziq his camel? This desert adventure and the snake attack really were changing her brother in extraordinary ways. Duncan wasn't a nervous, paranoid kid anymore. *He's way tougher and braver,* Zagora thought, *and kind of, well, likeable.*

Occam hoisted her onto a bony-ribbed camel and adjusted her foot straps. Once everyone was ready, the camels plodded out of the square, their driver, Occam, walking ahead of them, leading them down a sandy track through a grove of cypress trees. She looked back to see Razziq, walking barefoot, with a euphoric expression that she knew mirrored hers.

The trees melted away and Zagora was lurching and bumping over sand, almost falling off her camel as she tried to take in the sun, the dunes, the brilliant blue sky. Too late she realized she'd left her sunglasses, camera and sunscreen inside her backpack. She'd been too distracted to get them out.

From under the brim of her hat she looked at her father and thought him spiffy (his word) in his khaki outfit, sunglasses and pith helmet. He sat astride a nasty-tempered camel, which kept trying to chew his foot though it couldn't quite reach. The camel halted every few yards, jolting him forward, but Dr. Pym didn't seem fazed. *That's because my dad knows how to handle ornery camels,* Zagora told herself.

Grunting and spluttering, the camels trailed up and down the dunes. Whenever a wind sprang up, Zagora's camel twitched its ears and moaned through its teeth. Distant mountains shimmered beneath a zinc-colored sun. Zagora felt the heat burning through her clothes and searing the tops of her hands. There was no shade, only a harsh brightness that hurt her eyes.

Nothing, she told herself, *nothing is more real than this.*

She felt sorry for Duncan, hunched over his shabby brown camel, arms locked around its neck. Sometimes he seemed so vulnerable, frightened by animals and by being in the outdoors. He'd always been a high-strung kid, and she'd taken advantage over the years, sneaking up on him, telling spooky stories, scaring him out of his wits—her way of paying him back for being brainy and superior. Now she regretted it.

Riding along in silence, she thought of a perfect

name for her camel: Sophie—after her teacher, Mrs. Sophie Bixby. Both had the same quizzical eyes, round and amber, and the same thick eyelashes. Yet despite her euphoric state, Zagora was a little worried. Sophie wheezed noisily as she trudged up the dunes, legs wobbling and spit flying from her mouth. There were ragged patches on her neck and flanks, and she seemed to be painfully thin. Why hadn't Badi al Raman taken better care of his camels?

Zagora couldn't think of anything more terrible than Sophie keeling over, dead as a doorknob, with her still sitting on top.

ᘓᕲᕲ ᕲᕲᕲ ᕲᕲᕲ

Hours later, Occam found a small patch of grass surrounded by steep dunes, and Razziq announced that this would be their campsite. Zagora couldn't believe they'd be spending the night there. It seemed so wild and untamed, like the drawings in Edgar's journal.

"Oh my aching you-know-what," groaned Duncan, catching his foot in the stirrup as he slid off. Occam caught him before he went flying into the sand.

Their father appeared to be exhausted. Seeing the dark circles under his eyes, Zagora wondered if this desert trek was going to be too much for him. Charles Pym

wasn't young anymore—he was, in fact, considerably older than her friends' fathers—and in recent years he hadn't been on many expeditions. Instead he'd spent his time lecturing, writing articles and playing *Desert Biome Madness* on his computer.

While Duncan unpacked his astronomy instruments, Zagora and Razziq helped Occam set up three small tents and a blue-and-white-striped tent, giving the place a festive air. Then Occam set out clay pots and utensils and lit a roaring fire to begin preparing dinner. As the sun vanished behind the dunes, they all sat in a circle in the sand, dipping bread into a communal clay pot of tagine, scooping up vegetables and tender hunks of lamb.

"I can't wait to meet Pitblade Yegen," said Zagora as Occam passed around a dessert of oranges with cinnamon and honey. "I'm going to ask if he's bumped into any of the Azimuth tribe."

"I'd love to know," said her dad. "This really could be a eureka discovery, thanks to you."

She grinned at him, though she wasn't sure what *eureka* meant. As she bit into an orange, savoring its sweet taste, she saw pinpoints of light in the distance flickering through the bruised darkness—probably the fires of nomads.

"Those fires are along the border," said Razziq. "Algeria is not far."

"Algeria?" said Duncan. "Isn't that place supposed to be bad news?"

"Not to worry—those are Moroccan soldiers camped over there," said their father, assuming his blustery chief inspector's role. "We're safe."

Duncan took a bite of his orange and looked at Zagora, his expression doubtful. Their dad had always been a master at bluffing.

Zagora heard the haunting sound of the desert wind, low and distant. Sparkling grains of sand swirled before her eyes. Peering into the distance, in the approximate direction of Zahir, she could see an outcropping, faintly illuminated. She quickly realized she was looking not at rocks, but at oryxes, standing along the rim of a dune, erect and dramatic against the violet-black sky. They seemed to be glowing with light from the desert.

It was obvious that the others couldn't see the oryxes: Zagora was the only one, and she wondered if she really did have desert sight, and if maybe it was growing stronger because she was finally *in* the desert. The light of the oryxes began to dim, and she watched their golden shapes melt away. Moments later they dissolved into the night, and she felt a sudden unease. Why were the ghost oryxes following her?

"Okay. Here's the plan for tomorrow, kids," said her father, rubbing his hands together enthusiastically. "Occam will have our camels ready at sunrise, and the three of us will head out straightaway. If for any reason we get separated—and the desert, as you know, is full of surprises—our meeting point will be the Tower of the

Enigmas." He handed them each a rough-drawn map. "I don't foresee any problems, but in the desert we have to be prepared for the unexpected."

Zagora studied the map—an exact replica of the one Pitblade Yegen had sent her dad—with feverish excitement. Her father had carefully written in distances and highlighted symbols representing their campsite, the excavated part of Zahir (including a palace) and the Tower of the Enigmas, overlooking the city. It all looked incredibly cool and adventurous.

"Can't Razziq come with us?" asked Duncan. "In case anything happens, like a snake attack?"

Their father shook his head. "Sorry, but we have only three camels and Razziq's needed here, to help Occam."

"Yeah, but is it true, what Abdul told us?" Duncan suddenly looked worried. "Is Zahir dangerous?"

Zagora and Razziq exchanged looks. *Too late,* she thought. *We've come too far. We can't turn back now.*

"I'm afraid Abdul has listened to Ali's irrational stories about spirits and curses for so long that he tends to confuse truth with fiction," said their father. "Don't worry, Duncan, I'd never knowingly lead you into danger."

"Okay, Dad," said Duncan, apparently satisfied with their father's answer.

Zagora breathed a sigh of relief. And yet she worried, just a little, that maybe what Abdul had said was true.

After the meal her father said goodnight to everyone and disappeared into his tent. She watched Occam scour the clay pot with sand, rinsing it with water from a tin can; then she wandered over to the camels, which were huddled next to the striped tent. She loved their hump-backed shapes and earthy smells; she even loved their stubborn, cranky natures.

Leaning against Sophie, she whispered good night to her golden-eyed camel and gave her a hug. The coarse hide bristled against her skin, smelling like dry grass. She wished she had a brush to make her camel's hair shine. Sophie gave a snort and Zagora giggled, picturing her in plastic glasses and a polyester dress, a piece of chalk in one hoof, writing lines from a poem by William Blake on the chalkboard, the way Mrs. Bixby used to do.

Yawning, she returned to her mat outside her tent. She and Duncan had decided to sleep under the stars so they could watch Nar Azrak. *He must be really tired,* she thought, seeing her brother asleep on his mat. *He didn't even set up his telescope!*

Occam sat by the fire, playing a sad quirky tune on

his flute. Notes flew into the air like smoky cinders, spinning off into the dark. She felt a thrill of anticipation, thinking how the next day they were going to Zahir and she would meet the intrepid explorer Pitblade Yegen, grandson of Edgar, lost eleven years in the desert. There were so many questions she was bursting to ask.

She noticed Duncan's flashlight by his mat and, checking that no one was looking, opened her backpack and pulled out Edgar's journal. Switching the flashlight on under the blanket, she began to read.

> As we draw nearer, I see golden oryxes in the coppery light, shimmering, transparent. They appear expectant, as if they have been waiting for me. Are these mirages, hallucinations, creatures composed of swirling sand?
>
> Zahir has surpassed my expectations. The ruins are filled with relics and artifacts: an archaeologist's treasure trove. The palace is still there, though it is half buried beneath the sand. Everywhere I turn, I catch fleeting glimpses of oryxes. Mohammed tells me it is possible I possess the gift of desert sight, which is the ability to see back in time, into the past of the desert. That would explain why I am seeing the oryxes: they are coming to me out of a distant time.

Oh my gosh, she thought, *Edgar Yegen had desert sight!* That was totally amazing, to think that maybe she and Edgar had both been born with this rare and special talent. She wondered if the ghost oryxes she was seeing were the same ones Edgar had seen back in the 1930s.

The flute music ended and Zagora watched the sky crack open into a vast, empty space, forbidding and mysterious, with no beginning and no end. Nar Azrak appeared, seeming even larger than it had the night before, blotting out the stars, its blue light filling the night sky.

❖ ❖ ❖

The next morning Zagora was woken up by what seemed to be a very bright light. It took her a few moments to realize it was the sun. But hadn't her father told them they'd be leaving at sunrise? Her throat was parched and her head was spinning. The image of Nar Azrak was still very clear in her mind.

"Oh man, I fell asleep before Nar Azrak even came up," said Duncan, rubbing his eyes. Zagora could see star charts scattered on the mat around him. "I didn't take any measurements."

She looked over at her father's tent. "Why isn't Dad

up?" she asked. "And I don't see the camels anywhere." No matter what direction she looked in, the horizon stretched out for what seemed like infinity.

"Looks like Occam overslept," said Duncan, pulling on his boots. "He was supposed to wake us up. The camels are probably foraging."

Their father's tent was empty; his BlackBerry lay in the sand next to his sleeping mat. Zagora brushed it off and tried turning it on, but it wouldn't power up. His backpack, she noticed, was gone.

"Duncan, Dad dropped his cell," she said, "and have you seen his backpack?"

"Maybe he went to look for the camels. That's the kind of crazy thing Dad would do."

Zagora, unconvinced, exited the striped tent, then walked around to the other side, hoping to find her father standing with a cup of coffee, gazing out to the desert. There was no one.

"Dad . . . Dad!" she shouted, starting to panic.

Razziq drew back a flap of his tent. "Occam says he heard someone come here in the night." He stepped outside, a worried look on his face. "Occam said it could have been a dream, but now he says maybe not."

Zagora felt queasy at the thought that someone might

have been there in the night—and now, suddenly, her father had vanished.

"There are many ways to become lost in the desert," said Razziq quietly. "Do not worry, Zagora, we will find him. Go, tell your brother he is gone. We must move quickly!"

She spun around and ran back to tell Duncan the bad news.

"Cripes, this is all we need," he muttered, turning their father's mat over with the toe of his boot. "Are you saying Dad has either disappeared or was kidnapped?" She could see white bugs jumping around in the sand. "What if he just wandered off in the night and lost his way?"

"I don't know." She bit her lip to keep from crying. *We're in the wild,* she thought, remembering a line from a book, *and the wild has teeth and claws.* "Anything could have happened!" Her dad had looked so tired the night before. What if he'd sleepwalked into the desert?

Glancing down, she saw a flash of blue beneath the mat. She reached into the sand and her fingertips grazed a small, smooth object. The Oryx Stone!

Duncan drew his breath in sharply. "Hey, what's that doing there?"

"I think it fell out of Dad's backpack," she said.

She had forgotten how heart-stopping the beauty of the Oryx Stone was. Points of light flew from its edges, and the oryx seemed to glide over its surface in a long graceful arc. Had her father accidentally dropped the stone—or had he thrown it into the sand to defy his abductors, counting on her and Duncan to find it?

THE UNEARTHLY GLOW
OF NAR AZRAK

A chaotic half hour later, Duncan and Razziq plodded off through blowing sand, while Zagora rode on Sophie, who had wandered back into the campsite. Occam was out rounding up the other camels. He'd promised to stay behind in case Dr. Pym returned.

Razziq insisted they wrap shirts around their faces for protection, explaining how the Tuaregs, fierce camel riders of the Sahara, wore the *cheche*.

"I saw Tuaregs in Marrakech," said Zagora. "The *cheche* scares off evil spirits, right?"

"This is true," said Razziq. "And it allows anonymity."

Hmm, thought Zagora, *scares off evil spirits and makes*

you anonymous. Both seemed like good ideas at the moment.

The air was thick and hot, the sun a pale glimmering orb. Sophie stepped briskly along, as if sensing the rider's anxiety, and Zagora tried to ignore the ache at the pit of her stomach. If only she hadn't slept so deeply, cozy under the rough blanket, dreaming about the oryxes. If only she'd been more alert, she might have heard the intruders—and maybe her father wouldn't be missing.

Around her neck hung the Oryx Stone, nestled against her skin. She wondered for the hundredth time how to charge up the magic inside. Did she need to whisper an incantation or rub the stone a certain way? She was frustrated that it hadn't given her any powers—especially now, when she needed all the help she could get.

"We have the map Dad drew for us," said Duncan in a confident tone, "so let's head for our meeting place, the Tower of the Enigmas. That's where he said to go if we got separated."

"Good idea," said Zagora, feeling a sudden thrill despite her fear. She was going to Zahir!

Peering through her *cheche* from atop her camel, she scanned the windswept dunes, hoping to catch sight of a weary lost archaeologist. Minutes ticked by and she saw only sand shimmering in the heat, rippling up and away. She remembered her dad sketching pictures of the different shaped dunes. Crescent dunes were the hardest to draw, he'd said, because they were constantly changing shape.

As Zagora pictured her father's earnest face, her heart fell. Where in this vast desert could he be? What if he'd been smuggled into a camel caravan headed for Algeria or Mauritania, countries on his Kummerly & Frey map with endless miles of uncharted territories? She told herself she would simply keep looking until she found him. No matter how long it took, she'd travel the desert far and wide to rescue her beloved father.

Leaning down, she gazed into Sophie's left eye, which was filled with the golden light of the desert. The light seemed to gather and burst, and everything became clear, every stone, every grain of sand. The warm desert wind brushed against Zagora's face and she felt time shift once again. Across the expanse of dunes she saw a line of camels winding through a canyon, and small boys herding goats on a green oasis, and a man with almond-shaped eyes carving glyphs on a fortress. None of the others saw these things, she was sure.

It's true, she thought. *I have desert sight.* And desert

sight, she realized, had nothing to do with the Oryx Stone. Desert sight, ancient and mystical, belonged to her alone.

As they edged down a dune, Sophie made a gargling sound and stopped walking. Then her legs buckled. She slowly lowered her body to the sand. Furious, Zagora jumped out of the saddle. The camel gazed at her with watery brown eyes, giving her the same look Mrs. Bixby used to give when kids did things that were sneaky or mean.

"I know you don't like this very much," said Zagora, "but we have to find our dad and we need you to carry our stuff, like the canteens and the medicine kit. Please, Sophie, get up."

Sophie fluttered her long eyelashes; then, grinding her teeth in annoyance, the camel lumbered to her feet. Zagora kissed her, shutting her eyes against the coarse hairs, and took a firm hold on the reins, leading Sophie over the dunes, the sand burning beneath her sandals. Looking back, she could see that the wind had already erased their footprints.

"Ahoy, mates, I see something ahead!" shouted Duncan as they topped the next dune.

Zagora gazed down into a searing canyon that cut through a scorched plateau, yellow and brown and violently bright. A sheer wall of black rock loomed out of the sand, pitted with scores of openings that made her think of empty eye sockets.

"I think it is possible we have lost our way," said Razziq, visibly upset. "This is what nomads call a place of dark spirits."

"You mean spirits of the *dead*?" asked Zagora with a shudder.

"It would seem to be." He looked at her, unblinking. "What you call ghosts."

"Ghosts aren't real, Razz, everybody knows that," said Duncan.

Zagora wasn't so sure. She gazed at the black rock, bleak and imposing, pocked with hollow caves and fissures, its high walls shutting out the low-angled sunlight. There could be scarier things than ghosts in those caves.

"I don't care about ghosts or dark spirits or any of that stuff," she said defiantly. "We have to go in there and check it out. Dad could be inside one of those caves!"

"They call places like this the badlands." Duncan shook out his shirt-turned-*cheche* and rewound it messily around his head.

"Yes," agreed Razziq. "Terrible things can happen in such places."

The three stood shuffling their feet in the sand,

exchanging nervous glances. Their quest, Zagora realized, had been turned on its head, and they were no longer looking for Pitblade Yegen. Now they were on a desperate search for their father.

"Even if bad things happen, it doesn't matter," she said. "We have to go into those caves, Dunkie."

For once her brother didn't make a wisecrack about being called Dunkie. "You're right," he said. "We need to find out if Dad's in there."

"Zagora, you should ride the dromedary," said Razziq. "Then you'll see the desert from a different angle."

Zagora put a foot in the stirrup and swung one leg over Sophie, the boys pushing her up on top of the camel. They were heading into dangerous territory, she knew, with no one to rescue them if things went wrong. But what other choice did they have? *Stay calm,* she told herself, *be brave. That's what Freya Stark would do.*

As Sophie plodded ahead, Zagora studied the cliff, with its looming rock caves and black weathered walls, images of hyenas, snakes and bats tumbling through her head. Was there such a thing as desert bats? Her father would know. He knew everything about the desert.

Suddenly she realized how terribly she missed him, and her heart began to ache.

The attack came out of nowhere, fierce and unexpected, as the three children approached the entrance to the caves. Clinging to Sophie, Zagora gaped in surprise as a group of skeletal figures suddenly leapt from inside the caves, lunging at them from all sides: mummy-like creatures with savage black eyes, rags hanging from gaunt bodies, waving long curved swords.

With guttural shouts the attackers surrounded the two boys, taking them by their arms and dragging them into the caves. Before Zagora could escape on her camel, spidery hands pulled her down off Sophie's back. "Duncan!" she screamed as her *cheche* flew off. "Razziq!" Swinging and kicking, she tumbled backward into the sand.

She heard the boys' voices echoing from inside the caves, followed by Sophie's frenzied whinny as the camel reared up, magnificent and brave, like a warrior. Next came the crack of a whip, and Zagora, flat on her back, watched a large hoof come down, striking her above the eye.

An intense pain shot through her head. Her vision blurred. Sinewy arms took hold of her, lifting her out of the sand, and she felt herself being carried to where it was cool and dark.

A wave of nausea passed over her as they set her down on the sandy floor and covered her with a blanket. Bone weary, she fell into a dreamless sleep.

Some time later, she awoke with a jolt, confused, with no idea where she was and only a vague memory of how she'd gotten there. Her left eye throbbed painfully and her stomach was churning. She desperately needed a drink of water. Remembering the Oryx Stone, she checked to see if it was still in place, relieved to feel its smooth shape beneath her shirt.

Rubbing her swollen eye, she looked around the chamber, trying to sort out what had happened. She seemed to be inside some sort of cave. But where were Duncan and Razziq?

Above her sputtered an ancient lamp, smelling of smoke and dripping oil, throwing shadows across the walls. The cold air filled her chest with moisture. She had a dim memory of Razziq saying there were dark spirits here. Her pulse began to race as she imagined hideous creatures with lopsided heads and spiked wings creeping out of the walls and crowding around her, pressing on her windpipe until she couldn't breathe.

There had to be a way out. Zagora lurched to her feet. The room tilted crazily when she took a step, and she realized she was too dizzy to walk. Sitting back down, she noticed a strange-looking drawing on the wall in front of her.

The images had faded over time, but she could just make out a spiral pattern of hands, each hand holding a small blue stone—with an oryx at its center. Fascinated, Zagora stared at the ancient drawing until her head began to ache. What did all those Oryx Stones mean? She could see that none of the hands were alike, yet it was impossible to decipher the meaning of the artwork. Her dad would know, of course—but she had to find him first.

Then from a dark corner came a low rustling. In the dim light Zagora saw a dog with matted fur and a stony expression slinking toward her, its hackles raised. She could hear the sound of her blood beating against her temples. The animal looked feral, alien—and somewhat crazed. Slowly Zagora stood up, her eyes flicking back and forth, looking for a weapon.

"Do not be afraid, Zagora," whispered a voice that might have been the wind or the soft crumbling of rocks. "You are safe here. You are in the Azimuth Caves."

A minty fragrance wafted through the air. Out of the shadows floated a tall, thin figure. Red hair framed the copper-colored face like a halo of fire.

"Mina!" she cried.

"Did I not say we would meet in the desert?" Mina

held out a small clay bowl filled with an acrid-smelling mixture that looked like pancake batter with grainy bits.

"What's in there?" asked Zagora, eyeing the bowl suspiciously.

"Mustard poultice, for your eye. Is it hurting?"

"Course it hurts," Zagora snapped. She frowned at the scrawny mongrel, now curled around Mina's feet. "Is that dog rabid?"

"It is not a dog, it is a jackal. But it will not attack unless I order it."

A jackal! Oh right, she had a stamp with a jackal on it at home. But this one looked aggressive—and she wasn't convinced it would follow Mina's instructions, since it seemed to have a mind of its own.

"Grandmother says I must follow the stone of the oryx," said Mina, sounding a bit annoyed about the whole thing. "And so I am here." She dipped one finger into the poultice and dabbed the ointment around Zagora's eye. Despite its weird smell, Zagora found it soothing.

"You mean you have to follow me around everywhere?" asked Zagora. No wonder Mina didn't look too happy. "But . . . how did you know I was going to be here?"

Mina looked at her as if she'd asked a silly question.

"Did I not tell you Grandmother is a desert seer?" She sighed. "You still have the stone, yes?"

"Yes," whispered Zagora. Pointing to the drawing on the wall, she asked, "What does this picture mean? Why are all those hands holding the Oryx Stone?"

"This drawing is ancient, many centuries old. These are the hands through which the stone of the oryx will pass. That is why we call this chamber the Cave of Hands." She gave a cryptic smile. "You know, I think perhaps the stone is too much of a burden for you. Is this true? Perhaps *I* should take the stone to Zahir."

Zagora clasped the stone to her chest with a fierce protectiveness.

"I'm not giving the stone to you," she said through clenched teeth. "I'm not giving it to anyone."

Mina said nothing, her fingers moving deftly between the bowl and Zagora's eye. Then she set down the bowl, took a strip of dried meat from her pocket and handed it to Zagora. The meat was tough and sinewy, but Zagora wolfed it down anyway. The taste was disgusting; she hoped it wasn't anything too exotic, like lizard or hyena (or—she threw a furtive glance at the dog—jackal).

Mina gave her a cup of water and she drank it down, washing away the bitter taste. The water seemed to clear her mind. "Oh yeah, I remember now! Sophie was try-ing to fight those mummy guys off, 'cause she's a warrior camel, and she accidentally kicked me. Do you know if Duncan and Razziq are okay?"

Mina nodded and Zagora felt relief wash over her. "Where are they?" she asked, anxious to be with the others again. "I want to see them!"

"You must rest first," murmured the girl, frowning.

Unconvinced, Zagora leapt up, searching for her backpack. "You know, I really think I should be with them." She swayed dizzily, her mind in a muddle, then looked at the jackal. It was growling quietly.

"Very well," said Mina, her voice sharp. "I will take you."

Mina steered Zagora out of the chamber and pulled her through a cavernous space filled with strange echoes and flaming torches. The jackal followed. One cavern led to another and Zagora realized she was in a whole series of caverns.

"This is the Azimuth's secret place?" she said to Mina. "Here in these caves?" It seemed awfully sad to her, to live where it was damp and dark, surrounded by moldy stone walls.

"Yes. We are the forgotten. We are shadows of what

we once were." Mina's eyes glittered darkly as she slowed to a stop, the jackal pressed against her. "You must say nothing about these things to anyone. You must tell no one that the Azimuth are here."

"No one," whispered Zagora. Probably not a good idea to mention that she'd already told her father, Duncan and Abdul.

She had more questions, but Mina took off in a swirl of tattered robes. They plunged into heavy darkness, twisting and turning, ducking beneath crude archways, bumping into walls, the jackal a quick black shadow at Mina's side. At last they entered a vast cave strung with lanterns, its walls etched with squiggly shapes that Zagora knew to be glyphs. The domed ceiling was painted with stars, moons and whirling planets. Around the edges of the ceiling were tight little heaps of what looked like bats.

"This is the Chamber of the Cenozoic Moon," announced Mina, bowing her head. "Here we honor the ancients, ancestors who were stargazers and watchers of planets."

From the far end of the chamber came low murmurs and whispers—the ominous sounds Zagora had heard earlier in the caves—and she took deep breaths to calm herself. Through the flickering light she could see jackals like the one at Mina's side slinking along the walls, and the outlines of cadaverous figures, tall and forbidding.

The tall figures emerged from the shadows and she gasped, seeing their desiccated bodies, their rawboned limbs and gaunt faces. These were the mummy people who'd attacked her! Yet here in this cave they looked nothing like warriors. Their bodies seemed cobbled together from skin and bones, and around their eyes were delicate tattoos, which she guessed were scorpions. It seemed as if they were all talking at once, waving their arms in dramatic gestures, their voices sounding alternately angry, demanding, aggressive and cruel.

"Always they are arguing," said Mina. She gave a loud sniff. "Never can they agree."

"That's *them*!" whispered Zagora. "The mummy people!"

Mina glared at her with a stormy frown. Beside her the jackal growled deep inside its throat. "Not mummies." The girl pushed her face close to Zagora's. "They are Azimuth elders."

"They had swords." Zagora recalled their ferocious expressions. "I thought they were going to kill us!"

"The Azimuth attacked you because they felt threatened. You are strangers, and they were frightened. And fear," Mina added with a melancholy smile, "is what some of us have to live with."

Zagora saw the elders exchanging swift, panicked looks and retreating into the shadows, followed by the jackals. Mina's jackal darted away after them.

"Quick!" said Mina, pulling her through a doorway carved with moons, into a smoky torch-lit tunnel. They sprinted through a honeycomb of caverns until at last Mina pushed her through an entryway thick with cobwebs, into a dark cave.

"Zagora?" came a familiar voice. "Is that you?"

"Dunkie!" she shouted, seeing her brother's chunky frame emerge from the shadows. They threw their arms around each other and she found herself choking up. She didn't know what she'd do if she lost him, too.

"Oh man," said Duncan. "I thought they'd chopped you into tiny little—"

"Sophie kicked me and I got a black eye," she said, cutting him off. "I'm okay. Mina put some kind of mustard on it." She showed him her swollen eye and he grimaced.

"Zagora!" Razziq appeared beside Duncan and flashed his warm smile. "You are not harmed? No broken bones?"

"I'm good," Zagora said, hugging him. "My eye's hurt a bit, that's all."

"Your camel is down below, with the other dromedaries."

His words made her feel as if a great weight had been lifted. Sophie was okay!

"Those skull faces dragged us in here, but they didn't hurt us or anything," said Duncan. "They gave us meat jerky to eat, gahh!"

Seeing the others brought everything into focus, and Zagora felt a sudden longing for her father. A tear rolled down her cheek, and soon she was sobbing quietly to herself. The boys put their arms around her, trying their best to comfort her, and she gave them each a sorrowful smile. She sensed a fluttering above her head and saw Mina's small hand brushing away her tears with the frayed hem of her robe. *Mina's my friend, too,* she thought, *sort of.*

At last she stopped crying, and Mina motioned them forward with her hand. They all followed, ducking through small caves until they reached a crudely built door. With a theatrical gesture Mina flung it open, and blue light spilled over them.

"Nar Azrak!" cried Duncan.

Zagora rushed with the others to a balcony and, gripping the stone edge, gazed out over a line of dunes. Nar Azrak hung low in the sky, an immense globe wrapped in misty vapors, frighteningly close, turning the desert landscape blue. She could see the planet was noticeably larger than the night before, and far brighter.

"Every night Nar Azrak grows in size," said Mina in a tremulous voice. "It threatens a darkness foretold long ago by Azimuth seers."

"The Time of the Scorpions," said Zagora, recalling Abdul's somber words. "We know all about that."

Mina gave a grim nod. The others stood quietly, eyes fixed on Nar Azrak.

Then Zagora heard the sound of hooves thudding across the sand. Leaning over the balcony, she suddenly saw the Azimuth, in blue robes and turbans, faces covered, galloping across the dunes on white camels, waving scimitars and flaming torches.

"Azimuth warriors," said Mina proudly. "They wear desert *cheche,* like the Tuareg."

Zagora saw something huge and dark come out from behind a dune, running fast on numerous legs. Then there were tens of them, enormous shapes that slid from hill to hill. They were sharp angles against the sky, glinting in the blue light of Nar Azrak. Spare and menacing, with long spiny tails arched over their backs, the creatures moved on tall, stalklike legs, their unearthly shrieks echoing back and forth across the dunes.

They were scorpions, huge scorpions—giant scorpions!

She stared in dread and fascination while the Azimuth charged on their camels, shouting rallying cries as they approached the enemy. Two camels stumbled, tossing their riders into the sand. Moments later the scorpions surrounded them, their barbed tails raised to strike.

More Azimuth warriors surged forward, urging their camels on. Zagora flinched as one warrior sliced off a scorpion's claw. Another flung his torch, setting two scorpions on fire, and with shrill screams the creatures went up in flames.

"Always the scorpions come at night, under the light of Nar Azrak," said Mina.

"These scorpions," said Razziq in a horrified whisper, "they are . . . unnatural."

Terror, twisting and wormlike, wound its way through Zagora. How many of those things were out there, hiding behind the dunes, watching with black eyes? She thought back to the scorpion she'd dropped into Olivia's tea and the scorpions that had attacked Uncle Ali in his shop. Then a new fear took hold of her.

"Duncan, Dad doesn't know about the giant scorpions!" she cried. "He's lost in the desert and he doesn't know they're out there!"

They stared helplessly at one another while triumphant shouts drifted up to the balcony from below. Through tears and the smoke of burning torches, Zagora watched as the scorpions, shrieking furiously, scuttled over the dune and then vanished.

꧁ THE MEETING OF THE ORYX ꧂

After a rough night of tossing on a hard bed of sand and dreaming about scorpions, Zagora sat eating saffron cakes with Duncan, Razziq and Mina, talking about the monstrous creatures they'd seen the night before. Torches sputtered from the walls of a chamber that smelled of earth and fungus.

"Don't worry, Zagora," Duncan kept saying. "Dad can manage out there. He's desert-savvy."

That was true, but still she worried. Edgar Yegen had been desert-savvy, too.

"I was wondering, Mina," said Duncan, popping the last cake into his mouth, "did your ancestors worship Nar Azrak? I mean, was the planet some kind of a god?"

Mina threw him an icy look. "Not a god, no. Stones fell to the desert from Nar Azrak and the Azimuth used them to build a small pyramid. The Azimuth took from the stones a kind of magic—the power of Nar Azrak—and this magic protected Zahir."

"Hmm, that's sort of what I thought," said Duncan. "So the pyramid was aligned with Nar Azrak and all this planetary energy created a force field around Zahir. But when the Oryx Stone—also from Nar Azrak, right?—was stolen, the planet jumped out of orbit and the protective field around Zahir crumbled. In short, everything went haywire."

"Now Nar Azrak moves closer to Earth," murmured Razziq. "That is very haywire."

"Yes, that is what happened," said Mina. "Now it is time for you to go. Follow me."

Zagora stepped out of the caves into blinding sunlight, pleased to see Sophie, freshly brushed and fed, waiting for her. Blankets were thrown over her hump, along with water containers and woven bags.

"The journey to the tower is not long," Mina told them. "I have packed for you dried meat, figs, nuts, gourds of fresh water and . . . mustard poultice."

Zagora smiled. Her eye still hurt, but it was healing quickly.

"Follow the arc of the sun," instructed Mina, pointing down the canyon, "and keep following to where the sun goes down. Sometimes the path to Zahir is difficult, and you can easily become lost. Remember to take shelter before dark, because once darkness falls, the scorpions will be out—and they will be hunting, as they do every night."

Zagora swallowed hard. She knew they'd never stand a chance against giant scorpions.

"You go in search of your father," said Mina, fixing her black eyes on Zagora, "but do not forget the stone of the oryx. When you reach Zahir, you will know soon enough the power of the stone."

Zagora nodded. Maybe the stone needed Zahir to wake up its powers.

"If our dad turns up, you'll tell him we went to the tower, right, Mina?" said Duncan. "His name is Pym, Dr. Charles W. Pym."

"Yes, yes, I will remember," said Mina impatiently. "Now hurry. Go!"

The three children set off through the canyon, its walls pale yellow in the early morning light. Sitting atop her camel, Zagora glanced uneasily at the dune where they'd seen the scorpions the previous night.

"Adios, badlands!" shouted Duncan, grinning at Razziq.

Zagora waved at Mina as they headed west, watching her dwindle into a speck of blue.

"We have to make sure we go in a straight line," said Duncan. "I read that if you drive cross-country in the desert and miscalculate your direction by a few degrees, you can miss your destination by miles."

"That's not going to happen to us!" Zagora shouted down from the camel. "We'll just follow Mina's advice."

Every few steps Sophie hesitated, grumbling and creaking. Zagora nudged her neck with her foot the way she'd seen Azimuth warriors do, but Sophie refused to go any faster. Whispering into the camel's ear, she coaxed her on.

As the sun inched higher, beads of sweat rolled down Zagora's back. Everywhere she looked she could see miles and miles of sand, stretching to the far horizon— endless waves of star dunes, blown by African winds, changing shape from one minute to the next. Now she knew why her father always said that no map could chart the desert exactly.

The wind tore at her turban, blowing sand into her eyes, and the air turned a weird shade of yellow. She was finding it more difficult to breathe. The heat grew so intense it seemed as if all the oxygen were being sucked out of the air. As they crested a dune, a hot wind sprang up and a whirling blizzard of sand descended, engulfing the three of them in an instant.

She heard Duncan shout: "Holy mackerel, a sandstorm!"

"Stay together!" cried Razziq. "We must not lose each other!"

Fighting back panic, Zagora clung to Sophie's neck as whirlwind pillars of sand billowed around them. She remembered her father telling her that desert storms could bury a truck or a herd of goats in just a few hours. As they edged down a steep incline, the sand eddied and spun, darkening the air, turning Duncan and Razziq to shadows, and Zagora reached under her *cheche,* fingers grasping the Oryx Stone, trying to call up its unearthly superpowers.

Waves of sand flew by, enormous sheets of it, blocking out the sun, and she knew they could easily lose their way. What if the sand buried them completely? She imagined an archaeologist in the year 3000, digging beneath the sand and finding a puzzle of bones. He'd never know that her name was Zagora and that her brilliant father had been kidnapped. Her bones would be carbon-dated and displayed in a museum with a sign reading GIRL FROM 21ST CENTURY, MOROCCAN SAHARA.

Almost imperceptibly the light seemed to change, infused with a reddish tinge. A far-off wind echoed inside her ears. Before her a sparkling curtain of sand parted and she saw the oryx, sleek and elegant, moving up the side of a dune. Astonished, she watched it pause at the top of the dune and stand motionless, gazing down at her. Edgar had written that the oryxes seemed to be waiting for him to approach them. Was the oryx waiting for *her*?

"Keep an eye on my camel, I'll be right back," she said, sliding off Sophie and handing Duncan the reins.

"Are you crazy?" He grabbed her by the arm. "You're not going anywhere! This is a sandstorm!"

"Yeah, but I'm pretty sure there's an oryx up there on the dune!" she shouted, pointing ahead, although by now only blowing sand was visible.

"You should not go off alone, Zagora. It will be hard to find each other again." Razziq placed an arm on her shoulder, eyes gleaming behind his *cheche*. "In the desert a nomad never leaves his companions. It is the same for the three of us. We must stay together, no matter what happens."

"Sorry," she said, feeling embarrassed. "But I really did see an oryx."

"It was probably a mirage," Duncan told her, sounding like their father. "Wouldn't be surprising, since we're in the desert."

Razziq gave her a quizzical look. "I think Zagora may have a desert skill that very few people possess. Nomads speak of desert sight, a very special gift. Perhaps she sees an oryx that lived here many years ago."

"Seriously?" said Duncan, sounding doubtful. He thought a moment. "But I guess you know about these things, right, Razz?"

Zagora smiled. She'd always been jealous of Duncan's big brain and all those awards he'd won. He could chart distances of stars, balance equations and memorize formulas, and he was a whiz at fixing computer glitches. But mention magic or the supernatural and he would hyperventilate: the idea of invisible worlds was too foreign a concept.

And while Duncan had seen only dust and sand, *she* had seen the oryx.

"We must keep going!" Razziq shouted over the wind. "The storm is getting worse."

"This camel isn't cooperating," said Duncan, pulling on Sophie's reins.

"Even the dromedary is scared," said Razziq, stroking Sophie's muzzle. "Like all of us."

Struggling against the wind, they closed ranks and, gripping one another's hands, clambered uphill, heads bowed and eyes half shut. Raging gusts tore at their clothes, snarled their hair, unspooled their turbans and threw sand into their eyes, trapping them inside a void of whirling sand and howling wind.

Halfway up a dune, Zagora caught a glint of gold and felt a rush of excitement, seeing the oryx lift its elegant head and gaze into her eyes.

"Hurry, Zagora," said Duncan, his voice filled with urgency, "we have to keep going."

No longer able to resist, she pulled herself away and scrambled up the dune, ignoring Duncan's shouts, storming uphill, knowing as she went that she might be putting them all in danger. The sand formed a whirling tunnel around her, and moments later, she stood before the oryx—the same one, she was certain, that had appeared to her in the casbah of Marrakech.

The wild, staring eyes of the oryx drew her in closer, its supernatural light enveloping her. There was something fierce and mystical about the creature—a transcendent quality—and she knew she was falling under its spell. The oryx was not solid, but transparent, like a ghost—what Mrs. Bixby would have called *ethereal,* a word she reserved for only the most inscrutable things of this world.

Feeling a sudden inexplicable urge, Zagora reached for the Oryx Stone and lifted it up for the oryx to see, sensing the warmth and wonder of it, the ancient loveliness that was the stone.

"Look, an oryx," she whispered. "It's *you* they carved into this magic stone."

The oryx seemed to gaze at the stone with knowing eyes. Sniffing, it ventured nearer, as if it recognized something very old and very familiar. Deep inside the stone, a small fire burned brightly.

Then, unexpectedly, the diaphanous, smoky outline of the oryx began to darken. Zagora watched, open-mouthed, as the animal grew so dense she could no longer see through it. Its whorled horns, like polished roots of ancient trees, threw off a soft metallic light. The oryx stood before her, solitary and silent in the wind, snorting out dust through its nose—a living, breathing animal. The Oryx Stone had brought the oryx to life!

Alive, the oryx was even more beautiful, its movements exquisite. Zagora loved its wise face and sculpted horns, its eyes the color of the sea, and the way it turned its slender neck to lift its head. Standing motionless, she stared into those eyes, miles and miles into the center of its being, seeing right through to its goodness, its mystery, its wondrous beating heart, while the stone continued to glow in her hand.

Shouts came from below and the oryx wheeled around, kicking its legs, bounding gracefully over the dune, vanishing into the storm. Dizzying waves of sand blew past, and for a shining instant, time fell away, revealing a tower washed in silvery light, guarded by blue-robed men on white camels, sabers raised to the sky. Far below, Zagora could see a dusty wide road lined with tall columns, filled with camel caravans, goatherds and travelers on horseback.

The road led to a city with red stone walls. Ancient Zahir! She was seeing into the past again. Inhaling the smells of hibiscus and orange, the dusky scent of figs, she was stunned by the city's elegance: the towers and temples, the lush gardens and crooked streets, the palace of ocher and pink. Inside a great courtyard, a small pyramid of blue stones was being constructed.

Then the vision began to fade, its shadowy images dissolving, drained of all color and light, and the harsh blowing sand returned, swirling around her.

"Zagora!" shouted Razziq, running up to her, his turban flying apart. "We have been calling for you!"

"We thought you were lost," puffed Duncan behind him.

"I was talking to the oryx," Zagora said breathlessly. "And guess what, you guys. The Oryx Stone brought the oryx to life! It's real, it's not a ghost anymore!" She was shouting now. "The stone has the power to make the ghost oryxes real!"

Duncan looked at her, confused, but Razziq clearly understood.

"One day the oryxes will return to Zahir," said the boy, sounding a bit nostalgic. "An old legend, but many believe it is true. Perhaps this stone has such power."

"The Oryx Stone can bring animals to life?" said Duncan, scratching his head. "Wow."

"I saw the tower!" said Zagora excitedly. "And I saw Zahir—ancient Zahir! It was incredible!"

Razziq looked at her silently with his dark brown eyes. At last he said, "Then it is true, you have the gift."

"Did you say the Tower of the Enigmas?" asked Duncan. "Where?"

She spun around, pointing in the direction of Zahir, then felt a sudden stab of panic. Why wasn't she hearing

Sophie growling and spitting, the way she always did in the wind?

"Is Sophie okay?" she shouted to Duncan. Although he was only inches away, she could hardly see him.

A blurry hand lifted the reins and her mouth dropped open. The reins dangling from Duncan's hand were attached to . . . nothing! Where was Sophie? Zagora felt her heart leap into her mouth. The camel must have been so frightened by the storm that she'd bolted.

"The dromedary!" cried Razziq, turning and running downhill.

From below came a frenzied whinny.

"Sophie!" shrieked Zagora, hurtling down the slope after Razziq.

Razziq shouted back to her: "She's fallen in quicksand—she is sinking!"

Through cascading sand Zagora saw a dark shape, struggling and twisting, legs churning. Sophie had collapsed and was being pulled under. Covered up to her flanks, the camel tried to raise her head, but her efforts were futile. Her bottom half had disappeared and now the rest of her body was slowly sinking.

Seeing Zagora, she gave a high, frantic cry, thrashing her head violently back and forth.

Zagora stared in shock and disbelief, helpless. She felt a hand on her arm and, turning, faced Razziq. "Do something!" she cried.

"Don't go near there, Zagora," he said firmly. "Your dromedary has fallen into a sinkhole."

"But it's pulling her under! Sophie can't get out! You have to save her, Razziq!" She stared numbly as Sophie's tail vanished under the sand. "No!" she screamed.

Razziq put his arm around her shoulders. "We can do nothing," he said quietly, his face hidden by the blowing sand. "I am sorry, Zagora."

Sophie gave one last cry and Zagora sobbed in wild despair.

As Sophie's head slipped out of sight, Zagora and Razziq clung to each other like shipwrecked survivors. Zagora felt her heart shatter as the top of Sophie's hump sank from view.

The camel's furry ears were the last part of her to disappear.

TRADER, MAPMAKER, HUNTER OF ANTIQUITIES

Zagora sobbed all the way up the dune, struggling along-side Razziq through torrents of swirling sand. All she could see were Sophie's dark soulful eyes and twitching ears. She could still smell the camel's grassy breath, like when Sophie yawned, goofily showing her black gums and yellow teeth. Zagora had known from the beginning that Sophie was special, and she was certain that Sophie, with her keen camel intuition, had understood her deep passion for the desert.

Over the sounds of the storm, she heard Duncan call-ing to them, and she looked up to see a lumpy shape slogging downhill.

"What's happened?" he asked, sounding short of breath.

"The dromedary was swallowed into a sinkhole," Razziq told him in a solemn voice. "We could not save her, it happened too fast."

"Oh no," said Duncan, his voice quavering, "this is all my fault! I thought Sophie was right next to me, but with all the sand and wind, I . . ."

Zagora said nothing; she was too distraught to be angry with her brother.

"I'm sorry. I'm really, really sorry!" Duncan tried to console her, but she felt too numb to respond.

"We have to get out of this storm," said Razziq. "If there is a tower nearby, we must find it and take shelter. The storm could go on for hours."

"You're right, Razz, let's go." Duncan gently patted his sister's shoulder. "C'mon, Zagora."

She nodded, too weary to think anymore. Beneath the *cheche,* her face was wet with tears. Taking hold of their hands, she trudged on, images of her father and Sophie, as elusive as the shifting sands, tumbling through her mind.

Peering through plumes of dust, she caught glimpses of the tower, looming over them on a high plateau, its wind-scoured walls fading in and out of sight. Ranged in a circle at the base of the tower were at least a dozen oryxes, exquisite and terrifying. They matched exactly Edgar Yegen's description of them. Only, these oryxes were alive; their magnificent hearts were beating! *That's because the Oryx Stone is magic after all,* Zagora thought, *and the stone brought them to life.*

"I don't believe it," said Razziq. "I am seeing a tower—and I see oryxes!"

"Holy cow!" cried Duncan. "They're not extinct after all!"

Hands linked, they charged up the plateau in a burst of energy. Dark columns of sand slanted in the wind, swirling around them as they blindly made their way. Zagora knew for sure they were at the tower when she bumped into something solid: it was a door of rough-hewn wood, rounded at the top and embellished with glyphs, set inside an archway of stone.

"Where did the oryxes go?" puffed Duncan as the three huddled beneath the crumbling archway. "They weren't mirages, were they?"

"I think we scared them off," said Razziq.

Zagora wasn't so sure. Oryxes didn't scare easily.

"Right, then—time for the old heave-ho," said Duncan.

Together they pushed on the door, and with a loud creak, it swung inward. Zagora tumbled into a gloomy space with high stone walls, the others collapsing on top of her. Razziq quickly leapt up, kicked the door shut and bolted it against the wind.

She unwrapped her turban, sand flying everywhere. Her swollen eye was crusted with sand, but it no longer throbbed painfully, so she knew Mina's poultice must be working. Brushing sand from her hair and clothes, she stood up to get a look at her surroundings.

The tower had the feel of a desert outpost, or at least the way she imagined one, with thick curved walls and a desolate interior. Sand drifted across the bumpy cobbled floor, and high above, sand blew in through tall narrow windows. On the far wall a stone staircase corkscrewed up to a turret. Zagora had read in Edgar's journal that the tower was deceptively large, with hidden rooms underground, filled with mysterious glyphs and drawings. But none of those things mattered now. What mattered was finding their father.

Duncan and Razziq shook out their robes and turbans; their faces, caked with dirt and sand, were hardly recognizable. Razziq passed around a gourd of water—their last, Zagora realized, since their remaining supplies had gone down with Sophie—and they each took a drink.

"We'll search this place from top to bottom," said Duncan, looking around. "No clue is too small."

Zagora nodded in agreement. "And—and we . . . But Sophie's dead," she whispered, letting the reality finally sink in. "My camel's gone!" Overwhelmed by a terrible sense of loss, she let out a gut-wrenching wail and crumpled to the floor, weeping bitterly. "She's dead dead dead!"

Razziq knelt down beside her and placed his small hand in hers. She kept crying, thinking how she'd never see Sophie again. The wind moaned through the tower, drowning out her sobs.

After what seemed like hours, it was over; she wiped her eyes and nose on her sleeve and stood up. "Sorry," she said. "I'm ready to look for Dad now."

Razziq drew a sharp breath. She followed his gaze to the far side of the tower, where a light flickered through an opening in the floor that she hadn't noticed earlier.

"Someone's down there," she whispered, too frightened to move.

The others stood frozen in place. She could almost hear their hearts beating in unison. Holding her breath, she crept toward the light—it was coming from a trapdoor someone had left open—and stared down a flight of crooked stone steps. The smell of smoke drifted up.

Duncan sniffed; then he started to smile. "I think someone's cooking something down there." But his grin quickly faded. "Guys, I don't know if this is safe. We don't know who's down there. Maybe one of us should go first—you know, like a scout."

"But we're supposed to be like nomads," argued Zagora, "and Razziq said nomads never leave their companions. We go down together or nobody goes."

She felt drawn to the warmth of the strange light—and the possibility that their father might be down there.

"Our quest is different now," she went on. "We're not looking for Pitblade Yegen anymore. We're on a mission to find Dad, and we won't stop until we find him."

"Yeah, but we can't just walk into a room full of kidnappers and ask for our father back," said Duncan. "There could be smugglers down there, plotting dastardly deeds."

What kind of talk was that, *dastardly deeds*? Then Zagora remembered that her brother had recently finished a book called *The Smugglers of Truro*.

For a moment the wind ceased howling, and from below came a disembodied voice, high and raspy. The three stood listening. It reminded Zagora of the voices she used to hear crackling through the airwaves on Aunt Agnes's shortwave radio.

"I know this song," said Razziq, his eyes bright. "It is an old nomad song."

"Listen, guys, here's what we do," whispered Zagora. "We sneak down, the three of us, totally quiet, and keep to the walls. We check it all out, and if it's not safe, we turn around and head back up here. Simple." She looked at Duncan, imagining the wheels turning inside his head: *click, click, click.*

Duncan wiped his sweaty face with the edge of his shirt. "That's what Dad always says," he grumbled. "He'll say something's simple when it's not simple at all." He glanced at Razziq, then back at Zagora. But Zagora was not going to give in.

"Okay," he said at last, his face pale but resolute. "I'm ready. Let's go."

♣ ♣ ♣

They stood beside the trapdoor, breathing in smells of spicy cooked food and staring down into a dark murky space. Diffuse light illuminated the stairwell. The steps looked like they might lead to a dungeon, but Zagora tried not to think about that. Glancing at Duncan, she felt a surge of affection, thinking how hard he was trying to be brave.

They nodded at one another, gripped hands and started down. As they descended the crooked steps, the air grew cooler, and the smell of burnt food became more intense. Down and down they spiraled, until the steps ended. Ahead Zagora could see a passageway lined with rough stone and archways unfolding, one after the other, a dim light streaming through them. Was she really up to this? What if they were attacked? How would they protect themselves?

She motioned for the others to crouch low. Heads down, they slunk through the archways, keeping close to the walls, sand muffling their footsteps. In the grainy light, everything seemed alien, misplaced in time. She strained to hear the voice again, but everything was quiet. On the walls she noticed faded drawings of galaxies and constellations, colored with what her dad would describe as natural dyes—reds, yellows, blues. Her brother paused every few steps, tracing a pudgy finger over a star or a planet.

The last archway opened into a small domed chamber walled with shiny black stone. Zagora recognized it from Mrs. Bixby's Earth Science lessons as volcanic rock. There were no windows; smoke rose from a small fire and wafted up through a makeshift chimney. The three stared apprehensively into the shadows and flickering light.

With a start she noticed a lone haggard figure, hunched by the fire. As if sensing their presence, the stranger began singing off-key.

"What do you think?" she whispered, staring wide-eyed at the others. "Does he look like a kidnapper?"

Duncan shrugged. "He looks harmless, but who knows?"

A faint smile crossed Razziq's face. "This man sings Arab folk songs. He doesn't appear dangerous, but we should keep our distance. It is possible he knows something."

"I'm going for a closer look," said Zagora, trying to put on a courageous front. "I'll be right back." She flattened herself against the wall and inched her way around the perimeter of the room, hoping the smoke wouldn't make her cough.

As she drew nearer to the figure, she could see a silver dagger at his waist, and she began to make out vague facial features. Beneath the softly wrapped head cloth, two eyes burned strangely. Around the face, light quivered. Zagora thought of mythic beasts and angels, of dark beings dropped secretly to Earth. As she stepped bravely

forward, ready to introduce herself, Duncan let out a
hair-raising scream. Startled, the man leapt up, waving
the dagger, and Zagora froze, her heart thumping wildly.

"A rat!" shrieked Duncan. "A rat ran over my foot!"

Oh no, thought Zagora, *we're done for!*

Tall but stooped, the man began shouting in Arabic.
Zagora saw Razziq jump out from behind the archway;
keeping one eye on the dagger, he began speaking to the
stranger in a slow, calm voice. The man fell quiet, and
after a few moments, he set the knife down on the floor.

Duncan loped over to Zagora. "That rat was—"

"You almost got us killed!" she hissed at him, trembling with fear.

"This man asks what we are doing here," said Razziq
in a loud voice.

Zagora felt a twinge of excitement. The stranger must
be connected in some way to Zahir, or why would he be
here? Maybe he was a watcher, a kind of gatekeeper, like
she'd read about in olden-day books. He was bound to
have seen travelers passing through the city.

"Tell him our father was kidnapped and we're looking for him," she said in a shaky voice. "Our dad promised to meet us here—tell him that, too."

"Ask if he's seen any ne'er-do-wells or unsavory
characters," added Duncan.

Ne'er-do-wells? What the heck century was her brother from? she wondered. Oh yeah, it was probably another phrase from *The Smugglers of Truro.*

"This man sees nobody for many weeks," translated Razziq. "But in the desert, he says, strange things can happen, and sometimes people disappear."

Thinking of her father, Zagora felt a pain, raw and sharp, deep in her chest.

The stranger tossed something into the air. A lizard impaled on a stick, charred from the fire, landed at her feet. Zagora saw what looked like tooth marks along one side and her stomach did a slow flip.

"Spotted lizard," said Razziq. "He says to eat this: high protein, to keep you strong."

To her surprise, Duncan picked up the lizard and lifted it to his lips, but he didn't bite into it. *He must be starving,* she thought. She had lost her appetite completely. The man threw over a beetle, its wings crushed, but neither she nor her brother touched it. Beetles were good-luck signs, but a chewed-up one probably didn't count.

The stranger crooked a thin finger, motioning them closer, and they shuffled warily toward him. As they closed the distance separating them, Zagora began to see the man's features more clearly: sunken eyes; papery skin;

a long, bony face. A jagged scar sliced through one eye-brow.

"You are English?" he asked, and she looked at him in surprise. "I hardly recognized the language. It has been a long time since I've heard it spoken."

Zagora listened curiously to the stranger's odd, clipped accent. "We're from America," she said, feeling a bit less scared knowing he spoke English. "We're here on a quest."

The smell of burnt lizard was beginning to make her feel nauseated. Suddenly, more than anything, she wanted to be home, sitting at the kitchen table, joking with her dad and Duncan, eating pizza with everything on it. She wanted to be reading *Tintin* or losing all her Boardwalk hotels to Duncan in Monopoly. She wanted things to be the way they used to be.

"How did you find your way here?" asked the stranger. The scar on his face was deep and ferocious and it gave her the shivers. It was the kind of scar a desert explorer would have—maybe one who'd been attacked by a scorpion.

"An or-oryx," she stuttered. "We were lost in the sandstorm, then all of a sudden I saw an oryx. It led us to the tower."

The man's breath rattled excitedly. "You saw an *oryx*? Well, well. How extraordinary."

Zagora was proud of having encountered an animal that was rare, and in most places—including Morocco—gone forever. "I know oryxes are classified as EW—Extinct in the Wild, that is," she went on, feeling more confident, "but I really did see the oryx. It was sort of . . . ethereal."

The man smiled at her, and she could see his teeth were discolored.

"Razz and I saw oryxes, too," Duncan piped up, keeping his distance from the man. "They were standing right outside this tower."

The stranger frowned. "You've all seen oryxes?"

"We think the oryxes are coming back, see, because of the—" About to say *Oryx Stone,* Zagora stopped herself in time: not a good idea to reveal that she was carrying something of value. "Um, because of the legend. The one that says the oryxes will return to Zahir."

At first the man said nothing, and Zagora worried maybe she'd said too much.

"My dad told me that when the oryxes return to Zahir, the city will rise again." She tried to sound authoritative. "But only after great chaos."

The man nodded. "Yes, I know this foretelling. The nomads often talk of it."

"So . . ." Duncan gave a little cough, the way their father always did when he wanted to steer the conversation in a new direction. "Who exactly are you, if you don't mind my asking?"

"Trader, mapmaker, hunter of antiquities," came the dry, creaky voice, sounding as though it had not been used in a very long time. "'Round the decay of that colossal wreck, boundless and bare,'" he recited. "'The lone and level sands stretch far away.'"

"I know that poem!" said Zagora, amazed to hear familiar words in a place that was so foreign. "Mrs. Bixby read it to our class."

"'Ozymandias,'" breathed the man, sounding a bit more, well, friendly. "Shelley, of course."

In the firelight, Zagora noticed, his eyes seemed to be made from beaten gold. She was no longer frightened of him; in fact, she was eager to find out more. There was, she decided, something almost *mystical* about this stranger.

"Then you're a cartographer," said Duncan. "You draw maps—maps of the desert, right?"

"I have done that, yes," said the stranger. "Exquisite maps of the Sahara."

"So, you're not, um . . . *dying* or anything?" Zagora blurted out. She immediately regretted saying it, afraid she might have offended him.

The man ran a finger over his cracked lips. "Not dead yet." He didn't appear insulted.

Zagora saw a look of infinite sadness cross his weather-worn face. His expression was etched with misery, and she suddenly felt a kind of pity for him. She watched him put something into his mouth and heard it crack between his teeth.

"Care for one?" Licking his dry lips, he held out a handful of insects. "Fried purple locusts. Quite succulent." He waved a skewered locust in the air. "I'm not terribly fond of beetles, they leave a bitter aftertaste."

"This guy's crazy," Duncan hissed into Zagora's ear. "Remember what Dad told us, about the desert and madness going hand in hand? Here's proof."

"He's not crazy," she whispered, though she remembered her father saying the desert could drive a sane man to lunacy. "He's just . . . *different*."

The stranger leaned forward, eyes glistening. "You say your father was kidnapped?"

"We believe somebody came to our camp two nights ago and took him," said Zagora. When she talked about her father, it felt as if something sharp were stuck at the back of her throat. *This is too painful,* she thought, looking at Duncan.

"We went looking in the desert but we took a wrong turn," Duncan continued. "We slept in some caves and today we walked into a sandstorm and Sophie fell down a sinkhole."

The man blinked in surprise. "Sophie?"

"Our camel," said Razziq, throwing Zagora a sorrowful glance.

"A pity. Camels are very loyal beasts."

"Sophie wasn't a beast," said Zagora, indignant. "She was my friend!"

"Yes, of course." When the stranger moved, dust puffed off his clothes and his turban. "Now then, about this missing gentleman. What is his name?"

"Dr. Pym," said Duncan, his voice cracking.

"His friends call him Charlie," added Zagora, noticing a funny expression on the man's face. "Charles W. Pym, PhD, DSc. He's a desert expert and he specializes in glyphs and symbols and he's really, really brilliant—you could say he's a genius."

"Charlie Pym?" Locusts clattered to the floor as the stranger lifted his head in surprise. "But Charlie's supposed to be on his way to Zahir to meet with me. He should be here by now!"

⫷ SENTINELS OF THE STONE ⫸

"*You're* Pitblade Yegen?" Zagora stared in disbelief at the man's long beard, the white hair straggling from underneath his soiled turban, the face etched with lines of sadness.

"The real Pitblade Yegen is our dad's age," Duncan whispered to Razziq behind his hand.

Zagora didn't know what to think. The stranger looked put together from sticks and dust, as if he might blow away at any minute. It didn't seem possible that he could be their father's age. Yet the thought that he might actually be Pitblade Yegen unsettled her—because it meant the desert had turned him into an old, old man. Was this really what desert life did to you? Maybe it was time to scratch "desert explorer" from her career agenda and consider becoming a park ranger or an ice cream truck driver.

"I saw a photo of you in the desert," she said, "and you looked—"

The man raised a shaky finger. "Much younger? Ah yes, I was once that, too. But eleven years is a long time." His lips curved into a weary smile. "The desert always extracts a price."

"Nomads have a saying," said Razziq. "Something like 'One man enters the desert but a different man returns.'"

"My dad always says the desert changes you." Zagora couldn't take her eyes off the stranger's deep scar. "No matter how strong you are, no matter how smart." She couldn't decide if the man was a lunatic or a genius. Maybe he was both. "No matter how brave."

"Charlie's had plenty of experience with the desert, I'll grant you that." The man who called himself Pitblade gave a dry chuckle. "What I admire about your father is how equally at ease he is with both academics and nomads. A rare talent."

"I know," said Zagora, beaming. "He's my hero." Then she blurted out, "How did you get that scar?" She blushed, aware that it hadn't been a very nice thing to say.

"It is rather fierce-looking, isn't it?" he said mysteriously. "Come, listen, I will tell you my story."

They gathered in a ragged circle around the dying embers of the fire. Zagora kicked away a pile of beetle shells and sat down, anxious to hear what Pitblade Yegen had to say.

"Eleven years ago I came to Morocco to carry out archaeological excavations at Zahir," he began. "We needed help deciphering glyphs, so I invited your father. A few weeks into the project I hired a small plane to fly over the site. A sandstorm blew in and we went down: my leg was crushed and I received this gash." He traced the scar through his eyebrow. "The pilot was not so fortunate."

There was a brief silence; then he continued: "I crawled out of the plane to safety; then I passed out. When I awoke, I had lost my memory. Nomads found me wandering and nursed me back to health. For eleven years I traveled with them through the desert, unaware of my true identity. Then, two months ago, I was thrown by a camel and struck my head on a rock."

Zagora touched her swollen eye, remembering how

painful it had been to be kicked by Sophie. She listened intently as the man went on: "I was unconscious for two days, and on the third morning I sat up in my tent and all my memories came flooding back. Naturally I headed straight to Zahir, in the wild hope that my team had finished the excavations."

"Our dad told us the Moroccan government shut it down," said Duncan, sounding less skeptical, as if maybe he believed this really was their father's missing friend.

As for Zagora, she felt suddenly certain that this was Pitblade Yegen.

Pitblade nodded, sending up little clouds of dust from his turban. "Sadly, most of Zahir remains buried beneath the sand, with the exception of the casbah, where the palace stands—that was the area we'd excavated. Finding Zahir uninhabitable, I made my way here, to the Tower of the Enigmas, and sent a letter to my cousin Olivia asking her to contact your father."

Zagora exchanged knowing looks with Duncan. This probably wasn't a good time to tell Pitblade his cousin had been trying to convince people he'd gone mad in the desert.

"Did you send the message to your cousin by falcon?" asked Razziq.

"Yes, of course," said Pitblade. "It's the best way."

Zagora gave Razziq a sympathetic smile, remembering the wounded falcon.

"Look, Charlie Pym was my best friend," said Pitblade. "And I want to tell you . . . he had something of mine that I gave him for safekeeping."

"The Oryx Stone," said Duncan with a glance at Zagora. She stiffened, waiting for him to say she had the stone, but to her relief, he kept silent.

"Ah, the mystical stone of the oryx," said Pitblade, his tone rapturous. "One look and you realize it belongs not to this world, but to another. The holy seers of Zahir carved into it the sacred oryx, laying upon the stone a desert enchantment. The Oryx Stone is much beloved by oryxes—and despised by scorpions."

"Is that why there were so many oryxes in ancient Zahir?" asked Zagora.

"Precisely." Pitblade's eyes shone like burning glass. "Oryxes flocked to Zahir by the hundreds and the scorpions kept well away, for centuries. But the theft of the Oryx Stone changed everything. Zahir's protective barriers collapsed, the oryxes vanished and, most terrifying of all, the scorpions began to change."

"Hmm, I had it right," said Duncan. "I figured the Oryx Stone and Zahir were connected."

Zagora knew this was her chance to give back the stone, but she was suddenly gripped by a fierce possessiveness. She admired Pitblade Yegen, especially the way he bordered on being a visionary. And the stone was his—sort of. Or did it belong to the Azimuth? Mina's grandmother had said Zagora was the one who must return the stone. It was all pretty confusing. Zagora told herself she'd give up the stone when the time was right, but not a minute sooner.

Duncan gulped. "You say Zahir is uninhabitable?"

"Scorpions," said Pitblade darkly. "Giant scorpions have overrun the excavated ruins of Zahir—and they have grown increasingly treacherous."

"Oh cripes, I hate those things," croaked Duncan.

Zagora thought of her father and her heart skipped a beat. "Does my dad know about the scorpions?" she asked anxiously. "He must have seen them when he was here eleven years ago."

"Back then the scorpions were not so large, perhaps the size of young sand foxes, and we scared them off with torches." Pitblade met her gaze. "Your father has plenty of experience in desert survival. Charlie is totally unshakable."

Hearing his words, Zagora felt the weight inside her chest lift slightly.

"I found a box of photographic glass plates in my grandfather's attic, slides he'd taken of scorpions in the 1930s, and even then they must have measured twelve inches or more," Pitblade went on. "But I had no idea there were so many of them—or that over time they would grow to such unnatural proportions."

"These scorpions, do they have a lair?" asked Razziq. Zagora could see he was growing more nervous; no doubt he was remembering the frightening stories he'd heard about Zahir.

Pitblade stroked his beard. "Ah yes, they've built a nest for themselves beneath the city."

A nest? Zagora felt the top of her scalp prickle.

"Do you think the scorpions mutated?" asked Duncan. "Maybe they got bombarded by subatomic particles or zapped by radioactive cosmic energy!"

"Hmm, my grandfather had a similar theory. He believed the scorpions absorbed Nar Azrak's energy from the stones of the pyramid," said Pitblade. "There are several varieties of scorpion, the most lethal being the deathstalkers: narrow, flat heads; thin, lanky limbs and a very strange color—clear yellow or green, depending upon their surroundings."

Zagora could see Razziq was looking sort of glassy-eyed. *I bet he's sorry he came with us,* she thought. *He thought this would be a super-awesome desert adventure, but we've dragged him through sandstorms, kidnappings and giant scorpion attacks.*

"In the daytime the scorpions are dormant inside their nest. I believe that's because they rely on the energy of Nar Azrak to activate them. After sundown, it's another story: they come out each night just as Nar Azrak rises." Pitblade stared into the dying embers, eyes burning like two coins. Zagora thought how mysterious he looked, but he also seemed tormented. "I am convinced the scorpions of Zahir killed my grandfather."

The three children all fell quiet, processing this information. Zagora had hundreds more questions to ask, but suddenly her thoughts jumped back to her father.

"Hey, what about my dad?" Her voice was desperate. "We have to find him!"

"Oh man, you're right, Zagora!" Duncan turned to Pitblade. "You haven't seen any suspicious characters passing through here, have you?"

"No one has passed this way," came the reply. "But last night I did notice something unusual. I was up in the turret watching the sun go down and I thought I saw a light go on in the casbah—possibly in the palace."

"Bingo!" said Duncan, the way detectives did in the TV crime programs Zagora often watched with him.

She felt her heart begin to race.

"I'll take you to Zahir tomorrow, if the storm has ended, and we will search for your father." Pitblade rose slowly to his feet. "I trust you have no objections to taking an underground route. My eyes cannot tolerate bright sunlight, you see. In the desert I lost not only my memory, but most of my normal vision as well."

The children exchanged startled looks. Was that why his eyes appeared to be golden? wondered Zagora. He'd obviously suffered through some dreadful experiences. The more she thought about it, the more she understood why he and her father had been such great friends.

Pitblade Yegen was eccentric, daring and probably brilliant, too—just like her dad.

ᘒ ᘒ ᘒ

Zagora, ravenous, sat with the boys, munching sesame flat cakes, which Pitblade produced from a woven bag he'd hidden behind a rock. While she ate, she watched him navigating stiffly around the edges of the chamber, running his hands along the walls.

"Why didn't you give him the stone?" Duncan whispered into her ear.

"It's complicated," she told him. "I'll explain later." Meanwhile, she had plenty of questions she wanted to ask her father's old friend. "So I guess the Oryx Stone is . . . *magical*," said Zagora, biting down on something hard and bitter. She hoped it wasn't a beetle. "It's got powers, right, because it's connected to Nar Azrak? And all those outer space symbols we saw in this tower, they must be magic, too."

"You're confusing astronomy with astrology," said Duncan, grabbing another flat cake. "Astronomy isn't *magic*, it's mathematical. Stars and planets have their own inner logic, but magic's not part of the equation."

Pitblade thought a moment. "I'm not so sure I agree. Astronomy can be compared to Islamic geomancy, a method of divination using a complex system of sand patterns. It's mathematical but it is also embedded in ancient beliefs and traditions—and magic most definitely plays a part."

Zagora watched Duncan scratch the top of his head, looking unconvinced.

Suddenly and without warning Razziq sprang to his feet, dropping his cake on the floor.

"Scorpion!" he shrieked.

Zagora went rigid with fear. Sliding around the archway was the tip of a huge claw, followed by sticklike legs. A narrow head appeared, curling around the side of the arch; an array of cold glittering eyes seemed to be boring into her. For a brief mad moment she thought she heard it say her name.

"Follow me," said Pitblade, taking off at a limping run. "Quickly!"

Despite his poor eyesight and damaged leg, he moved nimbly—at least, it looked that way to her. They scrambled after him to a door of wood and silver set into the wall she hadn't noticed before.

"I cannot believe this," he said, leaning his shoulder into the door. "The scorpions are getting bolder by the day." He pushed a bit harder and the door opened a crack. "Hurry!" he ordered, ushering them into an inner room.

Ready to duck through the doorway, one foot inside, Zagora heard a clacking noise behind her. She glanced back and saw the creature scuttle into the room. The sight of the scorpion held her frozen, her stomach clenched in fright. Uncoiling its tail, it looked intently around, waving enormous pincers, its eyes glistening like chips of black glass. The scorpion was even bigger than the ones she'd seen at the Azimuth Caves.

Even more terrifying was the weird sensation that the creature was searching for *her.* Dark, complicated thoughts rushed into her brain, filling her mind with an abstract knowing, like an origami unfolding inside her head. She could hear strange sounds as the creature began speaking in an unknown language—or perhaps it wasn't a language at all—yet she understood its message clearly. "Relinquish the treasure; it belongs not to you. Relinquish the treasure and all will live; hold on to the treasure and all will die. . . ."

It was talking about the Oryx Stone!

"No!" she shouted, surprised by her own ferocity. "I'll never give it up!"

She reached for the stone and the scorpion went completely still. For a moment there was a deathly silence. Its ancient segmented body seemed to grow taller, more menacing, and Zagora swallowed hard, trying not to panic. The Oryx Stone grew warm in her hand, as if drawing light from some far, unreachable place.

From the depths of the stone an intense light emerged. She raised the stone above her head and a bolt of fire shot across the room, striking the creature. Two of its front legs melted away, and with a furious hiss, the scorpion darted out of the chamber.

Zagora, shocked by what she'd just seen, gave a gasp as Pitblade pushed her inside and shut the door, bolting it behind them. They clambered down the crumbling stairs, into a pitch-black chamber. At the bottom she huddled next to Duncan and Razziq, her heart beating so hard she could scarcely breathe. The darkness enfolded her, pressing down like a weight.

"The scorpion can't get inside here, can it?" wheezed Duncan. "I mean, maybe it has friends . . ."

"Don't worry," said Pitblade. "There is one door to this chamber, and I've bolted it."

But Zagora worried just a bit. That creature out there was *smart*.

"What concerns me is that the scorpions are growing more brazen." Pitblade gave a dry cough. "I've often heard them at night outside the tower, but this is the first time one has ventured inside. Tell me, what would you say was the size of that one?"

"It was big," said Duncan. "Maybe the size of a small horse."

Zagora shuddered. *Probably even bigger,* she thought.

"What happened up there, Zagora?" asked Razziq. "We heard you shouting."

"It was coming for me, so I held up the stone," she said without thinking, "and this weird light came whooshing out of it and melted the scorpion's legs."

She heard Razziq give a loud gulp.

"Are you kidding?" said Duncan. "That sounds totally like a science fiction movie!"

"Did I hear you mention a stone?" asked Pitblade in a quiet voice.

Zagora clapped a hand over her mouth. She hadn't meant to let on that she had the stone! How could she have spoken so thoughtlessly?

"Zagora?" Pitblade's voice floated out of the darkness. Suddenly miserable, she hung her head.

"Want me to tell him?" asked Duncan. Without waiting for an answer, her brother burst out, "She has the Oryx Stone!"

Zagora cringed against the wall, waiting for Pitblade Yegen to hit the roof. She couldn't blame him: she'd been totally dishonest about it from the moment she'd met him.

"But before you blow up at my sister, Mr. Yegen, I want to say something," said Duncan. "First of all, it was Zagora who found the Oryx Stone after our dad was kidnapped, and she's guarded it through a surprise attack in the desert and a sandstorm and her camel falling through quicksand, and I know this sounds crazy, but she says the stone made the ghost oryx come to life, though I'm not too clear on that last part."

Pitblade coughed into the silence. Zagora squeezed her brother's arm to let him know she appreciated his speaking up for her. It made her feel sort of, well, humble.

Duncan was turning out to be a true defender and fellow explorer and friend, all rolled into one.

"What he says is true," said Razziq. "Zagora has guarded the stone."

"Extraordinary," said Pitblade, and Zagora thought she saw his eyes flash gold. "Your unwillingness to give up the Oryx Stone has great significance, Zagora Pym, as does the fact that in your hands the stone gave life to an oryx—indeed, to many oryxes—and frightened off a scorpion."

Confused, she blinked at him through the darkness. What was he talking about?

"We are not out of danger yet, but I daresay we are nearer to rescuing Zahir," he said cryptically. "Have you ever heard of the Sentinels of the Stone?"

They all murmured "No," and Zagora felt her emotions ping-ponging from relief to surprise to intense curiosity. *Sentinels of the Stone* sounded like a term from Middle-Earth in *Lord of the Rings*.

"The Sentinels of the Stone comprise a secret society that goes back centuries," explained Pitblade. "The theft of the Oryx Stone was foretold in Xuloc's time, by Azimuth seers who predicted the fall of Zahir. They also foretold that the stone would have protectors as it made its way back to Zahir, to fulfill a prophecy called the Circle of Four that predicts a battle between oryxes and scorpions."

Zagora listened intently, hardly daring to breathe.

"These protectors, called Sentinels, have but one task—to guard the Oryx Stone—and their insignia is a tree of hands. The drawing represents the hands through which the Oryx Stone will pass, from its disappearance until it returns, once and for all, to Zahir."

"A tree of hands?" said Zagora excitedly. "I saw that drawing in the Azimuth Caves! It was a weird twisty pattern on the wall of a cave—all different hands, holding the Oryx Stone."

"That is truly remarkable." Pitblade was quiet for a moment. "You see, my grandfather was a Sentinel, as well. Sadly, he never realized that it was his destiny to harbor the stone from evil forces."

"Maybe he was too busy being an explorer," suggested Zagora. Still, she wondered: if Edgar Yegen had known about the stone's power, would he still be alive?

"Perhaps," said Pitblade, sounding a bit melancholy. "I learned about the Sentinels of the Stone from the nomads I lived with, and once my memory returned, I realized that I too was meant to be a Sentinel. That is why I asked your father to bring the Oryx Stone."

"I kept thinking the stone would give me

superpowers," said Zagora. "But it's a different kind of magic, isn't it?"

"The stone merely serves to bring out the inner strength of its wearer," answered Pitblade, "a strength they might be unaware they possess."

Zagora fell quiet, thinking. Was he saying that she had inner strength, like the kind a desert warrior would have? Did that mean she could survive the desert on her own, whether she had the stone or not?

"Your job, Zagora, is simply to watch over the stone. The Oryx Stone was passed to Edgar, then to me, and now it appears that it has been entrusted to you."

Her breath quickened.

"*You,* Zagora, are the next Sentinel of the Stone!"

༄༅ THROUGH THE UNKNOWN PORTAL ༄༅

Zagora saw a pencil-thin beam cut through the dark as Duncan clicked on his flashlight.

"Hey, my titanium Teknik-mini!" he said. "It was in my pocket all this time. Cool, huh?"

The flashlight illuminated the space around them, throwing shadows across the walls and ceiling. Zagora realized the chamber was far bigger than she'd imagined.

"What is this?" asked Razziq.

It took her a few moments to make out what he was pointing at, but as her eyes adjusted, she began to see faded murals on the rock walls.

"Mystical desert art, this is, painted by Xuloc, ruler

of Zahir," said Pitblade, sounding to Zagora like a museum curator. In the dim light, his eyes were the color of old bronze. "With my poor vision I've not been able to study them, but I know from my grandfather's journal that these drawings depict scenes from the past—and perhaps from the future, as well. All around them you can see the Oracle Glyphs, which your father came here to decipher. He's an ace at cracking glyphs."

"Yeah, my dad's a real glyph-cracker," said Zagora, blinking back tears. Her heart felt brittle, as if it might break into pieces. She wanted desperately to find her father. Maybe there were clues about his captors somewhere within this ancient artwork.

"Duncan, shine your light this way!" she shouted, bristling with curiosity and feeling more anxious than ever. A dark thought suddenly entered her head: what if there was a prophecy that said a brilliant scholar from across the sea would be kidnapped and sacrificed?

Pushing the thought away, she followed Duncan's tiny beam as it swept across the concave rock walls. The drawings, with their pale, airy colors, struck her as beautiful—and slightly haunting, too. Duncan angled his beam around wolves attacking an oryx (which made her a little teary-eyed), bandits marauding a camel caravan and figures dressed in what looked like ritual clothing. Xuloc, the Azimuth king, was depicted as a tall lean man with flowing hair and a braided beard, exactly the way she imagined a desert prophet.

"This is a glyph?" Razziq pointed to a squiggly line carved into the stone.

"Yeah. A glyph is a sort of symbol," said Zagora, marveling at the strange, inexplicable design. "My dad could decipher this glyph in a second."

Yet as she walked around, Zagora felt her high spirits quickly falling. The glyphs were impossible to figure out, and none of the drawings offered any clues to her father's whereabouts. Even more disappointing, she could see that Pitblade Yegen wasn't going to be of much help, either.

Duncan beamed his light on the curved sweep of the rock wall to the next drawing, where a large blue planet, vast and threatening, was about to cross in front of the moon.

"Nar Azrak," he said. "Hey, didn't Abdul say something about a lunar eclipse?"

"He did," said Zagora, but by now everyone's attention was focused on a drawing on the wall to the right of the eclipse. Duncan waved his beam over the lofty towers of Zahir, the oases filled with oryxes, the magnificent Palace of Xuloc. Everything she saw filled her with wonder.

Then a sudden thought came to her. "Do you have desert sight?" she asked Pitblade.

He shook his head somberly. "I once had desert sight, but when my eyes were damaged, I lost the ability to see into the past." He gave a crooked smile. "I know you have the gift, Zagora. All the Sentinels have it."

She was surprised at first, then realized it made sense. After all, a Sentinel would have need of some extra desert powers.

"Be forewarned," he added. "There is a certain vulnerability that goes with the gift. The scorpions will quickly sense that you have it. And, feeling threatened, they will go after you—just as they went after my grandfather. Stay on your guard and do not let them near you."

"Yeah, well, okay," said Zagora, swallowing hard. Mrs. Bixby used to say even the best things on earth had a downside, but being targeted by scorpions seemed pretty extreme.

She watched Duncan's beam flicker and go dim.

"Uh-oh," he said, moving the light to the left of the eclipse. "One last look and I'm turning the flashlight off."

Zagora's throat tightened as she studied the bleak

desert landscape, painted across the wall in dark slashes. There was no Zahir in the drawing, and no people or oryxes, either. There were no stars, no moon. High overhead loomed Nar Azrak. Strange and terrible, it hung over the dunes, which were swarming with giant scorpions.

"The Time of the Scorpions," murmured Pitblade. "That's what this drawing is about."

"But what do these pictures mean exactly?" asked Duncan. "Here's Zahir on one side of the eclipse, and on the other side the scorpions are running amok in the desert. Are both scenarios connected to the lunar eclipse?" He scratched his chin. "Any ideas, Razz?"

Zagora watched Razziq move back and forth between the drawings, examining each one, as Duncan's light grew dimmer.

"What you are seeing here are *two futures,*" he said ominously, giving the others a sad, wise smile. "But of course . . . ," he added, "only one will happen."

༄ ༄ ༄

Zagora awoke on a bare floor, feeling the damp creep into her bones. Someone was shaking her.

"Zagora, wake up, we must prepare to go to Zahir." Razziq gave her another shake and she sat up, hand flying to her neck: the stone was still there. Events from the day before came rushing back—the sandstorm, losing Sophie, seeing the oryx and finding Pitblade Yegen, being chased by the scorpion into the cavern. And, oh yeah, she was a Sentinel.

Then she remembered her missing father and her heart plummeted.

Pitblade silently led them out of the dark chamber, into the room of volcanic rock, past the dead embers of the fire. Zagora followed him beneath the series of archways, up through the trapdoor, into the main tower. Here she could see sunlight, warm and welcoming, flooding through the tall windows.

"The storm is over!" cried Razziq, and they all cheered.

"Hey, guys, look," said Duncan, reaching into his backpack and pulling out a package of batteries. "We'll have light underground!"

Hmm, thought Zagora. Maybe stuffing that bag with all those extra things hadn't been so silly after all.

Pitblade gave them each a bowl of gruel sprinkled with pine nuts. While they ate, he studied a map of Zahir he'd drawn on a strip of goatskin, holding the rough fabric up to his eyes. Zagora could see him planning and calculating with the same furious concentration her father always had. A sob of longing caught in her throat and she brushed away a tear.

Moments later he joined them, helping himself to a bowl of gruel.

"Ah yes," he said, squinting at Zagora. "In this light you look very much like her, I can see that now. The wildness of your hair, those brilliant blue eyes, even your smile, so very much like Maeve."

"Maeve Pym?" she echoed. "My mom?" It had never occurred to her that Pitblade Yegen might have known her mother. "You think I look like her?" A fleeting image appeared inside her head: Charlie Pym, young and handsome, and at his side a tall, smiling woman whose blue eyes peered out from under a wide-brimmed hat—two faces in a silver frame. Her heart gave a little tick.

"As far as my poor eyesight can tell, I'd say you do indeed—and you have your mother's feisty nature, too," he added, clearly amused. "I can think of no higher compliment."

Zagora felt her face flush. "Did you know my mom very well?" she asked, eager to hear more. "Was she, like, amazing?"

"She was. And she loved adventure, just like you."

"I knew it," said Zagora. Smiling to herself, she drew her legs to her chest and hugged her knees. How wonderful to hear those words. She glanced at Duncan and he threw her a lopsided smile, radiating something she had only recently begun to experience: brotherly warmth.

They downed handfuls of pine nuts, the last of their breakfast, and Duncan hurriedly replaced the batteries in his flashlight. Then, throwing their packs over their shoulders, the three children followed Pitblade down through the trapdoor. At the bottom of the steps, he turned right, leading them through a crevice in the wall. They tramped down a narrow stone passageway to an enormous clay pipe covered in spiderwebs.

"This pipe is an ancient irrigation duct built by the Azimuth," he explained, "and will take us underground to Zahir. It does not connect in any way with the scorpions' lair, so you have little to fear." He looked pointedly at Duncan.

Without a word they followed him into the enormous pipe, where the air felt damp and sluggish and the heat was suffocating. Duncan waved his flashlight around so they all could see where they were going. The floor was littered with bones, piled layer upon layer, which Zagora tried to avoid stepping on. Once, she saw a large skull shaped like a horse's head—or it might have been a camel's. She gritted her teeth, walking faster. It hurt too much to think about Sophie.

Pitblade's tough demeanor impressed Zagora. After living with nomads, he told them, he'd become skilled at lighting fires and could make a flaming torch if necessary. That kind of thing could come in handy while fighting scorpions, Zagora was sure. She could see he was courageous, like her father—and maybe a little reckless, too. But of course, recklessness was the way of desert explorers.

"I know all this must be difficult for you," he said to her and Duncan as they made their way through the ancient pipe. "We won't rest until we find your father—he's my best friend. I'd do anything for him."

"I miss him," said Zagora, feeling weepy. "A lot."

"We'll find him," said her brother, and she felt the faint stirrings of hope. *Maybe we can do this,* she told herself.

"I expect you've met my cousin Olivia?" said Pitblade as they hurried along. "Brilliant woman, a world expert on scorpion and snake venom. Breeds scorpions to survive under extreme adverse conditions."

Zagora felt a chill of unease: he'd just described her dead scorpion.

"I hate scorpions," said Duncan. "Snakes, too. I was attacked by a desert horned viper, you know, but Razz here saved my life."

"It wasn't me," said Razziq humbly, "it was my falcon who saved you."

"You're very fortunate, Duncan," said Pitblade. "Horned vipers are deadly."

Zagora gave a shudder, remembering the snake, with its weird little horns, winding itself around Duncan's leg.

"Olivia's a controversial figure in Marrakech," Pitblade continued. "She's been accused of shady dealings with the underworld, supplying rogue states with snake venom, selling stolen artifacts on the black market, dabbling in the exotic pet trade, and—well, the list goes on. Whether the rumors are true or not, I've no idea."

"It was *Olivia*!" Duncan hissed into Zagora's ear. "Olivia put those snakes in our car!"

Would Olivia actually do something that extreme? Okay, she was angry at their dad for skipping town and not delivering the Oryx Stone, but was she ruthless enough to put snakes in their car—in short, to risk the lives of an archaeologist and his two kids? And how had she known their route to Zahir that morning? *That woman must have lots of people working for her,* thought Zagora.

"Do you think digging up Zahir is a good idea?"

Duncan asked Pitblade. "I mean, what if they turn it into a theme park? I can see it now: busloads of tourists, couscous stands, cheesy souvenirs, camel rides for the kiddies."

"I don't think that will happen in Zahir," Pitblade replied stiffly. "I plan to restore the ancient city—and also import oryxes and set up a farm so they can live in their natural surroundings."

Zagora had a sudden fluttery feeling inside her chest as she thought of the oryxes.

"This way," said Pitblade, running his fingertips down the sides of a low archway. "I will show you something quite unusual."

Curious and impatient, Zagora followed him into a vast cavern. Green mist drifted up, cool and soothing against her skin, and she heard rushing water below. He led them across a limestone bridge so narrow they had to go one at a time. Peering over the side, feeling a bit dizzy, she looked down into a river filled with shadows.

"This subterranean river has no name," said Pitblade. "The Azimuth called it the Unknown River, and for centuries it's been running through underground caverns, providing Zahir with fresh water. It is the source of the water you've been drinking in the tower."

"'When you drink the water,'" murmured Razziq,

"'remember the spring.'" He grinned at Zagora, his face ghostly in the mist, and she grinned back, thinking how lucky she was to have him for a friend. She wanted to give him a hug, but she felt too shy.

They descended a flight of moss-covered steps cut into the rock, then entered a cavern rank with bitter smells, its walls black with moisture. As her eyes adjusted to the grainy darkness, Zagora stared at the wet flow-stone walls and a ceiling dappled with yellow and orange fungi. Already she missed the dry open desert.

"Wow, primeval," said Duncan, sweeping his light over a small lake covered in algae.

"This underground lake is said to be bottomless," Pit-blade said dramatically as they skirted the edges of it. Zagora kept her distance from the water: there was no telling what might bubble up from deep inside a creepy green lake with no bottom.

They approached a vast, sprawling archway, its surface crusted with gray and yellow lichen, and Pitblade's voice fell to a dry whisper: "We have reached the Unknown Portal, the gateway connecting this cavern to the city of Zahir."

Zagora felt her heart leap. Zahir, at last! Following Pitblade Yegen through the portal, she noticed odd geo-metric patterns beneath the lichen: signs, shapes and abstract symbols. If she looked hard enough, she could see glyphs, each connected to the next, like joined-up writing across the stone. It all looked incredibly esoteric, as her father would say, but there was no time to examine any of it.

"These are fabulous," breathed Duncan, directing his light on the glyphs.

"We'll bring Dad here to see them," said Zagora. "He'll go insane."

She watched her brother's face fall, but he quickly pulled himself together. "We'll find him," he said through clenched teeth, his doggedness reminiscent of their father. "We will."

They hurried on, catching up with Pitblade and Razziq, who stood at the bottom of a wide stone staircase. Sunlight poured down. Zagora could hardly believe it: at the top of the stairs was Zahir! Seized by a wild euphoria, she raced up, eyes gleaming with hope and excitement, out into the daylight—and into the ancient city.

The light was so sharp it dazzled her, and she spun around to face the dusty, hollowed-out street lined with low, flat-roofed adobe buildings. On all sides of her rose steep walls of hard-packed sand, and she realized she was deep inside an excavation site. Feeling giddy, she breathed in the hot stone smells of Zahir.

Pitblade and the boys came charging up the steps, adventuresome and daring, in the swashbuckling spirit of *The Three Musketeers*. (She'd read the book in Mrs. Bixby's class.) Razziq stared, awestruck, at the ruins, and Pitblade, wrapped in cloths to protect his eyes, walked with a vigorous step.

But Duncan was a different story. He folded his arms, a look of extreme disappointment on his face. Zagora's heart contracted. Her brother had been so tough and determined until then.

"This is Zahir?" he said. "I thought it was going to be incredible." He turned to her, his face growing redder by the second. She could clearly see all his inner frustration surfacing. "This is just a bunch of old mud buildings beaten down by the wind. Everything's been eaten away by the sand! How will we find Dad in this petrified wreck of a city?"

"What were you expecting?" snapped Zagora, thinking, *He'd better not be giving up.*

"I thought Zahir would be inscrutable and cool," he said, his voice cracking a little, "like the Mayan ruins I saw on that National Geographic special last week. Those were fantastic."

"As I explained, only a small part of the city was excavated," said Pitblade with an air of impatience. "But that was eleven years ago, and ever since then, Zahir has been exposed to the ravages of the desert."

"Are we going to the palace now?" asked Zagora, eager to start the search for her father. "Do you know a secret way there, too?"

"I do," replied their father's friend. "It might not be the best way, but it is the way I know. Let's keep to the shadows so we will not be seen."

He hurried on, throwing wary glances to the side, the others close behind as he guided them through a puzzle of deserted alleyways. They stumbled down streets cut deep into the earth that looped and doubled around, until Zagora lost all sense of direction. The excavated site of Zahir was a honeycomb of clay walls, empty court-yards and overhung passages, with buildings one and two stories high, many with roofs caved in, sand flowing out through the windows and doors. Zagora kept an eye open for scorpions or assassins or anything unexpected that might jump out at them.

"Hey, do you guys feel static in the air?" said Duncan, shielding his eyes.

Zagora had noticed it, too: the air crackled with light, as if emitting electric energy.

"It is always this way in Zahir," said Pitblade.

"Oh man, I hope we're not trapped inside some kind

of magnetic force field," said Duncan. "Stuff like that happens, you know, and not just in movies and books." Zagora could almost see his thoughts spinning off in wild directions. "I mean, what if this place is one big freaky experiment—and we're the guinea pigs?"

No one said a word, and as they hurried on, a heavy dread settled inside her chest.

A PLACE OF STRANGE AND FRIGHTENING BEAUTY

"Ah, Zahir, a place of strange and frightening beauty, its hidden treasures lost beneath the sands," murmured Pitblade as they tramped through the ruined city. "The most unforgettable of ruins, and the most mysterious."

Zagora's heart grew heavy as she remembered her dad quoting the same lines from Edgar's journal.

"Vultures," said Razziq, pointing to a clutch of dark birds circling overhead.

"Maybe vultures attacked your cousin's falcon," she whispered, and he gave a mournful nod.

Winding through twists and turns, Zagora felt as if they were moving deeper into a dark maze from which

there was no escape. Her heart grew cold and frightened. Before, using her gift of desert sight, she'd seen the glimmering city of Zahir with its majestic walls, spiraling towers and warriors on white camels—and, beyond, the endless miles of dark red dunes and lush oases.

But this was the real Zahir: an empty excavation site with hollowed-out streets and ravaged buildings, dust-dry walls and harsh winds—and, deep under the ground, a deadly lair of scorpions. Twenty-first-century Zahir was sadder—and lonelier—than she'd ever dreamed possible.

At the end of a shadowy passage hung with twisted vines, Pitblade hesitated. Zagora noticed his eyes were watering and he struggled to keep them open. Unfolding his goatskin map, he held it close to his face. "Excellent. Not far to go."

They continued on. Walls of packed dirt leaned over the excavated streets, which seemed to grow increasingly narrower, closing in like a high-walled labyrinth. At last she came to a stop behind Pitblade, who was inspecting a tall semicircular gateway edged with glazed tiles in brilliant colors, with flowing Arabic calligraphy across the top.

She caught her breath as she stepped through the archway, seeing a crumbling marble staircase ahead. High above, at the top of the staircase, rose a massive building of dusty red stone, with magnificent portals and terraces and a great curving roof.

"The Royal Palace of Xuloc," announced Pitblade, bowing his head. "Built by holy seers."

Gazing at the sculpted towers, the rooftop pavilions and rows of arching windows, Zagora began to feel a faint glimmer of something dark and dangerous.

"There are more than two hundred rooms in the palace," Pitblade explained as they climbed the steps to a pillared doorway. "Xuloc imported wood, gold, ivory, onyx and marble from as far as Timbuktu, Calcutta and Venezia, but unfortunately thieves have looted the interior, leaving the scattered ruins of pavilions, galleries, gardens, stables and dungeons."

Zagora pricked up her ears at the word *dungeons* as she hit the last step, and she tried not to think too deeply about what that might mean.

Painted scrollwork decorated the palace doorway, which swept to a point at the top. Set inside were two monumental doors of carved and studded brass. She watched Pitblade's tense profile—long, narrow nose, glistening scar and grimy head cloth—as he twisted a scrolled knob, muttering something about "imperial opulence." The door swung inward with a groan.

Heart fluttering, she peered into a hallway of colossal proportions, sun pouring in through stone grilles on the windows, throwing a wash of golden light over everything. She stared at the elegantly tiled floor, the columns and archways, the panels carved into complex shapes. The high curved ceiling was painted with what looked like magical signs and symbols of gold, silver and blue.

"I don't know," said Duncan, stubbornly shaking his head, and she knew what was coming next. "I've got a really bad feeling about this place."

"Perhaps you should stand guard," suggested Pitblade. "Keep an eye out for anything unusual. It's possible your father—or his captors—will pass this way."

Zagora saw Duncan blanch at the word *captors,* but he was obviously relieved to be staying outside. "Okay," he said, retying his head cloth. "If anything goes wrong, I'll give a shout."

Pitblade gave Duncan a look, and Zagora wondered if he took Duncan all that seriously. As usual, it was hard to tell what Pitblade was thinking. She just hoped her brother would be safe waiting outside on his own.

"Stay with me at all times," Pitblade instructed her and Razziq. "The palace is vast and the layout is deceptive. Remain quiet and alert, on your guard at all times, and remember: no matter what happens, we must stay together."

Zagora nodded, watching Pitblade stride through the door, motioning for them to follow, and she felt a surge of panic mixed with exhilaration. Taking a deep breath, she told herself to stay calm.

She mouthed *See you later* to Duncan and crept with the others into the palace, her eyes adjusting quickly to the dim interior. With Pitblade in the lead, they scoured the empty windswept rooms, following stairways that twisted in elegant spirals. They tramped beneath ornate arches and vaulted ceilings, through courtyards and sunken gardens. Every surface she looked at—marble, tile, wood, stone—was covered in a thick layer of sand. Over windows and doorways she glimpsed worn designs, chilling and mystical, too faded to interpret.

With its odd-shaped rooms and sudden turns, the palace struck Zagora as a perfect hideout for kidnappers. Each time she rounded a corner, she felt her heart rise to her throat—she kept expecting to stumble on her father.

"Ah yes, the ancient kitchen," murmured Pitblade. "I know where we are now."

Zagora trailed him into a room of limestone and slate, yellow walls rising to a convergence of arches, a brick hearth set inside a deep hollow. She thought she smelled smoke, but there wasn't time to investigate: Pitblade and Razziq were disappearing through an archway.

Hurrying after them, she entered a small courtyard that ended abruptly at a high wall covered in dirt and dust. Obviously the excavation efforts had stopped there.

"The Pyramid of Xuloc once stood in one of these courtyards." Pitblade tugged on his sand-crusted beard. "Unfortunately the pyramid is believed to have collapsed beneath the sand years ago. One day I will excavate it, but I fear we may find only crushed fragments."

Zagora stood imagining the blue pyramid and the Azimuth elders strolling along the paths of star-shaped tiles, reading dusty scrolls and contemplating the endless dunes. It suddenly dawned on her that the air was charged with an electric energy.

Feeling her knees give way, she sat down, hard, on the tiled path. At the edge of her hearing were whispers, and an icy tremor slid through her. Her head echoed with soft, sibilant sounds—indecipherable words, but with a frightening force behind them. Scorpions!

Was she going crazy or could these bizarre creatures really think?

"Are you not feeling well?" asked Razziq, bending down and staring into her eyes.

"They keep talking to me!" She clamped her hands

over her ears. "I just want them to go away." What was it Pitblade had warned her about? Something about having desert sight and being vulnerable to the scorpions.

The boy's dark eyes studied her with concern. "We must go, Zagora. It is no longer safe here."

"We can't leave yet," she argued. "We've only searched a few rooms. This place is huge!"

"Hurry!" shouted Pitblade from the doorway, his voice urgent. "We'll return tomorrow."

"I feel strange, too," said Razziq, looking frightened as he pulled Zagora to her feet. "Soon the sun will go down, and the scorpions will come."

Feeling disoriented, she gazed at the sky. "Sunset is hours off . . . isn't it?"

"Night comes quickly in the desert." He tugged at her arm. "We must not let ourselves get caught."

With a last glance at the courtyard, Zagora followed the others back into the palace and rushed through a series of immense rooms, to the main hallway. Tripping over her sandal straps, she stopped and kicked off her shoes—easier than doing them up again. She could hear Duncan shouting from the entranceway, something about a car, and Pitblade and Razziq began to run.

She started to dash after them, but then she heard a voice. It was coming from behind a moth-eaten tapestry on the wall beside her. *Run!* she told herself. *The scorpions will get you!* But the voice was so close. Just a quick look behind the carpet; then she'd catch up and tell them—

Clutching her sandals, Zagora flung the carpet aside and rushed forward, bare feet sliding across the stone floor. To her surprise, she was tumbling head over heels down a flight of steps, bumping past a blur of yellow and red tiles, thudding all the way to the bottom.

Hobbling to her feet, she checked for broken bones— there didn't seem to be any—and stared at a windowless vestibule filled with blue light. The light was spilling out through holes in a silky curtain that covered a keyhole-shaped archway.

Above the archway hung an orange sign with the words CAUTION! BIOGENIC TOXINS. Feeling her skin start to crawl, she wondered if *toxins* meant scorpion venom. Beneath it another sign warned: ENTRY STRICTLY FORBID-DEN. Was her father a prisoner down there, locked in a room filled with toxins?

Zagora peered through one of the holes in the curtain, forgetting everything else, gazing into a sterile-looking room at trolleys of glass beakers and test tubes. Pinned to a corkboard were dead-looking scorpions, like the one she'd dropped into Olivia's tea. A nearby table held scientific instruments and medical equipment she didn't recognize, and in one corner a large fan rumbled. She saw strategically placed oil lamps and a shelf of vials containing a dark amber liquid—was it scorpion venom?

Running along one wall were shelves of glass boxes. Zagora sucked in her breath. Inside the boxes she glimpsed snakes, spiders and—her stomach twisted into knots—scorpions. Some of the boxes were filled with water, and floating inside were scorpions the size of rats.

She caught a sharp whiff of perfume: the scent of lime and lavender.

"You've bungled it, haven't you?" said a throaty voice she recognized at once.

Zagora froze, seeing Olivia Romanesçu, carrying a clipboard, pace up and down in a swirl of bright fabrics, hair twisted into a severe knot. Two men in dark glasses, one with a goatee and shaved head, the other with a pencil-thin mustache—definitely the thugs from Marrakech—stood at attention in crisp white suits and snakeskin shoes. She realized with relief they hadn't heard her fall down the stairs: the fan had probably drowned out the sounds.

The goateed man started to speak, but Olivia silenced him with a savage glance that chilled Zagora to the bone.

"If this Pym character doesn't have the stone," Olivia said icily, "then where is it?"

"We searched Pym and tore his backpack to pieces," said the pencil-mustache guy. "No dice: he hasn't got it."

"He could've sent it to Yegen by falcon."

"Then track down Pitblade Yegen at once and extract it from him!"

Zagora felt a sudden lump in her throat. *Pym character?* They were talking about her father! Was he being held hostage? Had they kidnapped him for the Oryx Stone? Tears sprang to her eyes and she began to tremble violently.

"As you can see, the generator's up and running. Now we have power." Olivia strode to a glass wall that opened onto a glowing blue darkness. "You'll need to move the ultraviolet lights closer to the scorpions' nest. After you've delivered the stone to me, unload the rest of the equipment. Be careful with the glassware. I've only a limited number of venom vials. And throw a few morsels to the dogs, poor things are ravenous."

Dogs? Venom vials? Scorpions' nest? Zagora could hardly think, her heart was beating so fast.

"Get going," ordered Olivia, "and be quick about it."

Goggle-eyed, Zagora watched the two henchmen

exit through a metal door. *I've got to warn the others!* she thought.

But as she turned to sprint away, a hand shot out through the curtain and gripped her arm.

"Wherever did you come from?" demanded Olivia, and a bolt of fear shot through her. "Of course, you're Charles Pym's daughter. Silly of me not to recognize you."

"Where's my dad?" shouted Zagora. "You kidnapped him and I want him back!"

Smiling, Olivia loosened her grip. "Oh yes, your father's here, but I've hardly kidnapped him. Charles Pym is working for me."

"My dad wouldn't do that in a million years!" yelled Zagora. "He thinks your experiments are totally outrageous, and anyway, he's not an insect scientist!"

Olivia released her grip. "Yes, but there are two projects," she said in a silky voice. "My work with the scorpions *and* my plan to unearth the meteorites. I've put your father in charge of excavating the pyramid. You see, collectors will pay enormous sums for desert meteorites, and the money I receive will fund my experiments. If I can perfect my painkiller medicine, you've no idea what a medical breakthrough it will be."

"I don't believe you," said Zagora, staring at her defiantly. "I want my dad back."

"The project is top-secret, which is why your father hasn't contacted you. We've just set up the generator and gotten things in working order." Olivia raised her finely plucked brows. "Come, I'll take you to see your father. He's only a hop and a skip away."

Zagora's mouth dropped. Her dad was here, in the Palace of Xuloc, working with Olivia? That didn't make a lot of sense.

"Your father hasn't stopped talking about you since he arrived," Olivia went on. "Zagora this and Zagora that . . ."

"Really?" She secretly felt pleased to hear that. And yet . . . something wasn't right. Her dad would never agree to work with Olivia: he didn't trust her! Her mind was in turmoil. She knew that sometimes adults kept secrets from kids, mostly to protect them, but her father would never just disappear without a word to anyone.

"Follow me," said Olivia, leading her up the tiled staircase and—pushing the tapestry to one side, dust billowing around them—out into the main palace hallway. Olivia's face was blank as paper, devoid of all emotion, and suddenly Zagora felt a sick horror. She wanted to be back with Duncan, Razziq and Pitblade.

She started to run, but Olivia was quick; the woman took hold of her hair, grasping it by the roots. Frightened,

Zagora sank her teeth into Olivia's freckled arm, snarling in a passionate fury, but Olivia pulled her hair even harder. Zagora kicked and punched and spat at her tormentor, but it didn't do much good. Olivia seemed immune to pain.

Dropping the clipboard, Olivia almost calmly took hold of the girl's shoulders and shook her, the edges of her rings pressing into Zagora's skin. She shook her so hard that the Oryx Stone came flying up from under Zagora's T-shirt.

She watched Olivia's greedy eyes latch on to it and realized, her heart falling, that she'd suddenly lost the stone once and for all.

"Scheming little rat, spying on me. How dare you?" hissed Olivia, with murder in her eyes. "Now then, what have we here?" With a deft hand she had whisked the stone on its leather ribbon from Zagora's neck. "My shrewd business sense tells me this little artifact will fetch a few coins."

Zagora stared at Olivia, horrified. It was heartwrenching to see the Oryx Stone in this woman's large fleshy hand. What was strange, however, was that the moment Olivia had snatched it away, the stone's brilliant blue surface had gone dark.

"Play my cards right and this could end up in an

auction house in London or New York." Olivia held the Oryx Stone up to her heavily made-up eyes. "And, if all else fails, there's always the black market. I'm no stranger there, either."

With her other hand, she'd pinned Zagora's arm behind her.

Pitblade will be here any minute, thought Zagora; *then she'll be sorry.* There was no way Olivia could keep the stone, because she definitely wasn't a Sentinel—at least, Zagora hoped not. Then a scary thought floated into her head: what if the wrong person ended up with the Oryx Stone?

"You're stealing!" she yelled, blazing with hatred. "You can't sell the Oryx Stone! Give it back!"

Olivia's eyes went wide, and Zagora's heart sank a little more. "Good heavens, is this the legendary Oryx Stone?" She placed the stone around her own neck. "I thought it would be brighter than this, more elegant, you know? Nonetheless, it's thrilling to acquire this valuable relic at last. You see, I need the Oryx Stone to carry on with my experiments. The scorpions are deathly afraid of it, so the stone will protect me—give me the upper hand, as it were."

"I don't care. I want my dad!" Zagora struggled to break away. "He'd better be okay or I—*I'll have your guts for garters!*" Her dad's expression *guts for garters* was the worst threat she could think of, though she wasn't quite sure what it meant.

Olivia gave a high, tinkling laugh that made Zagora even angrier.

"Razziq!" screamed Zagora. The pain in her arm was agonizing. "Help!"

Olivia clapped a hand over her mouth, wrenching her arm a little more and hissing, "Silence!" Moments later Zagora was being dragged through a door and up a spiral staircase.

"To think that all this time *you* had the stone," chuckled Olivia, hauling the girl roughly up the steps. Against her wattled neck the Oryx Stone looked dull and lifeless, the luster sapped from it. "Seems I've sent my men on a wild-goose chase."

Zagora struggled to escape again, but she was no match for Olivia. With each turn the steps grew steeper; some had worn away completely, and Zagora worried that Olivia's weight might crumble the rest.

Four stories later, Olivia dragged her to a wooden door. Zagora was terrified. Trapped like a fly, her precious stone gone, she was on her way to being imprisoned, or worse. Maybe she'd be stung by scorpions, or poisoned by snakes. On the other hand, at least she wasn't being taken down to some smelly dungeon. She could only hope that Olivia would throw her into the cell where her father was being held.

The door opened into a small chamber. Tearing herself from Olivia's grasp, Zagora rushed in, looking wildly around at the rough walls and broken tiles. There was no sign of her father. She ran to the window and peered through the grillwork, gazing hundreds of feet down into a courtyard. She was somewhere at the back of the palace, but it was impossible to calculate distances or plan an escape route: the building was too enormous.

A crushing despair rolled over her. There was no way out.

"Evil old bat!" she screamed. "I want my dad!"

"Dear girl, this isn't about you, and it certainly isn't about your father." Olivia licked her knife-thin lips. "This is about the beauty of toxins, the potential of scorpions and my future as an entomologist. These are groundbreaking experiments, and no one is going to stand in my way."

"You'll go to jail for selling meteorites," said Zagora, wondering if she was fast enough to dart around Olivia and down the stairs. "It's against the law!" Unfortunately the woman's large body was blocking the way.

"My goal is to save lives," snapped Olivia. "And to do

this, I've created a web of businesses—some legitimate, some less so—to obtain and move equipment, chemicals and the money I need. One day I may even be recognized as a visionary."

"You put snakes in our car. I know it was you!" shouted Zagora. Then she was struck by another thought. "And you put scorpions in Abdul's shop in Sumnorum!"

"Well, here's the thing," said Olivia. "I'm all for revenge and settling old scores. If someone makes a promise and doesn't follow through, I send them a message."

Zagora glared at her, despising the woman with all her being.

"Charles Pym promised to deliver the stone to my apartment," Olivia went on in a syrupy tone. "He deceived me—and that was his fatal mistake." The sweetness drained out of her voice. "I sent him a message he would never forget."

"One of your snakes attacked Duncan," said Zagora, seething. "He could be dead!"

"Your father should have thought of that before driving off in that overpriced rental car."

Zagora wanted to tear the woman's heart out. She flew at her in a blind fury, but Olivia stepped sideways and, with a sneer, pushed her down. Zagora went sprawling across the floor, sand flying into her eyes and mouth.

She lay still for several seconds, then rose to her knees, spitting out sand, determined not to let Olivia see her cry.

"Better think twice next time you consider dropping a scorpion into my tea—especially when it's one of my own. Oh yes, I've developed an extremely tough breed that quadruples in size when immersed in water." With a haughty sniff Olivia strode to the door. "You'll pay dearly for that."

Zagora sat up, fists clenched. "I don't care. I'm glad I did it." She leapt at the door as it slammed shut, but it was too late: the key was already turning in the lock.

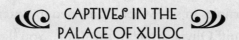

CAPTIVES IN THE PALACE OF XULOC

Zagora stood at the window, hot, angry tears streaming down her face as she watched the sky darken, and wondered if the others were safe. Nar Azrak was rising over the distant dunes and she could see it floating closer—terrifyingly close. She was bone weary, and after losing the Oryx Stone, she felt as if a piece of her had been taken. It was her task to protect the stone, making sure it didn't fall into enemy hands, but she'd failed, miserably.

She imagined her father with her on the night train to Marrakech, wearing his favorite yellow shirt with the blue parrots and talking excitedly about glyphs,

"I just want my dad back," she whispered, sobbing quietly. "That's all I want."

Blue light streamed into the room, suffusing the cob-webbed corners with an eerie glow. She brushed her tears away angrily, peering through the iron grillwork. Nar Azrak appeared to be even bigger than it had been the night before. Significantly bigger. *It really is coming toward Earth,* she thought, *just like one of Duncan's science fiction comic books.*

Down in the courtyard she could see shadows moving: long sinewy shapes, darkly luminous, crawling out from under the sand. Her throat went dry. Scorpions! Angular and jointed, they scuttled across the sand, tails raised, claws scything the air. Blood pounded in her ears as she watched them move to a feverish rhythm, flailing and shrieking. Feeling nauseated, she watched as dozens more crawled out of the sand. It was obvious that the otherworldly energy of Nar Azrak really had made them crazed.

Edgar Yegen had written:

> *Something ancient and terribly old lies buried beneath Zahir: the Pyramid of Xuloc, which I hope to unearth. Built from meteorites that fell from Nar Azrak,*

*the pyramid has been crushed beneath the sand, and
yet the energy of the stones is still there—and is feeding the scorpions with dark and frightening powers.*

All at once Zagora saw the scorpions go still, tilting
their heads. Hundreds of glistening eyes looked up at
the palace. They were staring at *her*! Their collective gaze
shook her to the core, and, heart thudding, she backed
away from the window, flattening herself against the
door. She was trapped.

A scorpion slid past her window, followed by another,
as they swarmed over the palace walls. She heard a scrab-
bling sound as a creature the size of a small deer, with a
barbed tail and hooked claws, slithered onto the windowsill. It was a clear shade of yellow, with a narrow flat
head and lanky limbs, exactly as Pitblade had described:
a deathstalker!

Each of its eyes, she realized with a hollow terror, was
scanning the room. It was searching for *her*. Its massive
claw slid through the iron bars, twisting this way and
that, as the scorpion tried to wriggle itself inside. To her
relief, the ironwork was so intricately designed that the
scorpion couldn't possibly fit through, no matter which
way it turned.

"Get away!" shouted a voice from somewhere overhead. It sounded like her father. "Get out, get away! Out!" It *was* her father; she was certain of it!

"Dad!" she yelled excitedly. "Dad, where are you? It's me, Zagora!"

Her words were drowned out by the scorpion at the window, shrieking in frustration as it thrust its claws through the grillwork, stretching them unnaturally across the room, until they were only inches away from Zagora. Screaming, she fell to the floor, rolling over and curling herself into a ball.

More scorpions clustered outside the window, filling her head with thoughts—dark scorpion thoughts: *Come with us, be one of us, we will teach you every star in the heavens and reveal the spells of the moon and the planets. Follow us to the desert.*

She curled herself tighter and gritted her teeth. Clinging to the outside walls, the scorpions clacked their pincers in a mad fury.

We are molten gold, radiant, magnificent, destroying with fervor, our claws sharp as scimitars. Beneath the light of Nar Azrak, we will rule the desert. . . . Come, be one of us, follow us into our lair. . . . Follow us to the desert. . . .

Covering her ears, she began singing her father's

favorite Broadway tunes at the top of her lungs. After what seemed like an eternity, the scorpion thoughts died away and she stopped singing.

A distant voice floated down from somewhere above, calling to her, like a dream from long ago: "Zagora!"

"Dad!" she shouted. "Dad, it's me. I'm right here!"

There was no answer, and she shouted again, but there was no reply. Perhaps it had been a trick of the wind— or the scorpions, darting crazily up and down the outer walls. Wracked with anguish and fear, Zagora huddled on the floor and fell into a dreamless sleep.

໑๖ ໑๖ ໑๖

When Zagora awoke, she was lying on the floor and the chamber was filled with the pearly-gray light of morning. Rubbing sand from her eyes, she sat up, suddenly alert. From the other side of the door came a strange sound—the sort of sound a claw would make scraping against wood. Scrambling to her feet, she ran to the far side of the room.

Through the keyhole shot a long thin tentacle. At least, that was what it looked like in the murky light. The scorpions really were intelligent, just as Edgar Yegen had said—and now they'd figured out a way into the room! She stared in horror as the tentacle flicked back and forth. Holding her breath, she waited for the scorpions to burst in, waving their claws and stingers.

The door flew open. *This is it,* she thought. *I'm done for!*

Confused, she gaped at the small, ragged, hollow-eyed figure before her, which held a twisted wire in one hand. "Razziq?" She took a step forward, then lunged, hugging him tightly. "I thought you were a scorpion!"

"Scorpions do not appear in the day," he said, giving her a quick hug back. She thought he might be blushing, because the tops of his ears, showing through his messy hair, looked bright red. "This wire trips the lock." He held up a long wire. "My uncle Jamal showed me this trick."

"How did you find me?" she asked.

"I came back into the palace to find you and I heard loud voices. I saw a woman—very big, very angry. She was dragging you up a staircase."

"Olivia Romanesçu," said Zagora. "She's an evil scientist we met in Marrakech. And, oh yeah, she does experiments with scorpion venom."

Razziq's eyes went wide. Before she could say more, Duncan stumbled into the room.

"You're safe!" he wheezed, looking tired and upset. "I was afraid something terrible had happened to you! I shouted when I saw that turquoise spray-painted car go by, but you didn't come out with the others. I wanted to storm the palace! But Pitblade said no, it was getting dark fast and the scorpions would be coming out. We spent the night shuttered up in some smelly old camel barn." He threw his arms around her. "I'm just glad you didn't get eaten by scorpions."

"Me too," she said, hugging him back.

"Zagora! I am pleased to see you," said Pitblade, towering up behind Duncan and Razziq. Beneath his ragged beard she noticed a crooked smile. "We've all been terribly worried."

His words gave her a warm feeling inside, and she realized that Pitblade Yegen was much more than a leader and explorer; he was also her friend.

"I was so scared," she told them. "Scorpions tried to get in through the window—a deathstalker almost got me with its claw!" She tried not to panic at the memory. "But it was too big to fit through the bars." Her heart lurched as she remembered that the scorpions could *think*.

"Who locked you in here?" asked Pitblade.

"It was Olivia," said Zagora. He stared at her, uncomprehending. "Sorry to give you the bad news, but your cousin's breeding scorpions and doing weird experiments. She's got a laboratory downstairs. And she's going to sell meteorites on the black market!"

"Do you mean that nonstop-talking crazy scorpion lady we met in Marrakech?" asked Duncan.

"Yes! Olivia has the Oryx Stone. She stole it from me!" Zagora felt herself growing angrier by the minute. "And she kidnapped Dad! She told me!"

Duncan's jaw dropped.

"Charlie is here, in the palace?" Pitblade's voice was barely audible.

"Yeah, and last night I heard him shouting at the scorpions. At least . . . it sounded like my dad." She looked at her brother. "He shouted my name—just one time—but I didn't hear him again after that."

"Maybe he was too weak," suggested Duncan.

She gave a little shudder, remembering the scorpions, and hoped her dad was okay.

"Think carefully," said Pitblade. "Where exactly was the voice coming from?"

Zagora tried to collect her scrambled thoughts, remembering her fear, and the unearthly light of Nar Azrak, and the scorpions shrieking outside her window. *Concentrate,* she told herself. She could hear the moaning of the wind and the cracking of the walls, the muffled beating of her heart.

"Upstairs." Her voice was barely a whisper. "Yeah, his room is directly over this one." She suddenly sensed a new emotion growing inside her, giving her strength. It was hope.

"Let's go!" shouted Duncan. "We'll tear this place apart until we find him!"

They charged out of the room, racing down a hall of tiles arranged in geometric designs. Zagora saw Pitblade looking around anxiously, and her heartbeat quickened: Olivia could turn up at any moment!

At the end of the hall they stood before an archway of delicately carved wood, painted with symbols—some Zagora suspected were evil eyes. Four wooden panels lined the archway.

"Where are the stairs to the next floor?" asked Duncan. "They should be here!"

"You must use your power of desert sight," said Razziq with a solemn look at Zagora. "I can think of no other way."

She tensed. Ever since they'd come to the palace, images had been flashing through her head, but nothing clear had appeared to her, only a kaleidoscope of colors, textures, sounds and movement—what she guessed to be echoes of the distant past.

"Do it, Zagora," said Duncan. "Use your desert sight to find Dad!"

I've lost the stone, she thought, *but I still have desert sight. That's my power.*

She closed her eyes and stood perfectly still, letting images and sounds and colors pass through her, trying not to think but just to stand there and breathe, letting the past pull her in. Before long she heard the desert wind, low and haunting, and all she could see was shimmering sand.

At the edge of her vision she glimpsed a veiled figure wrapped in pale striped robes, carrying a basket, hurrying through a side door of the palace, rushing up a staircase, along a darkened passage, to an archway of finely carved wood. Making certain no one was watching, the pale-robed figure leaned over and pushed on the bottom right panel, then disappeared inside.

The image faded. Zagora blinked a few times, then fell to her knees, pushing against the bottom right panel. Hinges creaked and it swung inward.

"A hidden door," murmured Pitblade. "Well done, Zagora."

She threw him a quick smile and dove through the space, tumbling into a small chamber where light fell through a window of green glass. A delicate staircase spiraled upward. When she saw it, her heart leapt.

"Pitblade's keeping a lookout, just in case," said Duncan, scrambling in after her, Razziq close behind.

The three children sprinted up the staircase to a great wooden door inlaid with copper, bone and colored glass and edged in round-headed nails. High on the door Zagora saw a brass doorknob shaped like a hand.

"Oh man, we'll never reach that," groaned Duncan. "We'll have to break down the door."

"No, no," said Razziq, calmly moving past Zagora. "Lift me up. I will open the door."

"Right," said Duncan, bending down. "Let's do this in a methodical way."

Zagora watched Razziq scramble up onto her brother's shoulders; then Duncan slowly straightened his back. She knew that in the past it would have been unthinkable for Duncan to lift Razziq—he just wouldn't have been able to do it—but after spending time in the desert, Duncan had grown leaner and stronger.

Pulling the wire from his pocket, Razziq closed one eye. Zagora watched him twist the wire through the keyhole beneath the hand-shaped knob, moving the wire up and down.

"Dad!" shouted Duncan, his face taut with anxiety.

"Dad, are you in there?" He banged his fist on the door, almost shaking Razziq off his shoulders.

Zagora heard a rustling on the other side. She was so excited she could hardly breathe. Razziq gave the wire another twist. There was a soft click and Duncan lunged forward, kicking the door open. Razziq jumped off his shoulders.

"I will go back now to stand guard with Pitblade," said Razziq. Before Zagora or Duncan could say a word, he was gone.

Peering into a shadowy chamber, Zagora saw light streaming in through a high window, illuminating walls covered in symbols, a ceiling curved like the inside of an eggshell.

"Dad?" she whispered.

From the shadows a parched voice startled her. "Zagora?"

"Dad!" she cried as a lone figure with tousled gray-flecked hair, cracked lips and stubble on his face limped toward her, looking exhausted and confused. Seeing her father again, Zagora thought her heart would break.

"But . . . it can't be you," he mumbled. "I must have a fever. I'm seeing things."

Mute with shock, Zagora looked her father over, half expecting to see a man who was frail, stooped and gaunt, as wizened as a desert prophet. But no, he still looked more or less like the Dr. Charles W. Pym she knew, standing before her holding a tattered book to his chest. She squinted to see the title: it was his old favorite, *Morocco on the Run.*

"Your eye—what's happened?" he murmured. "You've hurt your eye, Zagora. . . ."

Before she could answer, Duncan barreled up behind her. "Dad!" he bellowed.

Their father, bewildered, gazed back and forth between them. "Then you *are* real!" he said.

There was a stunned silence and Zagora felt a knot at the back of her throat, making it hard to swallow. "We're not mirages, Dad," she said, starting to cry. "It's really us." Unable to control her emotions any longer, she leapt at her father, throwing her arms around his neck. "Dad, Dad," she sobbed, burying her face in his shirt. "Dad, I really missed you!"

"I thought I'd lost you," he said, hugging her. "However did you find me?"

"We looked all over the desert!" She hiccupped. "Then we came to the palace and Olivia tricked me and locked me up, but last night I heard you yelling at the scorpions—"

"I've been so worried about you both." He stepped

back, smiling bravely. "I knew you'd find me. I never gave up hope."

Zagora smiled back. "Me neither, Dad! We were going to search the desert *forever* until we found you—right, Duncan?" She turned to her brother, who stood with arms dangling, looking awkward. "It really is Dad, Duncan," she said. "He's going to be okay."

With a gut-wrenching sob, her brother stumbled over and gave their father a bear hug, lifting him off his feet. "Whoa, Duncan!" Dr. Pym said, laughing out loud. Wiping a tear from his face, he threw an arm around each of them. Zagora, standing on tiptoes, kissed her father's bristly cheek.

"It was Zagora who saved us. She was really brave," said Duncan, trying to stay collected. "She was determined to find you, Dad."

Zagora grinned. She was finally getting used to the new Duncan.

"Duncan was brave, too," she said, beaming. "He was amazing, Dad. Duncan Pym is the bravest kid I know!"

"I'm so proud of you both," said their father. He hugged them again, then suddenly let go with a gasp. Zagora saw him staring over their heads in surprise. "*Pitblade? Is that you?*"

The two old friends embraced, laughing heartily and

thumping each other on the back, but to Zagora's dismay there was no time for talk of the desert or reminiscences. Razziq appeared and Dr. Pym shook the boy's hand. Within moments they were all heading downstairs, worried that Olivia and her henchmen might turn up at any minute. *We're like fugitives,* thought Zagora.

As they crouched along the walls of the palace, bodies tensed, she whispered to Duncan: "Olivia's going to blow a gasket when she sees we busted Dad out of his cell! But we'll show her a thing or two, right, Duncan?"

He grinned back at her.

Zagora was still furious about having lost the Oryx Stone. And at that very moment she resolved to find a way to get it back.

◖ THE PROPHECY OF THE GLYPHS ◗

The palace doors rattled as Pitblade threw them open, making Zagora's heart jump, but all was quiet outside. Her father seemed a bit overwhelmed, so she took his arm and guided him down the palace staircase, trying to avoid the crumbled parts. Then, blinking like moles, they plunged into the dusty maze of excavated streets. The only signs of life were vultures circling overhead. All she could see was blowing sand and the ravaged remains of a forgotten city.

"Did Olivia's goons kidnap you, Dad?" asked Duncan as they hurried along.

Their father gave a weary nod. Zagora was concerned:

his eyes looked like two poached eggs. "Her two guards came in the night," he told them, "bundled me into an old car and drove me to the edge of Zahir. Mad as hornets when they discovered I didn't have the stone."

"A turquoise 1960s car, right?" said Duncan. "That's the one that's been following us!"

"It was too dark to see much, but the car was definitely retro." Zagora's father turned to her. "You found the Oryx Stone, did you, where I dropped it in the sand?"

"Yep, we did," she said, throwing Duncan a look. She didn't have the heart to tell her dad that the stone was gone, snatched away by that witch Olivia. A scary thought drifted into her head: what if, by losing the stone to Olivia, she'd jinxed one of Xuloc's prophecies—or sent future events in a different direction?

Her father rubbed his whiskery chin. "I was entombed in that miserable cell—ghastly, really—and every night the scorpions turned up outside my window, trying to get inside."

Zagora felt a fresh wave of hatred for Olivia.

"I'm terribly sorry," said Pitblade, and Zagora realized that the revelations about Olivia must have been a shock for him. "I had no idea my cousin was capable of such despicable behavior."

They descended belowground, through the lichen-crusted portal, past the bottomless lake, over the stone bridge spanning the Unknown River, where green mist enveloped them. At last they entered the subterranean pipe that led back to the tower. The steps of the journey—portal, lake, bridge, pipe, tower—reminded Zagora of the steps in a board game she and Duncan used to play at Auntie Agnes's house.

As they tramped through the crumbling clay pipe, bones crunching underfoot, she blurted out, "Listen, everybody, I've got to tell you something weird about the scorpions." She couldn't keep this unsettling discovery to herself any longer; it was too frightening. "The scorpions can *communicate*! It sounds crazy, but they've been trying to put thoughts inside my head."

To her surprise, no one laughed.

"Intelligent scorpions?" Her father threw her a curious look.

"What language were they speaking?" asked Duncan. "Like, *scorpion language*?"

"It's not a language, it's more like the scorpions send messages into your head." She wiped her nose with the back of her hand. "They try to lure you to their nest—and they can sense a human's presence."

"Hey, remember my theory about the scorpions mutating?" said Duncan. "See, not only are their bodies bigger—but their *brains* are bigger! That explains why they can communicate."

"They tried to trick me," said Zagora. "They tried to get me to go down to their lair."

"Never forget, you are vulnerable to scorpions," Pitblade reminded her. "Because you have desert sight, they will go after you. They want the stone so they can destroy it—and they will destroy you in the process."

"Yeah, I figured that," said Zagora, thinking how devious the scorpions were.

"You have desert sight?" Her father looked at her in surprise. "How remarkable! No wonder you've always been drawn to the desert, Zagora."

She smiled at him, still amazed by the fact she had this unusual gift. And it made her feel extra special seeing the way her dad beamed at her.

Dr. Pym turned to Pitblade. "There were glyphs in the room where I was locked up: Oracle Glyphs. They kept me sane, actually, because I passed the time deciphering them. They mention an eclipse foretold centuries ago, when Nar Azrak will pass before the moon."

"The lunar eclipse, Dad, remember?" said Duncan. "Abdul told us about it."

"Of course. I'd totally forgotten. The glyphs warn that

during the eclipse, the moon could fall away and the sun be extinguished—and the world will change forever."

"The Time of the Scorpions," said Razziq.

They all fell into a pensive silence as they made their way back to the tower.

⚬⚬ ⚬⚬ ⚬⚬

As Zagora was bounding up through the trapdoor, into the Tower of the Enigmas, she stopped in her tracks. Light slanted through the windows and a warm wind blew in, bringing with it the smells of the desert. There was a strong scent of mint in the air. Before her stood a small figure wrapped in dusty robes, face veiled with an indigo-blue cloth, desert warrior–style, only one eye showing. Taking in the sand-coated toes, the ankles ringed with scorpion and oryx tattoos, she knew it could only be Mina.

The others crowded behind Zagora as Mina flung back her veils, hair flying, revealing a thin dark face and a stormy expression. Mina gave her a sullen look, as if Zagora were an insect she'd like to squash. *Uh-oh,* thought Zagora, *this doesn't look good.* But at least Mina hadn't brought that mangy jackal with her.

"I come from the Azimuth Caves, where there is

much chaos," Mina began. "The elders cannot agree on the ancient foretellings." Her scorpion tattoo glistened eerily. "Some say the prophecy of the Circle of Four is false, and that the Time of the Scorpions will never happen. Others are fearful, and say the Azimuth must return to their city." She looked at them with dismay. "But there is no one to lead them to Zahir."

Zagora had a somewhat unpleasant feeling, remembering the elders. The Azimuth had been a crazed, haggard bunch, knocking her off Sophie and dragging the boys into the caves. On the other hand, as warriors fighting mega-scorpions in the desert, they'd been pretty impressive.

"They are bringing my grandmother back from Marrakech," Mina continued. "She is the matriarch, the oldest of the elders. And she is a desert sorceress, a seer from the line of Xuloc. She has ancient knowledge."

"Pardon me, but are you talking about Azimuth elders?" said Dr. Pym, nearly choking on his words. "Then what my daughter told me is true: there are actually members of the Azimuth tribe living in the desert? In the world of archaeology, this could be the most important discovery of the past quarter century!"

"Meet my dad, Mina," said Zagora, astonished all over

again that she had her beloved father back. "And this is our friend Pitblade Yegen."

Turning to Dr. Pym and Pitblade, Mina bowed her head slightly, touching the tips of her right fingertips to her forehead. Seeing Duncan and Razziq, she gave a solemn wave.

"As it happens, I've recently deciphered the glyphs that predict the eclipse of Nar Azrak," Dr. Pym said to Mina, his voice taking on that scholarly edge Zagora admired. "They indicate that in order to regain their lost city, the Azimuth must be in Zahir when the eclipse takes place. If not, there will be a cataclysm of epic proportions."

Zagora shuddered. *Cataclysm* was a word she associated with earthquakes, volcanoes and interplanetary wars. She thought of the ancient drawing downstairs that showed two futures, and of Razziq saying that only one could happen.

"I understand," said Mina, looking angry and frightened. "But I do not know how to convince them." Zagora wanted to comfort her, but she felt a deep antagonism coming from Mina.

"Do the glyphs say Nar Azrak's going to crash into the Earth?" asked Duncan.

"I am afraid it isn't as simple as that." Zagora could tell her father was organizing his thoughts and regaining his composure. He was almost back to his old professorial self. "Some glyphs were too worn to decipher, yet one thing was evident: the Oryx Stone is at the heart of the prophecy. It must go back to Zahir." He smiled at Zagora. "Thank heavens the stone is safe."

Feeling her heart wither, Zagora exchanged anguished looks with Duncan and Razziq.

"I am afraid the Oryx Stone has fallen into the hands of my cousin Olivia Romanesçu," said Pitblade. "We no longer have the stone, Charlie."

Mina hissed through her teeth in surprise: "You have lost the stone?"

Looking into her furious eyes, Zagora wished she could shrivel up and disappear. Her father's face fell, and she realized that she'd let him down. In fact, she'd failed them all.

"It's my fault!" she said in despair. "I'm the Sentinel. I was supposed to be guarding the stone and I let that old bat Olivia snatch it away!"

"Then there is no hope," said Mina. "The elders have lost their ancient powers; their connection to Nar Azrak is broken. They have no leader, no magic. Without the stone of the oryx, Zahir is lost to them."

"I disagree. I think there's still hope," said Dr. Pym. "We must retrieve the stone and bring the Azimuth to Zahir at once."

"Hey, guys, remember Abdul told us the eclipse would take place in five days?" said Duncan. "I've kind of lost track but, um, I think it's happening tonight."

Dr. Pym sucked in his breath, counting back the days, and said, "You are correct. We may be too late."

"Not if we move fast," said Pitblade, turning to Mina. "If we go to the Azimuth Caves—Charlie and I—do you think we could convince your tribe to return to Zahir?"

Zagora glowered at Pitblade, infuriated by his suggestion. She'd only just gotten her father back from the clutches of that madwoman Olivia and now they were going to the Azimuth Caves?

"Are you crazy?" she shouted. "My dad can't go to the caves. It's way too dangerous, and besides, we just rescued him from being kidnapped and almost killed by scorpions!"

"Zagora, I understand your concern," said her father, his voice taking on a deeper resonance. "But I can do this—really, I can."

"I don't know, Dad. . . ." Zagora bit her lip, trying not to cry.

"It is imperative that I go. I am the only one who

can translate the glyphs," he went on resolutely, standing straighter. "If the Azimuth will believe anyone, it will be me."

As he spoke, he fully transformed into her archaeologist-extraordinaire dad: the glyph expert who traversed remote ergs and ruins, the explorer whose love for the desert was as boundless as the Sahara itself.

"Perhaps the Azimuth will listen to you," said Mina, her face suddenly animated. "Tell them how you deciphered the glyphs. Tell them to bring weapons to defeat the scorpions."

"Bring fire," said Duncan. "Right, Dad? You said scorpions fear fire."

"And tell them about the two futures," added Razziq. "Very important."

"Yes, we'll mention all those things," said Pitblade. "Do not worry, Zagora. I'll be Charlie's backup man, as well as his translator."

"We can't let the scorpions take over!" Duncan shouted with a fierceness that caught Zagora by surprise. He sounded sort of like a desert warrior.

"I will lend you my dromedary. He is a racing camel and strong enough to carry the two of you—and he knows the way to the caves." Mina bowed her head. "You will be safe with him."

"Mina, you're not going with them?" said Zagora.

The girl shook her head. "I am to stay here, with you. It is a promise I made to Grandmother. I am not to let you out of my sight—not even for a moment."

⚬⚬ ⚬⚬ ⚬⚬

Zagora stood in the doorway, watching her dad and Pitblade Yegen gallop off on Mina's camel, and felt her heart crumple. It was difficult to part with her father after she'd just gotten him back. And seeing Mina's camel had revived painful memories of Sophie.

"Don't worry, Zagora," said Duncan. "Dad's tough—tougher than he looks."

"Yeah, he's a desert warrior." Zagora sniffed. "I hope Pitblade will be okay, because bright sunlight hurts his eyes."

Duncan gave a philosophic sigh. "They'll manage."

"I know, I know," she replied, but she felt all kinds of worries gnawing at her.

"You lost the stone, Zagora," said Mina accusingly, coming up from behind, her eyes flashing. "How could you let such a thing happen? I would never have lost the stone of the oryx. I would have guarded it with my life!"

"I didn't *let* it happen," said Zagora, fuming. "Olivia grabbed the stone away!"

"Hold it right there, Mina," said Duncan. "Okay, there's been a mess-up, I admit." Zagora sensed he was using debate club tactics. "But this Olivia is a mad-scientist-megalomaniac-psychopath who won't stop at anything, so it's not fair to blame my sister."

"But Zagora failed as a guardian," said Mina. "She does not deserve the stone."

Zagora was furious. "You don't deserve it, either!" she yelled. "You make things up! Like talking to bees and taming scorpions and seeing through an oryx's eyes—none of that stuff is true!"

"I am the one who should be protecting the stone." Mina spat out the words. "Not you."

"Cool it," said Duncan, placing a hand on each of their shoulders. "We can't waste our time arguing. We've got to go to the palace and get the stone back."

Duncan's right, thought Zagora. *We have to go to the palace.* Her dad had said he and Pitblade would deal with Olivia, but it was obvious they were running out of time. It made sense that the four children should go back for the stone.

"We'll eat; then we'll plan our attack," he continued. "This is the way we do things now, okay?"

Zagora thought her brother was brave to stand up to

Mina, especially since Mina had her fist balled up, ready to punch whoever got in her way.

Duncan added, "Let's raid the stockpile Pitblade left us. He won't mind. We need grub to charge up the gray matter."

Scowling, Mina unclenched her fist and Zagora let out a breath of relief. Duncan, always awkward in social situations, had somehow defused their quarrel in less than a minute.

The four children sat in the tower munching figs and oranges, discussing a strategy to rescue the Oryx Stone. Razziq gave them gruel with crunchy nuggets on top. Zagora hoped they were pine nuts, but she had a sneaking suspicion they were locusts: a meal Pitblade Yegen would heartily enjoy.

"Er, Mina, mind if I ask you a question?" said Duncan. "What's with the scorpion tattoos? I mean, everybody hates scorpions. Why would you tattoo one on your forehead?"

Zagora had often wondered the same thing.

"Every Azimuth has scorpion tattoos, to show we are not afraid of scorpions," explained Mina. "We have scorpion names, too. I am Mina Ash-Shaulah, 'raised tail of scorpion': my mother gave me this name to protect me."

How strange, thought Zagora, *being named after your worst enemy.* Her enemies at home, Mr. Porter-Jones and a school bully called Ivan Grubb, paled in comparison.

"We have to go after Olivia," said Zagora, peeling an orange. "It's the only way we can get the stone back." The others nodded. When she bit into the orange, its bittersweet tang made her eyes water. "We're a team, like desert explorers and *Mission: Impossible* guys and nomads all rolled into one, so we can do it."

"No one is braver than we are," said Razziq.

"No one is braver than the Azimuth," added Mina, her eyes bright.

"The scorpions are really smart, Mina," said Zagora, spitting out a slice of orange peel. "They can communicate with humans—and they can sense when humans are around. It says in Edgar's journal that they were intelligent back in the 1930s!" *Oops,* she thought, *I didn't mean to say that.*

"You read Edgar Yegen's journal?" Duncan looked up with a puzzled frown. "I thought Dad lost it."

Why didn't she think before opening her mouth? The journal had been her special secret. "I found it in Dad's desk drawer, so I borrowed it." She stood up, gazing at the walls, wishing he'd stop looking at her like she was a criminal. "It's really old, and beetles have chewed the pages."

Running her hands along the wall, she walked slowly around the chamber. "Edgar wrote about all these amazing things he saw in the desert, but the problem was the scorpions were stalking him and, well, I think Pitblade was right. The scorpions killed his grandfather." A tear slipped down her cheek. Why was she crying when she didn't even know Edgar Yegen?

Maybe it was because she could hear his whispering voice in her ear, as if Edgar were beside her on this desert journey. And perhaps too it was because she'd inherited Edgar Yegen's role as Sentinel—a role that no one had explained to him. Yegen had died in ignorance of his destiny, unaware of the Oryx. He'd never realized the Oryx Stone's true power.

"But we almost missed the plane because Dad decided at the last minute to look for the journal," said Duncan.

"I know," Zagora said quietly.

It was almost by accident that she noticed a crumbling niche set into the wall, obscured by shadows. Feeling a ripple of excitement, she moved closer. What she thought were thin cracks she now realized were the wavy lines of a drawing, and she recalled Edgar's words about some drawings being hidden within the stone architecture of the tower.

"Duncan, the flashlight!" she shouted, brushing away the cobwebs. "Quick, I found something!"

They all rushed over, crowding together as Duncan flashed his beam at the wall. In the glare of the flashlight, Zagora could see the faded outline of a map of Zahir, in colors that she was sure had once been brilliant.

"Look, Nar Azrak crosses in front of the moon," said Razziq.

Zagora studied the eclipse, yet she felt drawn to the small pyramid, mysterious and glowing, depicted in a courtyard behind the palace. Light streamed down from Nar Azrak, illuminating the pyramid with a wash of eerie blue.

Feeling almost giddy, she whirled around to face the others. "Everybody says the Pyramid of Xuloc was lost under the desert," she said. "Some archaeologists say invaders wrecked it. Some say it was crushed under the sand. But you know what? I don't think any of that's true. I think the pyramid's still there—except it's hidden somewhere." She had a fierce certainty that she was right. "So we'll go to Zahir and find it."

"We're with you," said Duncan, nodding his approval,

and his words of encouragement made her feel stronger and tougher.

Mina pointed to a small oval on the pyramid. "Is this the Oryx Stone?"

Zagora leaned in closer. "Hey, I didn't see that." Her fingertips fluttered over the drawing and everything went dark—except for the stone, which glimmered brightly.

"Who is this girl?" Now Mina was pointing to a small wavy-haired stick figure at the top of the pyramid, reaching for the Oryx Stone.

"It looks like she is taking the stone," said Razziq.

"A *girl* stole the Oryx Stone?" Duncan zoomed in with his light.

Zagora saw three stick figures at the bottom of the pyramid, looking up at the girl, as if cheering her on. She stepped back, trying to piece it all together, and recalled Edgar's words:

> *Yesterday I happened upon a foretelling I recognized as the Circle of Four, set within a niche in the tower wall, hidden in the shadows where no light fell.*

"Wait a minute," she said. "What if that girl isn't stealing the stone? What if she's *putting it back*?"

A hush fell over the group.

"What if this isn't the past?" said Zagora. "What if it's the future? Those kids at the bottom of the pyramid . . ." She paused, struck by an amazing thought. "I think they're us. *We're* the Circle of Four!"

"The girl at the top . . ." Razziq's voice was barely audible. "She is *you*, Zagora."

Zagora touched the stick figure with the long, rippling hair, and a tingling went through her. As she turned her gaze from the glowing pyramid, she felt everything click into place.

"Oh my gosh, I think you're right, Razziq," she whispered, overcome by a sense of awe. "*I'm* the one who's supposed to put the stone back."

◖◖ TAKE BACK THE ORYX STONE ◗◗

Zagora watched Razziq assemble the torches, rolling pieces of palm tree bark into cone shapes and inserting sticks into the centers. They had all agreed that torches would be the best weapons for fighting Olivia and her henchmen—or scaring away the scorpions, if it came to that.

"Not difficult." Razziq's agile fingers wrapped wire around the cones, securing them at the bottom. "Uncle Jamal taught me how to make these."

Before leaving, Zagora sneaked one last look into Edgar's journal.

The scorpions are restless, creeping outside the tower, watching our every move. They are unbelievably large—and cunning. Mohammed grows more nervous by the day. I told him the scorpions are trying to communicate with me. He did not seem surprised.

I cannot help thinking I was brought here for some higher purpose, and yet that purpose has not shown itself to me. Perhaps I will never know.

I have given Mohammed instructions that should anything happen to me, the stone and journal will be returned to Malta and given to my grandson Pitblade. He is a fine young boy with a curious mind and—who knows?—he may one day follow in my footsteps.

Reading these last pages, Zagora felt a deep sadness, knowing that Edgar was doomed. He never did find out he was a Sentinel, charged with guarding the Oryx Stone. Still, it was heartwarming to think of the many ways he'd influenced his grandson. And he'd wisely entrusted Pitblade with the stone.

When the torches were ready, the four trooped outside into the searing heat. Mina hoisted a broom of goat hairs over her shoulder, saying they might need it. Razziq asked them to form a circle and shield him from the wind. Zagora watched him kneel down with an old bottle and hold the thick glass bottom over one end of a torch, waiting patiently until it caught fire. One by one, the torches were lit and passed around.

Energized by their mission to rescue the stone, Zagora stepped forward. "Okay, we go straight to the palace and find that old warthog Olivia and make her give us the Oryx Stone. We do it fast so her thugs don't catch us, and if we see a scorpion, we use our torches. Got it, everybody?"

The others nodded determinedly.

Gathering her courage, Zagora waved her torch in the air and shouted: "Take back the Oryx Stone!" The words rang out like a warrior's cry.

"Take back the Oryx Stone!" shouted the others.

Yelling and cheering, their torches raised high, the children marched across the sand, a dry desert wind howling at their backs. Down, down they went, on a slow, rugged descent into the valley, headed for the ruins of Zahir, covering their torches with their hands as they strode through whirling dust and the fierce glare of the sun.

Zagora felt the wind lift her hair so it floated out behind her. Her breath came fast and shallow; her heart thundered inside her chest. *We belong to the desert now,* she thought as they merged into the silence and mystery of the shifting sands.

The wind echoed in her ears and she gazed into the light as the desert unfolded around her: half-buried fossils, abandoned stone tools, tracks of caravans, slices of strange and beautiful rock—mementos from the distant past. Straight ahead, as if floating above the sand, the rose-colored walls of ancient Zahir, silent and mystical, spread out before her.

Keep calm, she told herself. *Be brave. This journey, this mission—this is what I was meant to do.* She now felt like everything depended on her.

By the time they reached Zahir, their torches were still burning: a good omen. They entered the excavation site by climbing down a wooden ladder that had miraculously survived the past eleven years. Once inside the excavated casbah, they closed ranks, keeping in a tight knot as they navigated through tunneled-out streets, where the light seemed darker, the shadows more threatening.

Zagora grew increasingly wary, watching the vultures swoop down. A growing unease sat like a stone in her stomach. *Am I asking too much of everyone?* she wondered, feeling tendrils of dread winding through her. *We're just kids.*

They edged along bumpy earthen walls, down passages that forked left and right. She knew the palace wasn't far now. Heads bowed against the wind, they stumbled past ravaged towers and buildings, twisting down narrow streets, until at last they came to a tall semicircular gateway, edged with brilliantly colored tiles and Arabic calligraphy flowing across the top.

Side by side, they walked up the staircase to the Royal Palace of Xuloc.

"Hey, everybody, we can do this," she said as they stood looking up at the enormous palace doors. "We're smart and we're tough, and we're not scared of anything."

The others stared back with resolute expressions.

"I am not afraid," said Razziq. "I'm ready for battle, like the Round Table knights."

Mina and Duncan gave conspiratorial nods.

Zagora held up her guttering torch, where a tiny flame still burned. "Okay, it's now or never," she said, twisting the ancient door handle. "Our mission is to rescue the Oyrx Stone, and nobody's going to stop us."

Half falling off its hinges, the door clanked open and Zagora strode into the sand-blown hallway, waves of panic rolling over her. Torches held high, the others followed her inside. The palace was deathly still, except for the low moaning of the wind. Inside her head, the image of the Oryx Stone burned like a kindling fire.

"Follow me," she said. "Olivia's laboratory is nearby, so we'll go there first."

Halfway down the hall, she lifted the dusty tapestry, and one by one they ducked under it. "Careful, the floor is slippery," she told them as they tramped down the yellow-and-red-tiled staircase. Remembering how Olivia had tricked her, Zagora felt angry all over again, but she was determined not to make the same mistake twice.

At the bottom of the stairs, they stared at the dark windowless vestibule and bright orange signs.

"'Caution! Biogenic toxins, entry strictly forbidden,'" Zagora read out loud, just in case Mina and Razziq weren't able to read English.

Blue light spilled out through tears in the curtain that hung from the archway. Scarcely daring to breathe, Zagora tiptoed forward, step by wary step, and peered through a large hole while Duncan, Razziq and Mina raised their torches and the goat-hair broom, ready to strike.

Seeing no signs of Olivia or her bodyguards, Zagora motioned for the others to follow, and bunching up together, they crept silently through the curtain and into the laboratory. Their clothing and skin turned blue and she said, "Don't worry, that's the ultraviolet lights."

"Look at those cages," hissed Duncan, pointing to the glass boxes. "Oh man, scorpions! And snakes!"

But Zagora was more concerned about the strange sounds coming from the other side of the glass wall. Running over, she peered through the glass at a honeycomb of caves, illuminated by blue floodlights. Her stomach did a slow turn as she watched the sharp-edged, angular shapes moving in and out of the caves.

"The scorpions' nest!" she breathed, and the others hurried over.

"They are awake," whispered Mina.

Duncan scratched his head. "What the heck is Olivia up to?"

"Ah," said Razziq. "These creatures think they are in the light of Nar Azrak, yes?"

"You're right, Razz," said Duncan. "Maybe she believes that by using this light, it may make them stronger. And smarter. That the light from the planet is what they've been feeding off of to grow!"

"Olivia told me she needs the Oryx Stone for her scorpion experiments. She knows they're afraid of the stone and she says it'll protect her," Zagora told them. "That's because she's doing these creepy experiments with the giant scorpions. She wants them to get bigger!"

She covered her mouth with her hands as a brown scorpion of immense size clattered swiftly toward her. It was easily six feet long, with four pairs of legs, huge claws and a barbed tail tipped with a stinger. Two shiny black eyes darted back and forth on the top of its head, and at the corners of its head were five more pairs—all staring at her with menace.

She felt drops of sweat trickle down her face as the creature came nearer to the wall. With a violent movement, the scorpion whipped its tail against the glass. Mina screamed and dropped her broom. Zagora's breath came in panicky gasps as the scorpion rose on sinewy legs, thrashing its tail, slime dripping from its mouth. Then it flung its entire body against the glass wall.

Razziq gave a terrified shriek as the wall cracked. Zagora saw another scorpion racing up behind the first, preparing to slam itself against the glass.

"Our torches have burned out!" cried Mina. "We cannot fight them!"

"They're breaking through!" hollered Duncan. "Run!"

The children tore off, clutching one another as they sprinted wildly through the palace, trying to get as far from the laboratory as possible. On the third floor they ran through high-ceilinged rooms of drifting sand, where nothing looked familiar, and for a moment Zagora felt she had lost her bearings. Turning a corner, she saw a flight of marble steps, shabbily elegant, and she led the others up, feeling as if they were all characters in a fairy tále.

They shambled into a room painted in bold yellows and greens, where she noticed signs of human life: thick carpets, oil lamps, a brass coffeepot on a tray. Peering through a double-arched doorway, she saw a room filled with Arabic designs, where a hot wind blew in through rounded windows. But unlike the other palace rooms, this one had shelves and trolleys stacked high with vials, beakers, flasks and petri dishes, and corked jars containing a dark amber liquid.

A voice, flat and deadly, broke the silence. Zagora's heart jumped into her mouth. The others came to a standstill behind her.

"Well, well, who have we here?" Bracelets jangling, Olivia Romanesçu heaved herself up from a table covered with glass slides and a large black microscope. "Little Red Riding Hood and her riffraff pals."

Insulted by her mocking tone, Zagora refused to cringe under Olivia's petrifying gaze. *Don't let her get to you,* she told herself. *Remember the stone.* She lifted her head high. "We're here to take back the Oryx Stone," she said in a loud voice, taking a step forward, feeling emboldened with the others behind her. "We're not leaving until we get it."

Olivia gave a throaty laugh as she gathered up her slides. "My, my, such bravado."

Zagora threw back her shoulders, the way she imagined Freya Stark would do. "The Oryx Stone doesn't belong to you. It belongs to the Azimuth." As she spoke, her eyes roamed the corners of the room, in case of a possible ambush. She hoped the others were watching, too.

"You've come too late." Olivia's lips twisted into an ugly sneer. "The artifact is on its way to Sotheby's."

"You're lying! You said you needed the stone for your experiments!"

"I've changed my mind. The London auction house is anxious to have it, given the sum it will fetch. I'll be a rich woman once it's sold."

Zagora wasn't sure whether Olivia was lying. Closing her eyes, she tried to focus her entire being on the stone, imagining it—spectral, opalescent and sublime. Opening her eyes again, she felt a warm current running through her, and she knew the stone was near.

"The stone's here," she said with sudden conviction.

Olivia's cheeks flushed crimson. "You're finished, all of you. Get out of here."

"We're not going anywhere," said Zagora defiantly as the others closed ranks protectively around her. She wondered how she could ever have considered Olivia glamorous.

"We're not leaving," Duncan said huskily.

Mina folded her arms and said, "We go nowhere."

"The Oryx Stone," Razziq stated firmly.

With an indignant huff, Olivia turned away from them. Zagora saw with alarm that she was heading for the bottles of dark liquid.

"She's going for the venom!" she shouted. "Stop her!"

She threw herself in front of Olivia, blocking a shelf of venom vials. With a look of cold fury, Olivia knocked her down. Zagora gave a cry of pain as her knee struck the floor.

Looking up, she saw Duncan barrel silently across the room, Razziq at his side. They charged in a wild frenzy, knocking over a trolley of test tubes, colliding with Olivia just as her hand grasped one of the vials. With a shriek of alarm, Olivia pitched forward, curling her body and landing with a thump. The vial smashed on the floor. The boys tumbled around her, Duncan calling her an old witch, Razziq yelling in Arabic.

"Watch out for the venom!" warned Zagora.

A small object rolled across the floor, and she saw sparks of light flying into the air. In an instant Olivia's hand shot out, her large fingers closing around it.

"She has the stone!" cried Mina, jumping up and down. "She has the stone!"

Wincing with pain, Zagora stood up, her head light as a puffball.

Razziq leapt at Olivia, kicking and punching, trying to wrestle away the stone. Olivia sank her fingernails into his neck and he staggered back, clutching his throat. Enraged, Zagora sprinted across the room, ignoring her painful knee. Olivia threw a punch, knocking the breath out of her. Zagora lurched sideways, crashing into a shelf of beakers.

"Leave my sister alone!" yelled Duncan.

Struggling to her feet, she watched her brother hurl himself at Olivia, tackling her to the floor, knocking over glass tubes and bottles. Then she saw Mina spring catlike into the air. Squeezing Olivia's fist with her wiry hands, Mina ordered, "Drop the stone." Her voice was sharp and angry. Zagora stared at Mina, awed and a little afraid, hardly daring to breathe.

Olivia tried to swing at the girl, but Duncan seized the woman's arm, pinning it behind her back.

"No?" said Mina with a cold smile. "Then we take it."

The girl expertly pried the woman's fingers off the stone, faster than Zagora could have imagined possible. Then again, Mina was probably a pro at this sort of thing.

Olivia stared at Mina with loathing in her eyes, unable to move because Duncan and Razziq had taken hold of her arms.

"Long live the Azimuth!" shouted Mina, holding up the Oryx Stone.

"We take back the stone!" hollered Razziq, and they all whooped. Zagora felt delirious with relief. They'd done it!

Looking triumphant and wild, her face incandescent, Mina strode over to Zagora with the stone and dropped it into her hand with a regal gesture.

"Hold on to it with your life," said Mina in a solemn voice, "and never let it go—until you must. For what happens this day in Zahir will be remembered until the end of time."

As the Oryx Stone fell into Zagora's trembling hand, ice-blue sparks flew out, and she stood marveling at its luminous glow. "Thank you," she said, her heart warming to this high-wired girl with scorpion tattoos. "I'll remember you, too, Mina—no matter what happens."

Mina smiled crookedly.

Puzzled, tired and exhilarated, Zagora looked down

at the Oryx Stone, lying in her open palm, brimming with ancient spells and enchantments. The stone was a mystery, an enigma, a gift from the universe. The stone, she realized, was their reason to hope.

"I'll have your heads for this!" bellowed Olivia, lumbering to her feet, arms swinging.

Zagora noted with satisfaction that Olivia's hair was tangled into clumps on her head and one sleeve of her jeweled dress was in tatters. Like Frankenstein's monster, Olivia lurched forward, and Zagora darted away, knocking over a trolley, sending vials crashing to the floor.

"Watch out!" screamed Zagora. "Scorpion venom!"

She could see Mina and the boys running up behind Olivia, grabbing the woman's hands and tying them behind her back, using a bungee cord she recognized from Duncan's cache of desert supplies.

Clutching the stone to her chest, determined never to lose it again, Zagora backed into another trolley. Glass cages fell, shattering across the floor, releasing a silver-green snake and dozens of tiny scorpions.

"Fool!" shrieked Olivia, trying to break free from the bungee cord. "Look what you've done!"

"Run, everybody!" shouted Zagora.

⚜ ⚜ ⚜

Clutching the Oryx Stone, Zagora forced herself to keep running, despite the pain in her knee, but it was hard keeping up with the rest of them. Sometimes she heard odd noises—once a high-pitched laugh that couldn't possibly be human—but she wasn't sure if the sounds were real. As she raced through the first floor, the rooms began taking on a familiar look.

Stealthily they moved through an archway to a room with yellow walls, which Zagora recognized as the ancient kitchen. Duncan stopped in his tracks, the others colliding into one another behind him. "What's that barking noise?" he whispered.

Zagora vaguely recalled Olivia's telling her goons to feed the dogs, but she'd been so upset at the time she'd forgotten about them. Through the doorway she saw four animals with rough mottled fur and dark muzzles, straining at thick chains. One yawned and she saw several rows of long, sharp teeth. Staring at their striped manes, their hefty shoulders and sloping backs, Zagora realized with a sinking feeling that these weren't dogs at all, but something far more dangerous.

"Hyenas!" whispered Razziq.

"*Striped* hyenas," said Duncan knowledgeably. "Look at those incisors!"

Zagora wondered what their chances were of getting

away without being seen. Her throat constricted as one hyena stuck its head into the kitchen and gave a low, anxious growl. The man with the pencil mustache appeared in the doorway and smiled as he caught sight of them. She froze, overcome by an unreal sense of horror as she watched the man reach down with gloved hands and unhook the chain, shouting commands in Arabic. With a bloodthirsty roar, the hyena sped toward them, quickly followed by the others.

Screaming in terror, the children took flight, sprinting up a wide staircase to the next floor. "I hate hyenas!" Mina yelled hysterically, grabbing Zagora's arm as they raced along an inner balcony. From somewhere below came a bloodcurdling howl, and the four scattered in all directions.

Suddenly aware that she was alone, Zagora took off down a sloping passageway, searching for another staircase, the Oryx Stone pressed to her chest. Too late she realized that the passageway went nowhere: instead it dead-ended at a door painted in shades of rose and mustard.

She heard another howl, this time much nearer. Panicked, she twisted the knob, pushing against the door, but it stayed firmly shut. She glanced over one shoulder and saw a dark shape careering around a corner. Fangs exposed, the hyena hurtled straight at her. She kicked the door in a frenzy. The hyena was almost on her. She kicked harder, and a searing pain shot through her knee. The air reeked of the animal's fetid breath.

How could she die now, just when they'd rescued the stone? One last kick and the door flew open. Zagora dove inside, slammed the door behind her and shot the bolt, almost sobbing with relief.

Leaning against the wall, her breath coming in short gasps, Zagora readied herself for the next attack. Snarling, the hyena flung its massive body against the wooden door. Splinters flew into the air. Then silence fell. Peering through cracks in the door, she could see a squared-off snout, a muzzle shrunken back around the hyena's sharp teeth.

She was no match for a hyena. It was far too ferocious.

As the creature thudded against the door, she saw a hinge fly off and heard a loud thump out in the hallway. The hyena let out a shrill, startled yelp. Unsure of what was happening, Zagora was too afraid to investigate. Her only thought was *That's it, next time he's in.* There was no way out except for a window. Climbing up onto the sill, she gazed hundreds of feet down—definitely too far to jump. Any minute the hyena would burst through.

The sky was slowly darkening. Wind whistled, low and ominous, around the palace walls. Crooking her neck, she saw Nar Azrak on the horizon. The eclipse was going to happen without her!

Regret and sorrow washed over her. She hadn't gotten it right after all. Holding the Oryx Stone, Zagora clung to the window frame, waiting for the end and hoping it would be quick, saddened that she hadn't said goodbye to her father or Duncan, or any of the others.

∞ THE SEVEN ARCHWAYS ∞

The door stayed closed and no hyena came racing through, attacking with savage teeth. All Zagora could hear was a threatening silence. From the windowsill she watched a handful of stars glimmering in the sky, amazed that her heart was still beating.

Thrumming with a mystical energy, the Oryx Stone glowed in her hand. The eclipse hadn't happened yet; maybe there was still time! She jumped off the sill and ran to the door, peering through the cracks, no longer sensing the creature's presence. Behind the door it was deathly quiet. Had the hyena given up and gone off with its pals?

Sliding back the bolt, she threw open the door. A heap of matted fur lay on the tiles. Curious, she crept forward, her stomach turning as she inhaled the cruddy stench of the hyena. She gazed at the dead animal with relief and disgust, marveling that it hadn't killed her. Its eyes had glazed over, and inside its mouth she could see double rows of long sharp teeth—probably engineered by Olivia.

From behind the dead hyena stepped a thin shadow, startling her. Ashen-faced, Mina stood holding an ornate brass urn, blood dripping from the bottom of it.

"I followed you," she said in a trembling voice. "The hyena tried to break down your door."

"Mina! Oh my gosh, you're so brave!" Overcome with emotion, Zagora threw her arms around the girl's shoulders. "You killed the hyena!" She'd read about "narrow escapes" in books before but had never grasped the true meaning of the phrase. "You saved my life!"

Mina hugged her back, and Zagora could feel her shaking. It took a lot to scare Mina.

"My grandmother tried to show me a path," said Mina, "but I was too angry to see it." She stepped back, fixing her intense gaze on Zagora. "I was angry at *you,* Zagora, because you have desert sight *and* you are Sentinel of the Stone—and I wanted these things for myself.

But I see now that my path is different. As long as you have the stone of the oryx, I must follow and protect you. I am—how do you say?—a guardian. Together we must keep the stone safe."

Zagora nodded, thinking how her words made perfect sense. "Being a guardian is a really important job," she said.

"We are friends, yes?" Mina smiled, her eyes wide with delight.

"The best of friends," said Zagora with a grin. "Friends forever."

Another quick hug, then they were running through the empty rooms of the palace, alert for hyenas, searching for the others as they raced from one floor to the next. Outside, the sky was growing darker by the minute. Wheeling around an archway, Zagora jumped in surprise as Duncan stumbled out from behind a tapestry.

"Am I glad to see you guys," he said. She could hear him struggling to breathe.

"You okay, Duncan?" she asked, worried about his asthma.

He waved his hand dismissively. "I'm cool. Everything's under control." He looked around. "Razz isn't with you?"

"No," said Zagora, and they exchanged anxious glances.

"Razziq is smart," Mina said confidently. "He's fast. They will never catch him."

Zagora hoped she was right. Razziq was fast, but could he escape a pack of wild hyenas? What about Olivia and her bodyguards? And the giant scorpions?

"A hyena chased me," she told Duncan. "It tried to smash down the door and it stank so bad I almost threw up. Good thing Mina killed it or I'd be dead right now."

Looking deeply impressed, Duncan turned to Mina. "You killed a *hyena*?"

The girl nodded. "This creature was unnatural."

"It had double rows of teeth on the top and bottom of its mouth," said Zagora.

"Sounds abnormal, all right," said Duncan. "One more of Olivia's—" He stopped in midsentence. "Oh no, I knew this would happen!" he cried. "They crashed through the glass wall!"

Through an archway, Zagora could see two huge segmented creatures, moving stealthily amid the marble columns of an inner courtyard, stingers raised: scorpions the size of horses.

"They're stalking us," whispered Mina.

Zagora watched them with fascination and dread as they moved in erratic circles around a dark shape on the tiles.

"They killed a hyena," whispered Duncan. "We'll get stung, too, if we don't watch out."

Zagora looked at the others with weary, frightened eyes, wishing desperately that Razziq would show up. Where was her dad? Why was everyone taking so long?

The scorpions had caught sight of them. A warped and frightening intelligence flickered across their eyes. Zagora's heart quailed. They were sending out thoughts to frighten her! *Relinquish the treasure; it belongs not to you. Relinquish the treasure and all will live; hold on to the treasure and all will die. . . .*

She began to shiver.

"Zagora, what is wrong?" whispered Mina.

"The scorpions are threatening me," she said. "They want the Oryx Stone!"

Mina threw her a ferocious look. "That will never happen."

"We risked life and limb to get that stone back," said Duncan. "You're not going to let those mutated arachnids take it, are you?"

Zagora swallowed hard. "Yeah, but if I let the scor-

pions have the stone, they'll let us go and they won't—"
She paused, not wanting to say *kill us.* "If I don't, we
might not get out of here alive!" The thought made her
go cold with fear.

"Do not be foolish," said Mina with disdain. "You
cannot barter with scorpions."

"Even if you give them the Oryx Stone," said Duncan, wiping his sweaty brow, "there's no guarantee they
won't sting us anyway."

Zagora met his tough blue gaze. *They're right,* she
thought. *What was I thinking? I'd be crazy to trust the scorpions.* She knew her dad would offer the same advice.
Charles Pym, Edgar and Pitblade Yegen, Freya Stark—all
of them had taken risks and stepped over the edge, flying
in the face of danger. Now it was her turn.

The Oryx Stone winked up from her palm. For centuries it had aligned Nar Azrak with the pyramid, creating
a barrier around Zahir, balancing the energy between the
earth and the heavens. The stone had been the glue holding everything together—until it was stolen. The scorpions feared the Oryx Stone not only because it could
harm them, but because it had the power to set things
right again. Hadn't Pitblade said the scorpions wanted
the stone in order to destroy it?

"Hey, those things are watching us!" hissed Duncan. "Man, is that ever creepy." He nudged his sister with his elbow. "Let's go, it's not safe."

Hands linked, the three took off.

"Nar Azrak!" gasped Zagora, looking out a window as they ran past. The rogue planet seemed to be growing larger, as if it were speeding toward Earth, about to engulf them all.

"Wait, stop!" cried Mina, slowing down, gazing at the scene outside. "I know it is my task to protect you, but I see my people coming. I must go—for a short time only. I will return soon, I promise."

Before they could protest, she sprinted down the corridor and vanished.

Zagora stood on her toes and stared out the window. "Duncan, there's a line of people crossing the dunes, and they're carrying swords and torches! The Azimuth are coming to Zahir!"

"That means Dad's on his way," said Duncan excitedly. "And Pitblade, too."

"We have to find the pyramid before the eclipse happens!" Zagora turned to her brother in a panic. "Come on!"

They raced off, heading for the back of the palace. As they ducked into the kitchen, Duncan came to a screeching halt and Zagora felt the hairs on her head stand up. Beneath the archway stood Olivia, holding a chain attached to a snarling hyena. Her other hand gripped Razziq by the neck of his T-shirt. He looked as if he was gasping for air.

"Razziq!" she screamed.

"Let Razz go or we'll attack you again," threatened Duncan, shaking a fist at Olivia.

Zagora felt her stomach drop as the two henchmen rushed inside from the courtyard, their expressions dour.

"I'll let your little friend go free," said Olivia. "Along with my doggie friend here." She yanked the chain and the hyena snapped its enormous jaws. "Better yet, why don't we barter? The stone in exchange for your friend."

Zagora glared at Olivia, overcome by a hopeless rage, hating her with a furious passion. Duncan stepped forward, about to speak, when the guard with the mustache cried out. Zagora saw a tall shadow looming up behind him. Olivia screamed as a massive claw locked on to the man's arm and his eyes glazed over with fear. Hissing wildly, the scorpion dragged the screaming guard into the courtyard.

After that, everything went into warp drive. Hackles up, the hyena started barking, snapping the links of its chain and tearing away in a cloud of dust. The other guard turned on one heel and raced through the kitchen, almost knocking Zagora over as he disappeared into the palace. Razziq whirled around, kicking Olivia; cursing, she staggered sideways, nearly falling over, and Zagora cheered as Razziq broke free. Flying across the room, he dove into Zagora's and Duncan's arms and they all embraced at once.

A shriek cut through the air and the children jumped apart. Zagora watched in horror as two giant scorpions closed in on Olivia.

"Do something!" Olivia screeched, her face white with fear.

Tails rattling, the scorpions attacked. Olivia shrieked as they seized her arms with their claws and pulled her roughly through the doorway. Zagora and the boys bounded across the kitchen into the courtyard, where she could hear Olivia's muffled screams as the scorpions dragged her, struggling, down under the sand.

The courtyard fell silent. Zagora thought she might throw up. All that was left of Olivia was an emerald sandal, inlaid with gems, lying on its side in the dust.

"I don't believe it," croaked Duncan. "This is too horrible for words."

"They have taken her to their lair," Razziq whispered. "There is nothing we can do."

Was this a sort of rough justice, wondered Zagora, because Olivia had terrorized them and kidnapped their father? Not really, she told herself. Being taken by scorpions wasn't something she'd wish on anyone—not even her worst enemy.

The wind began to rise, whipping Zagora's hair into knots and tearing the fronds off the palm trees. The sky darkened and the wailing wind picked up sand in long trails. High overhead, feverish waves of mist swirled around Nar Azrak.

"Hey, guys, the eclipse!" said Duncan, spitting out sand. "We don't have much time."

"Everything is in your hands, Zagora," said Razziq. "Only you can find the pyramid."

Standing in the dusty courtyard, she imagined the desert she loved so dearly, trying to call up her desert sight. Before long she heard the familiar distant wind, low and haunting. Waves of shimmering sand swirled before her eyes.

Images came flying at her, moving so fast she could hardly follow. All at once she saw things that were bound to the earth and things that were not. She saw the vast expanse of the Sahara; secret words and mystical signs; tracks in the sand left by the oryxes. She could see a ragged band of travelers making their way over the dunes, belongings piled high on camels, following a tall man in white robes. Beneath the sky rose the golden-red walls of Zahir. In a vast courtyard, workers constructed a pyramid while an olive-skinned craftsman polished a perfect blue stone, an oryx carved at its center.

Next she saw stonemasons unpacking sledges and chisels, digging trenches near the pyramid and lining them with goat droppings, packing in layers of rock salt. Using cut blocks of stone, they shaped seven arches and a gateway, filling in the gaps with small stones. The gateway, inscribed with magical writings, was fitted with heavy wooden doors. When the arches were completed, they built an earthen dome around the courtyard so that the pyramid would be hidden from view.

Pictures whirled, confusing Zagora, and she was in a different time. A man with hatred in his eyes wrenched the Oryx Stone from its setting, and a chill fell over her heart. She saw Zahir thrown into chaos, and a future where Nar Azrak blotted out the stars. Gone were the oryxes and camels, the moths and lizards and nighthawks, the snakes, centipedes and wasps. All she could see, for miles in every direction, were scorpions.

But other futures were possible, too—if only she could locate the pyramid.

She turned to the others as if awakening from a

dream, the images fresh in her mind. "They hid the pyramid," she said excitedly. "See that wall over there?" She pointed to the far side of the shadowy courtyard, which abutted a high earthen wall. "There's a gateway through there and we have to dig it out!"

She saw Duncan and Razziq exchange quizzical glances, but neither questioned her. Duncan switched on his flashlight and they ran across the courtyard to the wall, which was covered in layers of sand and dust and dirt.

"Behind this wall there's a gateway of painted stone, covered with glyphs and symbols. I saw it, really I did," Zagora told them. "It's carved with crosses, dots and moons, and arrows and suns—and golden oryxes along the edges!"

"Magical squares," murmured Razziq, "and holy circles. It must be centuries old."

"How do you know all that, Zagora?" asked Duncan, his voice filled with admiration.

"I saw it with my desert vision," she said, her face flushed with excitement. Odd, but she felt sort of like a celebrity. "Next we have to find a way through the gate. . . ."

"Hmm." Duncan furrowed his brow in concentration. "If the gateway is made of stones, then there has to be a keystone. That's the main stone at the top of an arch-way, holding everything together. Remove the keystone and the whole thing will collapse. By taking it out, we might be able to get to the other side."

"Brilliant," said Zagora. Okay, maybe her brother was kind of dorky, but he was a whiz kid when it came to practical solutions.

Duncan propped up his flashlight on the ground, aiming it at the wall, and they began tearing at the stones and dirt, scraping away the layers of sand, until at last the outline of a low arch appeared. Around its edges Zagora could see faded symbols. Once they'd exposed the key-stone, they gently pulled out the small stones wedged in around it.

"Hurry!" said Duncan. "The scorpions will be com-ing out. . . ."

The mention of scorpions filled Zagora with a word-less terror. As she worked, it felt as if hours were passing, though she knew it was only minutes.

When a space had been hollowed out around the keystone, Razziq turned to Duncan and said, "You are the tallest. You should take out the stone."

"Okay, guys," said Duncan, "stand back."

Zagora held her breath as her brother gripped the edges of the keystone and pulled. Dirt flew out from around it. Grunting, he wiggled the stone back and forth, then slowly eased it out.

"Watch out!" he shouted, and they all jumped away.

Zagora saw the gateway quake; then came a muffled rumbling as dirt showered down. All the stones began falling at once, sending up dust as they thudded into the sand, followed by the remains of a door, black and rotted, which disintegrated as they hit the ground.

"Unbelievable," said Duncan, clicking off his flashlight.

"By the dunes of the Sahara," murmured Razziq. "Look!"

Zagora stared through the gap, astonished: seven archways unfolded before them, each one larger than the last, opening into a space that was filled with an eerie blue light.

"That's it!" she cried. "The ancient palace courtyard!"

She gripped the Oryx Stone and they raced through the archways, following the dim glow, watching it grow brighter and brighter, until at last they came to a space of lofty dimensions: a ceiling that looked fifty or sixty feet high and walls encrusted with strange, indiscernible designs. Zagora realized at once that this was a dome the Azimuth had built around the original courtyard.

High overhead, at the top of the curved ceiling, she

saw a large opening to the sky, through which a flood of blue light poured down from the planet Nar Azrak.

"Mega cool," said Duncan, gawking in disbelief. "Wow, this place is bigger than South Station in Boston!"

Most amazing of all was the steep three-sided pyramid, at least twenty feet high, rising out of the sand, floating and dreamlike, throwing its unearthly light against the walls of the earthen dome. The meteorites had been cut and polished to perfection, fitted together to create the pyramid. Zagora had never imagined that anything like this could even exist. The pyramid, spare and elegant, was much higher than she'd envisioned. It looked like a shining relic from another world.

"Oh, wow," she breathed. If only Edgar Yegen had lived to see this.

"The Pyramid of Xuloc," said Razziq in an awestruck tone. "Built by the ancients with stones from Nar Azrak."

At the top of the pyramid Zagora saw a small oval groove—the place where the Oryx Stone belonged. Her stomach gave a sharp twist. She was going to have to climb up there.

"You mean that pyramid's been hidden all this time and nobody knew it?" said Duncan. He turned to his sister, giving her a high five. "You found it with your desert sight—cool!"

Zagora felt delirious with joy and astonishment.

"Feel that electricity in the air?" Duncan went on. "You know, if the scorpions' nest is under the pyramid, it's no wonder they're so huge and demented. Think of all that intergalactic energy they've been ingesting."

But Zagora wasn't thinking about the scorpions. Eyes shining, she marched excitedly toward the pyramid, preparing to return the Oryx Stone. This was, after all, her destiny. The only hard part was going to be the climb to the top: high places always made her dizzy.

Then something unexpected began to happen. She could hear faint rustling noises, like seeds rattling, and as the sounds grew louder, she felt the air vibrating around her.

"What the heck's going on?" said Duncan, squinting at her through whirling dust.

Zagora saw the strange designs on the walls of the dome begin to move. Clods of dirt fell from the ceiling. Tiny stones crumbled off the walls.

"It's coming down!" she heard Razziq cry.

They weren't alone.

The walls of the dome were suddenly alive with scorpions.

THE CIRCLE OF FOUR

"Run for your lives!" shouted Duncan, grabbing Zagora and Razziq. She felt her brother spin her around as they made a swift U-turn and raced back to the seven arches.

We can't fight giant scorpions, Zagora thought in despair. *We're just kids.* She held the Oryx Stone to her heart, hoping it might give her strength against the creatures.

As she ran through the courtyard, the ground began to shake. The dome seemed to be breaking apart. She saw scorpions leaping off the walls in confusion, legs entangled as they hit the sand. Then they righted themselves and scattered in all directions.

"Faster, guys!" huffed Duncan, herding them away from a scorpion.

Mud, dirt and stones rained down. The dome was caving in!

The children raced as fast as they could, dodging claws and scorpion tails, trying to avoid the collapsing walls. From behind them came deep rumbles and crashes as sections of the ceiling fell to the ground. Then Zagora heard another sound, very faint, rising out of the desert. Cutting through the noise was the muffled pounding of hoofbeats, growing louder against the sandy earth, and suddenly she was filled with hope.

The three dove beneath the first archway, huddling together and gaping at one another in fear while the dome continued to spew dust and rocks. A fine dust blew over them, stinging Zagora's face as her breath came in short, painful gasps. With the dome almost completely down, she could see that they were in a courtyard the size of a football field, enclosed by low walls of rose-colored stone.

She heard the drumming of hooves, much closer now. An instant later she saw an oryx sail into the courtyard in a burst of brilliance that hurt her eyes. Then came another, and another, red sand billowing, all the oryxes with heads lowered and scimitar horns gleaming.

"The oryxes are returning!" Zagora cried, awed by the noble creatures with fearless hearts. "They're coming to take back Zahir!"

The scorpions froze, legs tensed to spring. There was a profound silence as oryxes and scorpions sized up one another. Then, all at once, they leapt into action, charging one another head-on—fighting, shrieking, colliding— and Zagora's ears rang with the noise of battle. Terrified, she watched the oryxes, slashing at the scorpions with their horns, and thought how brave they were, how magnificent.

At the far end of the courtyard, where two massive wooden doors had crumbled to the ground, Zagora saw the Azimuth appear, as if in a dream, and for a short while the skirmishing between oryxes and scorpions subsided. The Azimuth came storming in through clouds of sand. They were tall, spectral and warrior-like, wearing elegant purple robes looped over their shoulders, eyes burning with supernatural gazes. They streamed into the courtyard, some on foot, others on camels, carrying swords and flaming torches, led by a tiny birdlike woman in turquoise and scarlet, her face like carved stone. She moved with a regal stride.

"The Azimuth," said Zagora. "Look, there's Mina's

grandmother!" She could hardly believe this imposing woman was Noor, the gnarled old lady she'd met in Marrakech.

A slight, wiry figure jostled through the crowd, waving to her. "Mina!" she cried, and both girls began running.

As they reached each other, Zagora saw that her friend looked oddly changed. There was a flush of red on Mina's cheekbones and her hair hung in plaits beneath a gold headband. The blue silken robes she wore looked almost new, except for a tear down one sleeve. *Mina looks like a scrappy princess,* Zagora thought as she hugged her, inhaling her minty scent.

Duncan and Razziq came running up, and Zagora felt her eyes blur with tears.

"We're a team again," she told them. "Not even the scorpions can stop us now!"

The Azimuth warriors stood silently, contemplating the scorpions across the width of the courtyard, while the oryxes quietly surrounded the pyramid. Nar Azrak, Zagora noticed with sudden panic, was moments away from blotting out the moon.

Squaring her shoulders, she stepped forward, summoning all her courage. Duncan, Razziq and Mina closed in protectively around her. She stood tall, her blue eyes solemn, her dark wavy hair shining, the prophecy seared into her mind.

In a defiant gesture, Zagora raised the Oryx Stone high over her head. The stone flared, and light poured out of it, illuminating the faces of the bedraggled group, containing them inside a mystical circle. *The Circle of Four,* she thought, *that's us.*

"We're the Circle of Four, the four kids in Xuloc's foretelling," she said. She felt herself glowing with a mysterious inner light. "We're brave and we escaped hyenas and scorpions and we fought Olivia and we took back the stone." She lifted her chin determinedly. "The Azimuth are depending on us to save Zahir. Your mission is to stand against the scorpions until the stone is in place." Closing her hand over the stone, she shook her fist in the air. "Death to the scorpions!"

"Death to the scorpions!" echoed the others in unison, raising their fists.

Zagora turned and ran like the wind, arms flailing. She thought only of the prophecy. A high, hollow whickering filled the air and she saw deathstalkers moving toward the Azimuth warriors. Near the pyramid, darker, larger scorpions clustered in tight knots, lashing their tails and shattering the blue stones. Overhead, vultures gathered.

As she approached the pyramid, the oryxes charged the scorpions. She saw one scorpion escape, its twisted outline crawling up the pyramid, quiet as a ghost except for its hissing breath. Mina screamed, and Duncan shouted "Run!" just as the scorpion lunged.

Zagora jumped onto the pyramid and scrabbled up, her stomach knotted with fear. Gazing out over the courtyard, she saw two blue-cloaked figures, scimitars at their sides, emerge from the whirling sand on white camels, charging in through the crumbled gateway. The first rider was Pitblade Yegen, and the second was Charles W. Pym. Both looked like true desert warriors. Zagora was so happy she thought she might burst into tears.

She clambered higher, grasping the handholds carved into the stones, terrified of losing her grip and falling backward. Shouts from Azimuth fighters echoed throughout the courtyard, along with the clash of oryx horns and scorpion claws.

Scorpions clattered up the pyramid behind her, shrieking with rage. One leapt into the air and landed just below Zagora's feet, so close she could smell its moldy breath. It had jumped from the ground below! A second scorpion appeared beside the first, hissing wildly, followed by a third that sprang onto the pyramid, claws extended.

Zagora froze. They were closing in on her!

"Oh no you don't!" shouted a no-nonsense voice, and she blinked in surprise, seeing her father climb expertly up the pyramid, not bothering with the handholds, carrying not one but two torches, the scimitar at his side. The three scorpions came to a standstill. Zagora's heart filled with pride: her dad was risking his life to save her!

Looking more like an Azimuth warrior than an absentminded professor, Dr. Pym ducked as a huge claw whipped past his head. Zagora watched, hardly daring to breathe, as her father flung a torch, setting fire to one of the scorpions. It reared back with an anguished wail, sliding down the pyramid.

Where on earth had her father learned to fight scorpions?

Chewing on her knuckles, she watched him brandish his remaining torch at the two scorpions. As one of them advanced, he pulled out his scimitar and lopped off a claw; then he plunged his sword into the creature's crusty shell. With a shudder the scorpion pitched sideways, foam dripping from its mouth, and bumped down the pyramid. From below came a great roar, and looking down, Zagora saw the Azimuth tribesmen, waving their swords triumphantly.

"Keep going, Zagora, you're nearly there!" shouted her father.

Recovering her balance, she scrambled up, struggling higher, fearing that at any moment she might go hurtling down the side of the pyramid. With blistered hands and a pounding heart, she felt weak from head to toe. Hauling herself up by sheer willpower, she continued, inch by inch, listening to the frenzied clamor of oryxes and scorpions below.

She had a clear view of Nar Azrak, directly overhead, moving into the path of the moon. *Don't give up now,* Zagora told herself. *You're going to make it.*

From behind her came a crazed skittering, and twisting around, she saw a scorpion, far bigger than the others, surging up the pyramid. Terrified, she scrabbled frantically upward. A claw shot past, like a gleaming scythe, inches away, almost knocking her off.

The scorpion unfurled its poison-tipped tail. Reaching for the Oryx Stone, Zagora pressed her fingers around the edges, feeling it grow warm in her hand. She'd been concentrating so hard on climbing she hadn't had a chance to use the stone against the scorpions. When she held it up, it glowed with a molten heat, transforming into a sphere of fire far brighter than the stars overhead—brighter, even, than Nar Azrak. A bolt of light shot out and the huge scorpion went up in flames. *This is it,* Zagora told herself. *Nothing can catch me now.*

The moon was a thin sliver: in a matter of seconds it would disappear completely. She willed herself up the last few inches, her arms heavy as stones, her nerves screaming and her shoulders blazing with pain. At last she was at the top, suspended between the earth and sky. She took a deep breath, her gaze taking in the whole of the desert.

A deep serenity fell over her. She could feel the transcendent energy of the Oyrx Stone. It seemed as if the desert world was struggling to right itself. As for her, she knew she wasn't the same girl who had entered the desert just a few days before.

Lifting the stone, Zagora closed her eyes and murmured a series of words, all of them incomprehensible, and she sensed someone was speaking through her from another place and time. She felt the blood beating behind her eyelids as, in her own language, she whispered, "This is for you, Edgar Yegen."

Wedging her foot against the side of the pyramid, she leaned forward and set the Oryx Stone into the small hollow space, like placing a crown on the forehead of a high king. The stone fit perfectly.

At that instant a mass of dark blue exploded overhead. Zagora looked up to see Nar Azrak careering away from Earth at an almost impossible speed. The wind faded to a dull roar, the sand ceased to blow, the vultures flapped away and her hand was suddenly empty. Down in the courtyard the giant scorpions lay scattered and unmoving, like huge chess pieces turned on their sides. Even from this distance she could tell they were dead.

Desert peace and quiet prevailed. The moon and stars shone like desert jewels.

Exhausted but victorious, Zagora gazed down at Duncan, Razziq and Mina, her dearest companions in the world. Standing at the base of the pyramid in a half circle, they looked up at her, waving and shouting in triumph, the oryxes lined up behind them, radiant in the moonlight, their noble heads lifted to the sky.

༄ THE TOWER OF THE ENIGMAS ༄

Zagora stood on the turret at the top of the Tower of the Enigmas, gazing up at Nar Azrak. For hours, ever since the Oryx Stone had been returned, the planet had been growing visibly smaller. Duncan was certain that it was heading back into its old orbit. It must be true, she thought dreamily, because Nar Azrak was much dimmer, and the stars and moon were breathtakingly visible.

Pitblade Yegen was showing Duncan and Razziq how to work the astrolabe, and everyone was taking turns looking through Duncan's telescope, set up on a lightweight tripod he'd dug out of his pack. Zagora and the boys had exchanged tearful goodbyes with Mina, who had left with Noor to celebrate the Azimuth tribe's return to Zahir. Pitblade had promised to have the city excavated and ready to move into by the next summer.

Zagora gazed out at the city of Zahir rising mysteriously out of the dunes. From here she could see the Pyramid of Xuloc, glimmering in the dark, and she thought of her precious Oryx Stone, and how in this ordinary world there existed extraordinary things, just waiting to be found.

As they trooped downstairs for the evening meal, she thought, *The nights won't be scary or dangerous anymore, now that the scorpions are gone.* She sniffed, suddenly feeling hungry: the air was redolent of cheese and olives. They shared a meal of crusty bread, figs and melons, and as they ate, they talked about the scorpions and the Oryx Stone.

"We need never fear the scorpions again," said Pitblade. "Each of us played a role in returning the Oryx Stone—you especially, Zagora."

"Simply put," her father said, "you were exceedingly brave. I'm terribly proud of you."

Zagora beamed. She'd never really done anything important or meaningful in her life—until now.

The adults mulled over the unknown fate of Olivia Romanescu. Finding no trace of her or her henchmen in the palace, they of course feared the worst.

"I feel responsible for Olivia's dreadful actions," said Pitblade. Zagora saw a look of regret on his face. "She was my cousin, after all, and I trusted her."

"No one blames you. How could you have known her true nature?" said Dr. Pym. "Such a strange woman. While I was being held prisoner Olivia told me she'd glued a scorpion, still alive, to the envelope containing your letter to me."

"Good heavens," said Pitblade.

Zagora's father narrowed his eyes at her. "That was the scorpion you dropped into Olivia's tea, wasn't it? Hmm, quite wicked of you."

"Served her right, the old witch," Zagora muttered.

"Let me guess," her father said. "The scorpion was programmed to grow bigger the moment it made contact with water. One of her cutting-edge genetic engineering experiments."

"You had that creepy thing in your pocket all the way from Boston to Morocco?" said Duncan, wrinkling his nose.

Zagora nodded. Scorpions were now at the top of her list of the Most Disgusting Creatures on Earth.

Suddenly feeling shy, she turned to Pitblade and said, "I have something for you." Reaching into her backpack, she pulled out an ancient leather book, dust falling from its beetle-chewed pages, and handed it to him. His eyes misted over as he ran his fingers across the battered cover, and his face took on a faraway expression. *He's remembering his childhood,* she thought.

"Thank you, Zagora," he murmured, opening the worn leather cover. "You've no idea what my grandfather's written words mean to me."

Her father threw her a stern look, and she braced herself for an unpleasant scene.

"Why didn't you tell me you had Edgar's journal?" he asked.

Duncan and Razziq, sitting on either side of her, fell noticeably quiet.

Zagora felt a lump at the back of her throat. Why was she always messing up? "I just wanted to read it, that's all. I always planned to give it back. I'm sorry, Dad."

To her surprise, her father smiled. "When I was locked away in the palace, I had plenty of time to think about you and Duncan," he said. "I know you try hard to be good, and maybe I've been too hard on you—perhaps I should give you more credit for the things you do right. You have a generous heart, Zagora. That's what I love most about you."

She felt her cheeks burning. Blinking back tears, she jumped up and threw her arms around her father.

Pitblade leafed slowly through the pages of the journal. "If you only knew the hours I spent as a boy poring over my grandfather's words and sketches, fantasizing about one day becoming a desert explorer," he said. "He died when I was very young, yet I feel as if I knew him well—maybe because his words have stayed with me all this time."

"Me too, I feel the same way," whispered Zagora, sad to think she'd never meet this remarkable man in person. It was odd how Edgar's journal had become so real to her, more real at times than her life back home. She had come to regard Edgar almost like a fellow adventurer on her journey through the desert—an invisible companion through all the dangers she'd faced, advising and enlightening her along the way.

As the meal wound down, there was a knock at the door. Duncan jumped up to answer it. Zagora wondered who could be calling that late at night. A man in a turban and dust-covered robes, his face caked with dirt, staggered into the tower.

"Occam!" cried Razziq.

Dr. Pym rose to his feet. "Why, that's our guide!"

After they'd all welcomed Occam and offered him bread and cheese, he turned to Razziq, speaking in rapid-fire Arabic.

"Occam left our campsite to look for the two camels," Razziq translated. "On his way back, he was swallowed by the sand and fell down a dark hole with steep sides. There was no way to escape, and he worried that the sand might bury him alive."

"Geez," murmured Duncan.

Zagora leaned forward, curious to hear more.

"Occam shouted for help but no one came, so he played his flute instead. Fortunately a tribe of nomads passed by on horses and heard his music, and they helped Occam out of the hole." Razziq paused. "But before he was rescued, Occam realized he wasn't down there alone, because he felt something warm next to him, breathing on his fingers: an animal. Then he saw two big eyes—"

"An oryx?" whispered Zagora, though an oryx didn't seem likely.

"A camel." Razziq grinned. "A camel that had been pulled under the sand."

"What?" shouted Zagora, her heart thumping wildly. "Where?" Leaping up, she rushed out of the tower, stumbling into the moonlit night.

A few yards away stood a raggedy, bony-ribbed camel, munching on a prickly pear bush. The camel stopped chewing and raised its eyes.

Zagora nearly fainted. Even in the darkness, she'd

know those eyes anywhere. Big and brown, they were filled with the light of the desert, with extra thick lashes, just like Mrs. Bixby's—minus the plastic-rimmed glasses, of course.

"Sophie!" Tears blurring her vision, she stumbled over to her long-lost friend. "Is that really you?" She threw her arms around the camel's neck, kissing her weatherworn face.

"You still smell like Sophie," she murmured, kissing the camel's bristly fur, feeling a thrill of perfect happiness.

✺ ONE YEAR LATER... ✺

Zagora was on the last page of the biography of Helen Thayer, the first woman to walk across the Sahara on an ancient camel trade route, when she noticed her plane was starting down for a landing. Marrakech! That summer she was traveling solo to meet her father, who was already in Marrakech, after convincing him of how trustworthy and responsible she was now that she was twelve. Duncan, currently at a junior astronomers' camp, would be joining them in August.

Over the past year she'd received a number of letters from Pitblade Yegen. He had gone to see Mina's grandmother Noor at the Azimuth Caves, and Noor had treated his eyes with roots, herbs and what he surmised were desert spells. He was now able to see again, and—even more amazing—he'd regained his desert sight.

For the past four months, her father had been in Morocco with Pitblade, excavating Zahir. Aunt Claire had lived with Zagora and Duncan while they'd finished out the school year. Their dad wrote that the frequent sandstorms hadn't slowed them down and the giant scorpions had disappeared for good. Every week he sent photographs of relics they'd dug up in Zahir. The most exciting photo was of the tomb of Xuloc, unearthed when they'd destroyed the scorpions' nest beneath the pyramid.

Zagora couldn't wait to see all the treasures her father had found, especially a stash of coins stamped with the sign of the oryx. And Duncan had gone bananas when he heard about the astronomical instruments Pitblade had discovered in one of the palace rooms.

Please reassure your brother, Pitblade had written, while telling them about his plans to turn the palace into a museum, *that we will not turn Zahir into a theme park.*

A crew was rebuilding the irrigation ducts to water the oases around Zahir. Soon the city would be habitable again, with running water, electricity, shops, a small hospital and a school. The Azimuth, including Mina and her grandmother, were preparing to move into the restored buildings. The Azimuth Caves had been declared part of the World Heritage Trust and would forever be protected.

Pitblade had planned to import oryxes from Saudi Arabia, but there was no need for that now, because oryxes were flocking from all over northern Africa to the green oases of Zahir. In one letter, Pitblade attributed their sudden resurgence to the mysterious powers of the Oryx Stone, and Zagora was sure he was right. Razziq, hired for the summer as assistant oryx keeper, had attended the births of three baby oryxes.

Faithful to his promise, Razziq had returned to Maison Tuareg, where he found out that Uncle Ali had survived the scorpion attack. After Razziq explained in detail to Abdul the treachery of Olivia Romanesçu, Abdul had apologized profusely, inviting the Pyms to come to Maison Tuareg the next time they were in Morocco. Zagora was pleased to have Abdul as a friend again.

She would be seeing Sophie again, too. Razziq promised she could ride Sophie, because he said Sophie was really her camel, after everything they'd gone through. Zagora had packed a special brush to keep Sophie's fur shiny, along with her secret journal. The journal was genuine leather, just like Edgar Yegen's. Inside the cover she'd written *The Journal of Zagora M. Pym, Intrepid Explorer/ Desert Adventurer.*

Zagora stepped off the plane. In the airport, waiting among the crush of people for her luggage, she unfolded the newspaper clipping she'd cut out, and read it for the millionth time.

> *Members of a Tuareg tribe in a remote part of southeastern Morocco claim to have found the remains of a gigantic scorpion approximately six feet long. The creature is thought to have floated down an underground river and washed up inside an earthen tunnel. Police are investigating.*

Extraordinary things in an ordinary world.

She saw her father elbowing his way through the crowd, waving excitedly to her—as if she wouldn't recognize his silvery hair, or the yellow shirt with blue parrots she'd bought for him, to replace his old one.

For a moment she heard the desert wind, low and haunting, and a shimmer of sparkling sand fell before her eyes. Running to meet her father, she thought, *Here I am, in Morocco again.* For the last eleven months she'd dreamed of returning to Zahir—the ancient desert city with the name her dad said meant "obsession"—and now it was really happening.

The desert, she knew, was waiting for her.

And this time she would be ready for it.

CHRISTINE BRODIEN-JONES is the author of *The Owl Keeper,* a dystopian fantasy for middle-grade readers. She studied writing at Emerson College in Boston and has been a reporter, an editor, and a teacher. A journey to the Moroccan desert with her family sparked her interest in the mythology of the Sahara Desert and inspired her to write *The Scorpions of Zahir.* Christine and her husband, Peter, live in Gloucester, Massachusetts, and Deer Isle, Maine.